SCENT of DECEIT

SCENT of DECEIT

RINZI PETER PHOYA

authorHOUSE®

AuthorHouse™
1663 Liberty Drive
Bloomington, IN 47403
www.authorhouse.com
Phone: 1-800-839-8640

Published by AuthorHouse   03/16/2012

ISBN: 978-1-4678-9185-1 (sc)
ISBN: 978-1-4678-9186-8 (e)

~ CONTENTS ~

"Once he realises he is trapped, why doesn't the monkey let go of the bait?"

-Shaka Zulu

~ ACKNOWLEDGEMENTS ~

A SPECIAL 'THANK YOU' goes to some very unique people, without whom, less would have been achieved. To my lovely and wonderful wife, Sandra Phoya: for staying up late by my side, pouring yourself over the final manuscript and urging me on. You are such a genius by far and I'm the luckiest man alive.

To my two good friends, Chiyembekezo Kadangwe and Madalo Haji: for making your great minds available and seeing this project through. Despite the distance, we found a way to do it and we did.

Last but not least, to all my friends, especially those who have read some of my works. For continuously complimenting and praising my work, despite the obvious flaws; your kind words and positive criticisms always motivate and nourish my desire to write more. And it is your comments which gave me the strength to create this book.

Scent of Deceit is from me to you; for the precious time you invested in my work, a gesture which is greatly appreciated and will forever be remembered. I hope you will enjoy each and every page.

Rinzi Peter Phoya

~ DEDICATION ~

THIS BOOK IS dedicated to my two wonderful children, my source of pride and joy.

Yellenna Nia Phoya; my beautiful little Princess, you are such a priceless treasure. You are too young to comprehend. I hope time will come when you will be able to read this, perhaps pause and realise the endless love that I feel for you.

Nikolai Ray Phoya; you are what I always wanted in a son; I wouldn't have asked for a better image of me. You never cease to amaze me, always making me proud.

~ INTRODUCTION ~

SCENT OF DECEIT is a story about emotions of love, infatuation, heartache and what happens when certain lines are crossed.

Walter Lumbadzi is a successful businessman, a rising politician and a loving husband to Dr Tamanda Lumbadzi; a beautiful, educated and career oriented woman. Up until now, their marriage has been one long honeymoon. However, ripples start to appear when Walter meets a very gorgeous and sexy woman on Facebook.

Nomsa is a woman who has a chequered past and a secret that will put Walter and Tamanda's once loving marriage to the test.

The blurry line between love and lust gets further complicated by a gruesome double homicide, deceit, and cross-border dealings which involve politicians, the police and simmering family rivalry.

Will Walter manage to successfully hold on to his political ambitions and save his marriage?

"Love itself is what is left over when 'being in love' has burned away, and this is both an art and a fortunate accident. Your mother and I had it, we had roots that grew towards each other underground, and when the pretty blossom (flowers) had fallen from our branches we found that we were one tree and not two."   ~Captain Corelli's Mandolin

~ I LOVE YOU ~

THIRTY-NINE YEAR OLD Walter Lumbadzi was pacing up and down his expanse office. The black silk tie around his neck was loosened and the sleeves of his white—Yves Saint Laurent—shirt were rolled up to his elbows. The gold cufflinks were somewhere on top of his polished oak desk, next to the large flat computer monitor. The sleek Samsung mobile phone was pressed tightly to his right ear; he was astounded by what, his friend; Graham Malloch-Brown, the British high commissioner to Malawi, was saying on the other end of the line.

"Are you serious?" Walter asked; his mouth partly open in disbelief.

"Yes, my friend. Apparently your government has given me forty-eight hours to leave the country." Graham replied in a calm manner; his words, a proper British accent.

"They are expelling you out of Malawi because of a leaked cable?" Walter asked, shaking his head.

Still pacing the length of his office, he stopped next to a chair which had a T-shirt draped over it. He ran his free hand over it, feeling the texture of the fabric, without looking at it.

"Yes, apparently an email I sent to the Foreign Secretary in London did not go down well over here." Graham laughed, not making any attempt to hide the sarcasm.

"Graham, I feel uncomfortable talking sensitive issues over the phone." Walter cautioned his friend.

"Oh! I forgot about the rumour of the phone hacking machine. We need to meet before I leave for London." Graham said with a laugh; an attempt to disguise his anger at what was happening to him.

The Englishman had grown fond of Malawi and made some wonderful friends; he always knew that his diplomatic job will take him from country to country and that once in a while he would have to side-step political minefields. However, he hadn't expected to end his Malawian deployment in such circumstances.

"You are right, we need to meet. I will be coming over to Lilongwe today." Walter said in a subdued tone.

He walked towards the large window; taking in the panoramic view of Blantyre. He could just about make out the tall buildings in the distance, they were partly obscured by trees and haze coming from charcoal fires across the township of Mbayani.

"Are you coming down here for business?"

"No, Tamanda is returning from a seminar in South Africa and I have to pick her up at the airport."

"I guess I will see you then."

"No doubt."

"I have spoken to a few wealthy individuals in UK about your political aspirations. People are willing to step in if you show the initiative."

"Tell me more when I get there." Walter said, feeling a chill of excitement tingle his entire body.

"I sure will, and of course it will be nice to meet Tamanda, my wife was just asking about her last week."

"I'm sure the two women will talk us to death."

"Your lovely wife is such a breath of fresh air; don't you ever leave that woman Walter."

"Me, leave Tamanda? Are you out of your mind?" Walter laughed.

"Men, we are funny creatures. I don't know why women fall in love with us." Graham joked.

"Mmmh . . . you have a point there." Walter said, then lowering his tone, he spoke slowly; "About your connections in the UK, thanks in advance, Graham. I really appreciate that."

"I know you don't need financial assistance, but it does help to have friends in high places." Graham said; his tone changing from friendly banter to serious.

"You genuinely think I can do this, Graham?" Walter asked; trying to inject some subtleness in his voice.

"Let my friends at the IMF apply external pressure, and you just continue doing what you are doing now. Anyway, let's talk more when you come to Lilongwe."

"I will give you a call when I get there Graham. You take care, my friend."

"You too, Walter; I will see you later." The British diplomat said with a smile, before hanging up the phone the same time Walter did.

Walter was still standing by the window of his expanse office, on the third floor, looking outside; subconsciously fiddling with his mobile phone. He was not paying attention to the fleet of tankers or flat-bed trucks parked in a row along the massive warehouse, opposite the office complex. Neither was he interested in the dozen 40-foot shipping containers; stacked in a row of three high and four lengthwise on the concrete ground. His ears could not even pick out the cacophony of organised chaos taking place inside the large sprawling brick wall enclose compound; mechanics working on trucks, welders with their goggles-looking like aliens—holding blow torches. Young men were offloading some merchandise from two trucks into the large brick warehouse, whilst some were folding large tarpaulins; shouting, laughing and sweating in the afternoon heat.

Inside the air conditioned office, Walter was oblivious to all this, his eyes were focused past the brick that surrounded the walled compound; he was looking at the horizon, his mind still trying to discern the conversation he just had with the British high commissioner.

He then shook his head, looked at Blantyre; the biggest commercial city in Malawi. A smile creased his lean chiselled face; he turned around, slowly easing himself into his plush chair. He reclined himself; the smile on his face widening as his eyes focused at the sample white T-shirt draped over the seat on the other side of his huge oak desk.

The short sleeved garment, with political paraphernalia, had just been delivered three hours earlier and Walter couldn't get enough of it. His lovely set of teeth appeared to glow the more he looked at his own face, printed in colour, on the white fabric of the T-shirt. Underneath it, were the letters; *Walter Lumbadzi for MP* emblazoned in black font.

For the past four months, he had been pumping personal money into his political campaign. It was an ambitious and costly political undertaking being funded through his business empire *Lumbadzi Investments*; an amalgamation of businesses from import and exports, international road haulage, printing, and filling stations, of which he was its Chief Executive Officer.

Walter's *Lumbadzi Investments* had enough resources to absorb the spiralling cost of trying to unseat an incumbent MP, a seasoned politician riding on the strength of the ruling regime. He advised his accountants not to document how much money was being channelled into funding his political ambitions.

"I honestly don't want the heartache of knowing how hard this will hit me in the pocket." He had confided to his wife, Tamanda, a few months ago.

"Are you sure that's the reason or is it the fact that you don't want to leave a paper trail?" Tamanda, who knew her husband well, asked mischievously.

The ringing of the Panasonic phone on his desk startled Walter. With his eyes still admiring the T-shirt, he picked up the sleek looking handset off its cradle.

"Yes Hendrina?" He answered in a business tone; the smile of a short while ago, now replaced by a slight frown.

"Sir, it's your wife on line four." Hendrina, his twenty-seven year old secretary, said in a mellow voice.

"Thanks Hendrina, you can put her through." He said, leaning further back in his chair, his eyes switching from the T-shirt to the flat computer monitor, "and, Hendrina, will you please e-mail last month's budget figures to me?"

"Yes sir." Hendrina answered respectfully, her face beaming, before connecting her boss's line to his wife.

"Hi darling, can you hear me?" Tamanda's voice crackled on the other end.

"Hey sweetheart, yes I can hear you loud and clear." Walter said, a soft lazy grin creasing his youngish features, the frown disappearing in a flash.

"Great. I was wondering why I was struggling to hear Hendrina clearly." Tamanda said loudly, trying to speak over background noise.

"I don't know, maybe because she always speaks in a shy polite manner when it's you on the phone." Walter said, rocking back and forth, his eyes turning to the black and white portrait of his beautiful wife perched on his tidy desk.

"I thought I couldn't hear her because of this being an international call."

"That too sweetheart," he said repositioning the portrait; "notwithstanding the fact that the girls here at the office are scared of you." Walter teased, laughing when he heard his wife breathe in, on the other end of the line.

"Scared of me? They better be." Tamanda said in a mock threatening tone.

"How come you didn't call me on my mobile sweetheart?" He asked, sitting back upright.

He squinted, the frown returning as a result of what he was seeing on the monitor; the email with budget figures he had requested from Hendrina had just popped up. There was a huge mismatch between last month's actual expenditure figures and what had been projected the previous month.

"My mobile phone battery is dead; you know I can never memorise your mobile numbers at the rate you keep changing them, sweetheart."

"I haven't changed my number in six months sweetie." He said whilst his eyes scrutinised the figures on the screen.

"It's only been three months, darling."

"Three? I'm sure it's been longer than that!" Walter said, laughing whilst his brain took a mental note of the chart full of figures, on the screen. He was going to have a word with his accountant.

"Okay, even if it was six; is that what you call a long-run? I have had mine for years."

"I think I won't be changing this one." He said with a laugh, fully aware that his wife didn't believe what he had just said.

"Didn't you say the same thing about your last number?"

"I mean it this time. If I change my number again, I will walk barefoot for one week."

"Ha! That will be the week when pigs fly and elephants dance."

"Do I really change my number that often?"

"Too often; luckily for you sweetie, the office's land line is engraved on my mind just like our anniversary date." Tamanda said in a mellow voice, stressing on the word *anniversary*.

"Oh, I see . . . have you already left the hotel?" He asked, his frowning face inching closer to the monitor, pretending not to have heard the word anniversary.

"Are you dodging commenting on the anniversary remark Walter Lumbadzi?"

"Anniversary? Ours or your parents'?" He queried teasingly; he had just remembered that their anniversary was two weeks after that of his father-in-law and mother-in-law.

"Dad's and Mum's is today, you haven't forgotten about that, have you?"

"How could I? I thought that is the whole reason we are doing this Kamuzu International Airport thing, instead of you jumping on a connecting flight to Blantyre."

"Thanks for remembering sweetheart. I am at O.R. Tambo airport now; I came in early because I am supposed to meet some colleagues who are coming in from UK."

"You are where? You are not using Johannesburg International Airport?"

"Yes, it's one and the same; I thought I mentioned it to you when we spoke yesterday evening? You weren't listening were you?"

"Why do we Africans like changing names of our institutions and places . . . aarrgghh!" Walter laughed sarcastically before adding; "anyway, why are you meeting them at the airport?"

"Their flight got delayed for two days somewhere in Europe, courtesy of the Icelandic ash cloud."

"You mean to tell me they missed the whole seminar? Why do you have to meet with them anyway?"

"Since I am the leader of the African biomed team for the macrophages research that we are working on, it is a matter of protocol that I do a proper handover to the European team leader, an annoying Professor who also happens to be the only neurobiologist," Tamanda spoke flawlessly into the phone, her excitement apparent.

"What do you actually do at these seminars apart from drinking tea and doing handovers?"

"These are exciting times for us Walter; our Australian colleagues have made an astonishing breakthrough."

"Have they now?"

"Yes sweetie; they, or rather we, have found that tuberculosis is able to survive within microphages and that it is able to secrete an enzyme that disrupts pathways which are used to fight off harmful bacteria. By impairing and subverting the host's immune system, it ensures its survival while increasing the rate of proliferation . . . sorry Walter; I get carried away when I start . . ." Her voice trailed.

"Sweetheart, it all sounds like Greek; I have no idea what you just said, let's just change the subject and talk about what you are wearing." He said, groaning painfully to the amusement of his wife who started laughing on the other end.

"Ok, apologies for my Greek sweetie, I am wearing my grey suit; forget it if you think I will tell you what I have got underneath." Tamanda laughed loudly; teasing him.

"Aawww! That's not fair." He moaned like a little boy being denied his toy.

"I was calling just to tell you that I will be boarding in two hours, right after this meeting. Fingers crossed, I should be there around 4:30ish." Tamanda said, laughing at her husband's silly but cute moans.

"Is that how long it takes from Johannesburg to Lilongwe?" Walter asked jokingly.

"How long did you think the Jo'burg-Lilogwe flight took, sweetheart? Twenty minutes?" Tamanda said making faces while coughing playfully.

"I honestly thought it took longer. I swear last time I flew to South Africa it took me two days." He said, failing to hold a serious tone; he burst into a bout of laughter.

"Are you referring to the South Africa found on Planet Crazy?"

"No, I am serious sweetie." He said, still laughing hysterically.

"I love you Walter, my silly husband." Tamanda said against a backdrop of airport noise; she paused—waiting for the reciprocating *I love you too* before hanging up the phone.

"I love . . . I . . ." He stuttered, distracted by the beeping of his mobile phone.

He glanced at the sleek Samsung which was next to the keyboard, it was showing the name; *Land-Lord* on its small blue illuminated screen. His eyes bulged out with excitement.

"Hello? Are you there darling? Tamanda's voice reverberated through the office phone which was now balancing precariously between his shoulder and his left cheek.

"Yes sweetheart . . . sorry, I was saying that; I love you too." Walter stammered, trying to regain his composure whilst picking up the, still beeping, mobile phone.

It was a message coming from *Land-Lord*; a fake name he had saved in his phone directory to denote Nomsa. He had no idea what prompted him to use such a fake name. He could have opted for Nom or simply Salala, her surname, or something less ridiculous than what he had chosen; Walter mused whilst glancing at the text message.

"*Check your e-mail Lover Boy.*"

"Did I call at the wrong time darling?" Tamanda's voice came back on the other end of the phone startling him; the phone-receiver almost fell from his shoulder.

He couldn't believe he had actually forgotten that his wife was still on the phone.

"Yes, I mean no sweetheart . . . it's just this whole political campaign mumbo-jumbo." Walter spoke whilst grabbing the computer mouse; he clicked on the *e-mail* icon.

The computer screen changed from the spread-sheet containing budget figures to a fresh screen; a short e-mail from Nomsa.

"*For your eyes only Lover Boy, find attached something which will make you wish you were here with me.*" Nomsa's e-mail read.

He smiled, clicking on the 'open attachment' icon. The internet was agonisingly slow today. He impatiently tapped his right foot on the floor as an image started to form, pixel by pixel. It was the photo of Nomsa.

If Nomsa was to be compressed into two words; they would have to be *beautiful* and *sexy*. Walter's mouth was partly open as his eyes feasted on the chocolate goddess plastered all over his computer screen. He was looking at a female who possessed stunning angelic features, yet oozed an abundance of sexiness in a sinful way.

Nomsa had gorgeous big eyes that gave the impression they could see right through a person, yet they had a lazy look that never failed to arouse him. Her neck was very long, distancing her head away from the sexy ample breasts; a gorgeous set of lumps which were now covered under a red lacy bra. They appeared to be pointing at him from the screen. She was standing up with hands resting on her curvy hips. Hers was a height which would make any model faint with envy. Her black weave was long like sin, let loose to flow down past her shoulders like raging water off a cliff.

Walter found himself licking his dry lips as his brain tried to take in her voluptuousness; he was mesmerised by the curves which appeared to be chiselled by someone who had the devilish intentions of torturing men's eyes. The fact that Nomsa only had skimpy panties, matching with her bra and high heel boots, was enough to increase his heart rate. He felt a tug from somewhere below, similar to that experienced the first time he saw her.

With his left hand, Walter reached out, touching her full lips on the screen; they were doused in moderate red lipstick and deliberately curved in the most sensual smile. He started smiling subconsciously.

"Tamanda . . . I mean Sweetheart . . . can you call me back, something urgent just came up . . . politics . . . politics my dear, and then they are expelling Graham too." Walter fumbled for words, his brain struggling to engage with his wife in a normal conversation.

"You mean Graham, your British friend, the high commissioner? Why?"

"Yes, him darling, but I can't talk right now, let me . . ."

"It's okay sweetheart, I know how stressful and demanding this political campaign has been," Tamanda said softly, before adding, "I will see you at the airport when I land."

"Yes, you do that sweetheart." Walter said, not sure what he was saying, confused by the alluring photo of Nomsa which appeared to be beckoning him closer to the computer screen.

"Bye sweetheart . . . I love you." Tamanda said romantically, blowing a kiss into the phone.

"I love you too sweetheart." He said hastily; then dropped the phone back into its cradle, his attention fully on what he was looking at.

~ ADDICTED ~

APART FROM THE nicely tended bed of white lily flowers around it, there was nothing unique about this house. Like many houses along this winding stretch of dirt road, Nomsa Salala's two-bedroom house was small; splashed in cheap light green paint which was peeling off. The windows had thick ugly burglar bars and it had a corrugated rooftop without a ceiling inside; nothing to muffle the clattering noise of rain or lessen the scorching heat of the summer sun. However, unlike her previous home, this one had basic amenities inside.

The privileges of having an indoor toilet and shower came in form of not having to walk outside clasping a bar of soap and toothbrush every morning, losing dignity in the process. Prior to moving into this house, Nomsa used to wash in a small and smelly communal bathroom; shared amongst seven households in the deprived part of Ndirande Township. Now, she had her own toilet with a tiny window from where she could see the picturesque and breath-taking view of Chilomoni Mountain looming so close.

However, today Nomsa was not intent on this particular view or any other; with the lid down, she was using the toilet like a chair. With only a red bra, with matching red panties and velvet high heel shoes, Nomsa was still uncomfortable due to the unbearable heat from the scorching sun. Its intensity was made worse by the cheap corrugated roof; her thighs felt clammy, sticking to the plastic toilet lid. She wiped off beads of sweat from her forehead; her big eyes were staring lazily at the closed plywood door.

On the other side of the door, Nomsa could hear her two-year old child, Prince, crying loudly. She felt like covering her ears to muffle the toddler sounds. Her eyes felt like someone had sprinkled sand on them, she hadn't slept at all last night, not even a wink. Prince had been running a temperature. Throughout the night she had been pacing to and from the bedroom, kitchen and bathroom; applying cold-presses to the child's forehead, giving him fluids so as to keep him hydrated. By morning time there had been a slight improvement in Prince's condition. Nonetheless, she didn't feel comfortable leaving him with the neighbour; the lady who cared for him while she was at work. Nomsa rang her workplace that she would not be coming in.

Nomsa's motherly love towards her baby boy was undeniably strong. However, the child was a constant reminder of her past life, a past she detested. Prince was without a father, a bastard, a product of a one night stand; a business transaction where one achieved some sexual gratification and the other monetary gains. It was a past whose memories she tried to confine into the deepest recesses of her mind.

Nowadays, Nomsa was just grateful that she had exited the prostitution trade with her health intact; having been spared any sexually transmitted diseases. In an era where a lot of women in her trade never lived to see thirty, Nomsa had miraculously celebrated her 32nd birthday. Not only was she alive and well, but she was also looking stunningly attractive than girls ten years younger.

Perched on the toilet, her back leaning against the cool ceramic cistern tank, she stretched her long legs in front of her. Feeling its cooling effects against her bare back, Nomsa cocked her head to one side while looking at her slender legs.

However, her self-admiration was cut short. Renewed shrieks of Prince resonated from the living room.

"Mummy is coming Prince, baby!" She yelled, gingerly placing her feet on the floor, reminding herself what it is she was supposed to be doing.

All along, her right hand had been clenched into a fist. She slowly unclenched it, her long fingers trembling slightly. Nomsa took a sideways glance at her right hand; disbelief etched on face at the contraption she was holding. She bit her lower lip in anger for what she was about to do.

"Mummy is coming . . . I am coming baby." Nomsa sobbed more to herself, her voice not carrying beyond the closed door, its tone dropping to a whimper.

Tears started cascading down her cheeks, forming tiny rivulets, before seeping into her lacy red bra.

"I . . . I am coming baby . . ." She choked the words, her speech slurred as she slowly inserted the hypodermic needle into a protruding vein on her left arm.

About eighteen months ago Walter had, single-handedly, helped her quit prostitution. He had sorted her out with a decent job as a receptionist at an accounting firm belonging to one of his friends. She would have loved to work for Walter, at any of his many companies. She still appreciated the employment he got her at a company belonging to his friend. The job took her off the streets; however, there was still one vice that had maintained its stranglehold on her.

Drugs.

Despite the reassurances she gave Walter that she had kicked the habit, Nomsa hadn't entirely been honest with him. She had succumbed to a few relapses, like the one she was having now. However, because of shame and her love for Walter, she did her best to appear drug-free. It dawned on

Nomsa that being clean made him very happy; he genuinely cared for her in a way that was new and at times strangely nice. She couldn't afford to let him know that she was still using.

How could she let him know that she had deceived him? Guilt was eating at her, she hadn't expected their relationship to progress this far. He was too nice a man, if only she could be entirely honest with him. But how could she?

Nomsa started sobbing silently, her right thumb slowly squeezed on the syringe's plunger downwards. Her eyes were clamped shut; she couldn't bear to look at the clear liquid exiting the plastic medical contraption, entering her blood system. Her body was rocked with mild convulsions and she groaned as the drugs quickly spread throughout her system. There was an almost surreal calmness that descended over her. She welcomed it, her eyes rolling, her chin burying itself into her soft ample cleavage. She was floating out of her own body, the feeling was beyond delicious.

The beeping of her Blackberry, on the floor, disturbed her stupor; her head snapped right back, her drugged eyes struggling to get her bearings. It took much effort for her to figure out where she was. She had completely lost track of time and had no recollection of how long she had been sitting on the toilet. Her watery eyes were strained on the Blackberry, it appeared blurry and far. Blinking profusely, she struggled to discern the scribbling displayed on the flashing blue screen. It took her a few seconds to realise that it was a message from Walter.

Albeit her drug induced state, a smile spread across Nomsa's mouth; a text from Walter, the only man in the entire universe who meant something, never failed to make her smile. He was the person who had saved her from the brink and showed her that all men are not misogynistic.

She tried to read the text message, however the phone was too far down on the floor; the powerful drug had started working its magic. Nomsa's head was buzzing; the tiny toilet, all of a sudden, appeared expanse and delightful. She had to be hallucinating, it was a beautiful hallucination which she did not want to let go of. A smile formed on her lips as she was teleported to Walter's private and wonderful cottage in Salima. It was a different, but magnificent world.

A cocktail party was in progress; she had on an exquisite long strapless evening gown exposing her gorgeous shoulders. She was the centre of attention and her left hand was constantly and nervously massaging the expensive white pearls which adorned her neck. There were a lot of important and wealthy people; politicians and business elites, all of them addressing her as Mrs Lumbadzi. The men accorded her respect whereas the women were stealing envious glances at her. She had her arms intertwined with Walter's in a lover's style. It was a rich and happy world; so different far removed from hers, especially her childhood.

Nomsa grew up not knowing who her parents were. Her mother, so she was told, got pregnant out of wedlock at the age of sixteen; it was a difficult pregnancy and she died as a result of labour complications.

Nomsa was raised by her uncle; he was a mountain of a man, with a permanent frown and didn't condone to joyous banter in the house whenever he was around. His own children did their best to stay out of his way and Nomsa trembled with fear every time he called her name. He made it explicitly clear to her, from an early age, that she was the reason his sister was dead. He was very abusive to her and she was reduced to a status of a house servant. She was expected to do the cleaning and washing up, after his four children; making their beds when they went to school.

Nomsa's childhood was full of pain; she missed out on a lot of things—there were no birthdays and no Christmases, only misery. Her uncle, in collaboration with her auntie, decided not to send her to school, they constantly told her she was too stupid. Her auntie was always scolding her and slapping her; she was never allowed to eat at the dining table with the family, she was made to sit on the kitchen floor alone, eating their leftovers.

One day while the house was empty; her uncle surprised her when he came home in the morning; the wife was at work and the kids were at school. Nomsa still remembers his big body crushing on top of her, his sweaty palm clamping her mouth shut; muffling her desperate screams for help, while his other hand ripped the dress off her small body. She was only thirteen then.

Three years later at the age of sixteen, while everyone was away; Nomsa stuffed all her belongings in a plastic bag and ran away from home. She started selling her body to men who were willing to pay for sex; she needed the money for sustenance and to pay for basic numeracy and literacy classes.

The world she was dreaming of now, there was no pain no sorrow. Walter was there, making sure that she was safe.

Nomsa tried to resurface from the depths the drugs had plunged her; the Blackberry was still beeping between her feet. Somehow she surmised that in order to pick it up she had to stand up first; Nomsa steadied herself, getting up from the toilet. Her legs felt wobbly; she immediately toppled forward, banging her head against the door. Nomsa was surprised by the violence of the impact; her head snapped backwards and she landed back on the toilet seat with a loud crash which caused Prince, on the other side of the door, to stop wailing.

Grabbing her forehead with one hand, thankful that the drug had numbed her senses of pain, she slowly bent over; picking up the Blackberry with her left hand, Nomsa could barely read Walter's text.

"*You look delicious and dangerous in your red underwear . . . please send me another one without your bra.*"

She had to read the text several times, the drugs in her playing havoc with her eyes. She couldn't stop smiling though; mustering some energy to type a response.

"*You naughty boy, why do you want to see my legs?*" Nomsa typed and pressed the *send* button.

She waited for his reply, listening to the throbbing on her forehead which sounded like the beating of a distant drum.

"*I can see your legs Sexy Thing; I want to see your breasts.*" Walter replied.

Nomsa read the text, and instantaneously started laughing so loud Prince started crying again. She couldn't believe she had mistaken *legs* for *breasts*.

"*Send me a naughty picture of yourself first and I will send you one where I am completely nude.*" Nomsa's well-manicured fingers typed slowly, not too sure what she was typing.

The drugs in her system had resumed their magical wonders; everything started getting fuzzy again. She pressed *send* and abruptly got up with the urgency of someone who just remembered something important that needed doing. Steadying herself on the door handle, Nomsa exited the toilet, staggering like a drunk into her tiny living room.

Prince was strapped to the high-chair, still crying as the piece of bread she had given him had dropped on the floor.

"I am here baby . . . Mummy is here." Nomsa said apologetically, her eyes noticing her neighbour's black cat nibbling on the piece of bread on the floor.

"Shoo! Shoo!" She tried to scare the black furry creature by flaring her arms all over the place.

The domesticated cat, which must have come in through one of the open windows, did not bulge; it stood still looking at her, still nibbling on the piece of bread.

Nomsa angrily took off her left velvet high heel shoe; she steadied herself whilst clutching to the shoe like some sort of boomerang. With all the strength she could muster, she flung her shoe at the black feline, missing it miserably. However, she almost hit her baby's face. The throwing motion, drug dazed stupor, balancing on one high heel shoe, plus the horror of nearly maiming Prince all culminated into Nomsa losing her footing. She toppled forward; this time there was nothing to break her fall. She watched in horror as the hard polished floor rose up to meet her face. The impact was excruciatingly violent and jarring.

"Walter!" Nomsa uttered his name before passing out.

~ THE WIFE ~

A PUFF OF smoke erupted as the rear wheels of the Boeing 737 made contact with Kamuzu International Airport's asphalt, the longest runway in Malawi, at exactly 16:40. There was vibration throughout the cabin as the captain engaged reverse thrust; the powerful exhausts from the huge twin engines countered the forward motion, decelerating the huge plane. The engines whining noise halts all human conversation; seasoned fliers and novice ones bracing themselves in silence, a constant reminder that flying still remains a nerve-racking mode of travelling.

In her seat, Dr Tamanda Lumbadzi swallowed hard following the popping sound in her ears; she glanced sideways at the elderly Pastor sitting next to her by the window seat. He had his eyes clamped shut, either in prayer or fear, maybe both; Tamanda thought, looking at his fingers which were slowly relaxing their grip on the armrests as the plane started taxiing towards the airport terminal.

"Thank you dear Lord for bringing us safely back to Malawi. Amen." The Pastor murmured a silent prayer, breathing a sigh of relief and finally opening his eyes.

Tamanda smiled politely at the Pastor who was looking at her. He had been talkative since they left O.R. Tambo International Airport in Johannesburg; he had gone dead quiet when the plane started descending towards Kamuzu International Airport. He was scared of flying; he had confided to her just after taking off, two hours earlier.

"It's been a pleasure flying with you Pastor." Tamanda said with a smile, shaking the Pastor's extended clammy hand, before standing up to reach for the overhead compartment.

"May the Lord be with you my daughter, remember what I said."

"Yes Pastor, without God a marriage is like a strong castle built on sand." Tamanda repeated what the Pastor had been telling her during the flight.

She had been forced to endure his nonstop religious talk simply because they were sitting next to each other. Tamanda was not a religious person, she did not believe in the existence of a higher being; however she disliked being labelled an atheist. Brought up by strict catholic parents, her religious beliefs began to wane as she grew older, especially when she left Malawi for higher education in America. The more she delved into the world of science, the more she started gravitating towards Darwinism, the less she believed in the metaphysical.

At first she kept this a secret from her parents, although not for long; Tamanda knew that it was just a matter of time before the liberal American student in her was bound to come out. She remembers vividly the day this happened. She was sitting in her father's office, a month after returning from the USA, before he had retired as Chief Justice. As usual her proud father was going on about how proud he was that she was a qualified doctor; Tamanda was sitting on the other side of his huge disorganised desk, smiling and nodding her head.

"I knew God would open doors for you Tamanda my daughter." Her father said, sifting through the clutter on his desk, fishing out a bible from the pile of legal documents and books.

She knew her father was going to sift through the holy book so as to locate a verse which could authenticate what he was saying. Tamanda seized this opportunity to tell him what she had been putting off, since returning to Malawi. She could not let him get to the chapter or verse he was looking for or this would turn into one of his long sermons. She leaned forward in her seat, her left elbow on the edge of the desk, coughing slightly; her father paused flipping through the pages of the bible, looking at her over the top of his thick prescription glasses.

"Father, with all due respect, I disagree with what you have just said."

"Come again? Disagree with God opening doors to your doctoral degree?"

"Father, I studied day and night, I missed on a lot of fun. My success was through hard work, it had nothing to do with God." Tamanda responded, noticing the shock in her father's eyes.

"America has changed you my daughter, it has educated you. Bar that, it has also changed you." Her father said in a calm tone.

"Father, do you honestly think you became the country's most prominent Chief Justice because God wanted you to?" Tamanda asked, holding her father's gaze.

"My daughter, you are grown up now, some day you will find out how much God can do if we put Him first." Her father said, addressing her question.

Dr Tamanda Lumbadzi respected her parent's religiousness or that of anyone else. She was also thankful that they reciprocated the gesture and accepted that she had chosen a different path; that of Darwinism. She knew most of the theories behind evolution by heart and regarded herself as student of science. Hence the notion that we are all descendants of Adam and Eve, as far as Tamanda was concerned, was simply a myth on which creation is based. Her scientific mind found this, not only laughable, but impossible to prove factually.

During the flight, she had so much wanted to tell the Pastor that the strong love between Walter and her was due to the chemistry they shared, it had nothing to do with God, as he was insinuating. However, her strong Malawian upbringing forced her to sit tight, listening to the Pastor on how not including God in a marriage could bring a dangerous rot. If the Pastor had been one of her Christian friends from university or someone she knew, this could have turned into one long interesting debate. Instead, she nodded the whole way from South Africa. She was still nodding and smiling politely at the Pastor as they entered the skies of Malawi and started their descent towards Lilongwe.

She feigned interest; however, she was somewhere far and exotic with her Walter. The smile on her face had nothing to do with what the man of god was saying.

The captain did the whole ceremonial '*thank you for flying with us speech*'. The passive crowd of passengers could not wait to escape from the air-conditioned cabin, despite the boiling heat outside, just so they could see the welcoming faces of family members and friends.

Everyone was on their feet, helping themselves to their hand-luggage from the overhead compartments, the minute the 'seatbelt light' went off. Along the aisle, just in front of Tamanda, were two very talkative young men who were cracking jokes about Air Malawi.

"I am sure this captain took a shortcut." One of the young men said loudly, heaving out a big bag he had miraculously managed to squeeze into the overhead.

"The plane was too full that's why he wasn't stopping to pick up any more passengers along the way." His friend remarked, laughing loudly at his own joke.

Tamanda was dying inside with laughter. She managed to keep a straight face forgetting about the two comedians as soon as she got off the plane. She couldn't wait to see her husband and was already searching the sea of faces the moment she cleared customs. Her eyes kept darting towards 'International Arrivals' lounge gate where other passengers were already hugging, laughing and greeting their respective family members and friends. Dr Tamanda Lumbadzi tiptoed on her high heel shoes, craning her neck to scan through the sea of strangers, hoping to catch Walter's familiar tall frame, craving to see his handsome face.

"Where are you darling?" Tamanda whispered to herself, a slight frown creasing her beautiful face.

From the corner of her eye she noticed that a few people were looking at her. Tamanda was blessed with naturally good looks; was used to getting looks, especially from men. She was someone who took good care of her body; refrained from alcohol and was vehemently opposed to cigarettes. She rarely applied any makeup, perceiving it as a façade. She had nothing against cosmetics or women who were obsessed with beautifying themselves using powders, lipstick or mascara. Tamanda just didn't see the need. A bath, body lotion and a dab of her favourite Channel perfume, which wasn't too loud and vicious to the nostrils of others, was how she prepared herself every morning before meeting the world.

Thirty-four year old, Dr Tamanda was a product of private schools; the prestigious St Andrews in Malawi and Stanford

University in America. She was at the pinnacle of her career and madly in love with her husband; she once told him that she felt teenage love when she was around him and when she was apart from him.

Although the two of them weren't blessed with children, Tamanda felt like their marriage was one long honeymoon. Walter was the only man who managed to push all the right buttons and hit all the right spots. She found him sexy, attractive and funny. There was also a certain warmness about him which always sent butterflies fluttering in her stomach.

The fact that her husband was not religious made the two of them highly compatible. She had long figured out that he was neither an atheist nor a disciple of Darwin, like she was. Walter had not gone far with his education like she had; however, he was alarmingly intelligent and fiercely ambitious. Driven by the quest to make loads of money and create a name for himself within Malawi; he was so far exceeding on both fronts.

Walter was not a man who knew fear; although deep down, Tamanda knew that her husband was afraid of poverty. His poor background, which he rarely talked about, was a driving force in his quest for success. Most of her friends admired her and constantly commented what a stunning couple the two of them made.

She was also aware that after seven years of marriage and no child; some of those very same friends were talking behind her back that all was not well; she could not conceive. Why society was quick to point a finger at her was something she could not fathom; not that society was wrong. Tamanda was indeed infertile.

When she first discovered that she could not bear children, a year into their marriage, it had devastated her.

She remembers sobbing uncontrollably, soon after her Gynaecologist broke the news that she had Endometriosis. Tamanda, a doctor herself, knew what this entailed; her Gynaecologist didn't have to go into details. Her worry was Walter; would he understand? Would he leave her and seek a fertile woman, someone who could bear children for him. He always talked of how he wanted children to fill the many bedrooms of their mansion. He would often speak of how he envied her father; how he would love to have half the children his father-in-law had.

Sitting in her Gynaecologist's office, going through tissues to dry her tears, Tamanda was petrified of what was going to happen once she broke the news to her husband. Ironically, her infertility brought them fiercely closer. She had given him the bad news during dinner; averting her eyes, feeling guilty, her voice trembling. He paused, the silverware hovering over his plate, his unblinking eyes staring at her. He slowly set the fork down, then the knife, pushing the half full plate away from him; he stood up, took a few steps, until he was standing right behind her chair. He gently placed both hands on her shoulders, leaning over her ear;

"Everything will be alright sweetheart." Walter said softly, whilst rubbing her shoulder gently.

"I . . . I just feel as if . . ."

"Sweetheart, don't agonise over it, although it may be a good idea if this stays between us." He said, planting a kiss at the back of her neck.

"Oh! I love you Walter."

"I love you more sweetheart." He said gently pulling her up off her chair; he kissed her again, gently on the lips then carried her to bed, where they made passionate love.

In the early stages of their marriage, it used to hurt Nomsa seeing other couples having children, especially her own siblings. However, over time she got to terms with her condition; sometimes the two of them would joke how their house had seven master bedrooms. Childlessness stopped bothering her; after all she had young nieces and nephews to spoil, on top of a demanding career. Most importantly, she had a husband who loved her regardless, and she reciprocated those feelings tenfold.

Her husband was a nice man, always donating to good causes; renowned for generously funding some church and community programs, although, at times, such gestures were always a means to an end. Walter was very cunning, he viewed Christians as people who, one day will advance his political ambitions as voters or become customers to one of his many businesses.

"Doctor! Doctor Lumbadzi!" A familiar voice shouted from amidst the crowd of those welcoming their family members and friends, startling her from her daydreaming. It was the person she had caught staring at her. She turned around towards the source of the voice.

"Oh it's you Maxwell?" Tamanda quizzed with a slight hint of disappointment whilst trying to force a smile at their driver. She straightaway knew that Maxwell's presence was a tell-tale sign that her Walter hadn't come to welcome her.

"Yes madam, *Bwana* sent me to collect you; he had to go to the constituency for a meeting." Maxwell said with a smile, rushing in to help her with her pull-along suitcase.

"Thank you Maxwell." Tamanda smiled letting go of her suitcase.

She followed Maxwell outside the terminal to the sprawling car park. It was a nice cloudless bright day maybe just a tad hot; Tamanda noted as they zigzagged around other parked vehicles before coming to a stop behind an unfamiliar white Mercedes Benz.

She had only been gone for ten days, already Walter had bought another car; Tamanda observed, shaking her head in disapproval even though there was a smile on her face. Her husband would always have a discussion with her before buying himself a pair of shoes or a shirt. However, when it came to buying cars, he always made solo decisions and would often surprise her with his usual; "sweetheart, close your eyes, I want to show you something," remark.

"Walter, Walter, Walter." She murmured, barely audible for the driver to hear.

For some reason, her husband was a car fanatic; always obsessed with being the first to drive the latest thing on wheels in the country. She had lost count of how many expensive vehicles littered the parking lot outside their mansion.

Tamanda once commented jokingly that his obsession with cars was an extravagance which, with the ongoing economic quagmire and government austerity measures, might be perceived as unbecoming amidst the country's poverty. Walter didn't seem to mind though; simply telling her that he had worked hard for everything he owned.

She did not mind her husband's expensive hobby; he could afford it and she understood him. Nonetheless, she still felt uncomfortable, especially when friends or siblings came over for a visit. Tamanda and her siblings had been brought up in a family that shunned materialistic tendencies; as a result, her siblings tended to raise eyebrows at Walter's expensive acquisitions. They thought that he came across as someone who was trying too hard to prove a point that he had made it in life.

"I see that *Bwana* has bought another car for you Maxwell." Tamanda joked with the driver who was loading her luggage in the boot.

"This one just arrived last week madam, it drives like a dream." Maxwell said softly with a wide smile, his hand patting the open boot gently like it was living organism.

Tamanda shook her head, baffled that Maxwell had completely missed the underlying sarcasm in her remark. Men will always be boys; she mused, inhaling the familiar Malawi afternoon.

"I see, am sure it drives like a dream, isn't that what you said about the last . . ." Tamanda did not finish her sentence.

From the corner of her eye she noticed that Maxwell was trying to conceal something. She could tell that the driver was just as surprised as she was when silky female underwear fell out of a plastic bag which had been there before her luggage was loaded. His futile attempts to hide the pink lacy panties were halted by Tamanda's icy question.

"Maxwell, what are you doing?"

"I was going to . . . I . . . I don't know madam." Maxwell stammered, his hand frozen in the process of trying to conceal the female underwear.

"Who else has driven this car apart from you?" The warmth in her voice was replaced with ice.

"I think it was Samson, yes it was Samson, the other driver, madam." Maxwell stuttered, swallowing hard and avoiding eye contact with Tamanda.

"Samson? Is he the one who is assigned to the Toyota Prado?" Tamanda asked the driver in an interrogative voice.

Her eyes full of disgust at seeing the cheap looking skimpy pink underwear in her husband's car.

The two hour drive from Lilongwe's Kamuzu International airport to Dedza was devoid of music or any small talk. Maxwell avoided looking at the rear view mirror; he didn't want to make any eye contact with his madam. He kept his gaze firmly on the road in front of him, both hands firmly on the steering wheel.

Tamanda was preoccupied with the outside world; trees and electric poles which were zooming past. However her mind was somewhere else; she tried to focus on her parents' anniversary, except that she couldn't shake off the image of that underwear.

"Maxwell, the day Samson drove this car, do you know where he went?" Tamanda asked, watching Maxwell's reaction through the overhead mirror.

"To Salima madam, Samson went to the cottage in Salima." Maxwell responded slightly nervous; he sensed that she was observing him from the backseat and he shifted uncomfortably in the leather seat.

Tamanda noticed the driver's fingers gripping the steering wheel tighter than was necessary. She thought about to grilling him some more, but decided against the idea. She just had a long flight, on top of the marathon seminar, the never ending presentations and cocktail dinners; she was exhausted and saw no point in interrogating the driver on something which her husband could explain better.

"Just in case I fall asleep Maxwell, we are stopping at Dedza. I am visiting my parents." Tamanda said whilst reaching for the Daily Times newspaper she had just bought at the airport.

She looked at the front page headline; a smile cut across her serious face.

"*Walter Lumbadzi; Favourite to win Blantyre Urban Constituency.*"

~ CYBER MEETS REALITY ~

"THE MAJORITY OF Malawian politicians are technologically defunct." A friend, who had just returned from Europe, once told Walter.

"Most of them have never heard of Facebook; those who have, haven't got the aptitude or the knowhow to harness the power this social networking tool can deliver." His friend went on between sips of Carlsberg beer.

"Mmmh, is that so?" Walter remarked; prompting his friend to say more

"Yes, the argue that, the majority of Malawian voters do not care about Facebook, why then should they waste their time or energy interacting with people who will never even make their way to the polling station come voting day?" His friend said, downing the last contents of the green bottle.

"They do have a point, don't you think?" Walter responded in a manner he knew was going to provoke more from his friend.

Of course, he knew that there are a few politicians, whose names can be found on Facebook, despite the fact that they have no clue what they are doing. They post their photos, will keep on adding friends and won't even interact with those friends or supporters on their page.

"Theirs is a case of sitting in a powerful vehicle albeit not having a clue on how to get it started. The end result is that they are worse off than someone who is on foot." His friend had said whilst beckoning to the waiter for another bottle of Carlsberg.

That was three years ago, when Walter had this conversation with his friend; Facebook had not taken hold with the majority of Malawians.

In Walter's case, it was his wife who introduced him to Facebook. Because of her American exposure, Tamanda must have seen, from an early stage, the advantages of this social networking tool. She had propelled him to use the internet so as to take his business; *Lumbadzi Investments* to new frontiers. So, when he told Tamanda about his intentions of running for a political seat, she encouraged him to utilise the internet the same way he had done with his business.

"The internet phenomenon has, of late, shifted from being a predominantly instrument of commerce into the realm of politics." Tamanda said to him over breakfast a year after he had the Facebook conversation with his friend.

His wife went on to talk about how Barack Obama's victory was all down to the power of the internet; telling him to ignore those voices that say that Malawians are not technologically plugged in.

"It's not just Malawian voters you are trying to expose yourself to. There are people outside the country who would be willing to assist you in more ways than one, but they have to hear of you first. Market yourself sweetheart."

Tamanda was right, she was always right. Coupled with what his friend had told him; Walter approached the internet with a single objective, to harness its powers and sell himself to Malawians.

Within a month of launching his internet campaign, a group of Malawians in the diaspora, both UK and USA, came together. They contributed funds to purchase computers, laptops and printers for his cause which were then shipped to Malawi.

He assembled a team of tech savvy volunteers who he dispatched to canvass for him and also set up IT posts throughout Blantyre; equipped with at least one laptop, a printer and a mobile phone. With this new tactic, Walter's team managed to cover more ground than that of his well-known rival; the incumbent MP.

At these IT posts, people would come and liaise with his tech savvy volunteers on almost anything; from help with matters pertaining to funerals to transport for hospitals runs. Even those who wanted to contribute or offer assistance in distributing fliers flocked to these posts.

Walter's political machinery was getting real time feedback from his people and often responded accordingly. Even people who did not have access to the internet or didn't know how to use the internet were encouraged to visit these posts. They could interact with him through an intermediary; the person with the laptop. Ordinary people were able ask questions and he was responding to them straight away.

On some of his posts; laptops were connected to portable video projectors which would show movies interspaced with Walter's political campaign adverts. This was his cunning way of bypassing the state controlled radio and television station; both of which his political rival has access to.

All this was a bit chaotic at first and detractors were many. Nonetheless, the scheme took hold and Walter's name caught on like a bushfire.

There were one or two incidents in the early days of the scheme whereby two of his staff members manning a post were attacked; computers together with some peripherals were destroyed. The matter was reported to the police; nothing materialised. The following week two similar incidents happened; at one post, a laptop was smashed by hooded thugs and at another, a computer and a printer received identical treatment.

Walter decided that it was better to fight fire with fire; two days after the vandalism incident, a vehicle belonging to the incumbent MP was torched right outside his house. A message tied to a brick was thrown right through his living room window.

"Next time it will be your house."

From then on, attacks on his tech people or IT posts stopped.

Walter first met Nomsa on Facebook, soon after setting up a cyber-group for his political campaign. She was charming and witty, always commenting how all politicians were the same. He found himself interacting more with her. Despite not finishing his secondary school, it became obvious to him that Nomsa had not gone far with her education either. He picked this up by the way she constructed her sentences and the obvious grammatical errors. In a way she was like him; he thought to himself.

Nomsa was the opposite of his wife; Tamanda was blessed with academic intelligence. She was definitely not multilingual, not the person who would comfortably wade through Tamanda's biomedical world. Nomsa was not book smart, she was street smart.

It did not take Walter long to realise that growing up in a tough environment had moulded Nomsa into a very hard and resilient female.

Their increasing Facebook interaction eventually morphed from mere political chatter to intimate private chats.

"One of these days it would be nice to actually see you in person." He wrote to her, not sure why he wanted to turn cyber-friendship into something more; something tangible.

"I don't make it a habit of meeting with politicians . . . hahaha!" She responded.

"But you meet with men who are not politicians then?"

"Maybe if you weren't I would give it a thought."

"So if I told you that I am not a politician, you would have no qualms meeting me?"

"First of all; speak proper English, what do you mean by qualms . . . lol. Second; if you told me you were not a politician, even though you would be lying, yes I might agree to meet you."

"Even after I have told you that I am married? You would have no qualms with that?"

"There you go again with that 'qualms' word. Yes, even after you have told me that you are married, as long as you are not a politician, I would agree to meet you."

"That's interesting, me being married doesn't faze you but being a politician does."

"Hahaha, should it? Okay, you can bring your wife along. You can also bring Qualms with you so that I can meet all three of you . . . hahaha!" Nomsa had written back teasingly.

Two weeks after that interaction, Walter and Nomsa had their first face-to-face meeting. They had agreed their rendezvous to be at the secluded resort of Ku Chawe Inn, in the hills of Zomba.

The town of Zomba is the former capital city, before Lilongwe took over the mantle, which lies approximately 57 km from Blantyre. It took him forty minutes to drive from

Blantyre all the way to the town of Zomba, and another twenty minutes to drive up the meandering road to the exotic Ku Chawe Inn, a magnificent hotel perched on a plateau, six thousand feet, above the town of Zomba.

The scenery of overgrown green forest going up the winding narrow tarmacked road is one of the most breath-taking. However, Walter's mind was oblivious to all this; he was preoccupied with encounter ahead. During his slow ascent, common sense was urging him to stop the Range Rover, make a U-turn and head back to Blantyre; it was not too late to do what's right. His heart, on the other hand, was telling him the opposite.

The heart won.

Their meeting was meant to be a one-night stand, a fulfilment and manifestation of their steamy exchanges on Facebook; so Walter thought.

He had decided to get there twenty minutes early than their agreed time. For some reason he was nervous; he needed time to calm his frayed nerves.

Walter was by the bar, thankful that it was midweek and there was hardly anyone, except a few white patrons and the bar staff, who kept looking at him.

"I will have a Sprite with ice please." He said to the over joyous waiter.

With his recent announcement, that he was going to contest for a political office, his face was front page news. Perhaps his decision to come and meet Nomsa in the secluded mountain resort wasn't such a good idea; Walter thought as he calmly grabbed his glass and wandered outside, pretending to admire the scenic, lush greenery that cascaded from the peak of the mountain all the way down.

That's when he saw her; she was talking to a tall skinny man, probably a taxi driver, then she started strolling up the path from the parking lot. It had to be her, even if she hadn't told him that she was going to be dressed in a red dress and red high heels, he knew it was her. He was not sure whether to walk down the steps and meet her or stand there and observe.

Going down the steps and introducing himself was the manly thing to do and it was common sense; after all, he was the one who had initiated this meeting. He did not bulge; Walter was transfixed to his spot, awestruck by how beautiful she looked in reality. Cyber Nomsa was sexy; however the real Nomsa went beyond that term.

As soon as their eyes met, she flashed a warm smile; Walter took a moment; scrutinising her as subtly as he could. She appeared to be in her early twenties; he couldn't believe that throughout their Facebook interaction he hadn't asked her age. Perhaps he didn't want to invite a similar question from her; was he starting to be conscious of his age? No, he didn't ask her age because he was scared she might turn out to be too young. This would most likely thrust him into the realm of paedophilia.

Being married and doing what he was doing was problematic enough; however, doing it with a prepubescent girl came with consequences that would finish him off politically and socially. He shuddered at the mere thought alone. If she turned out to be way too young he would have had no choice but to terminate their relationship.

Looking at her now, he breathed a sigh of relief; certain she was in her mid-twenties. There is no way a sixteen year old would possess beautiful breasts of that magnitude; he mused, forcing himself to peel his eyes from her chest. He looked up at her smiling face.

"Walter?" She asked as she slowly walked up the steps to where he was standing; "or should I call you by your Facebook name, *Lumbadzi?*"

"It is my last name, however Walter will do." He answered; surprised that what he had planned to say to her the moment they meet had evaporated from his brain.

"I am Nomsa or you can call me by my facebook name; *Nomsa.*" She joked and could tell that he was a bit unnerved by her calmness.

"It is so nice to meet you Nomsa." He smiled, extending his hand.

"A handshake feels a bit awkward, wouldn't you say?" Nomsa smiled back, looking at his extended hand and not offering hers.

"Why? What do you mean?" He quickly dropped his hand, dipping it into his pocket on the pretext of searching for something.

"After all those steamy chats we had on facebook, I was expecting a hug." Nomsa purred, climbing the last step until she was on the same level with him.

"Oh, how silly of me . . . I was going to, but then I wasn't sure if . . ."

". . . If I would hug you back?" Nomsa finished the sentence for him, giggling.

"Yes." He said opening his arms; he wrapped them around her.

She felt soft and yet firm. Nomsa was warm and yet her touch gave him goose bumps throughout his body.

"Walter, I hug men all the time . . . but you, you are a bit tense, you don't do this often, do you?"

"No, I don't go around hugging men." He joked, thankful that his sense of humour had not evaporated together with his machismo.

That was as physical as it got on their first encounter. Instead of dashing off towards the room he had already booked, both of them were surprised with what happened next.

"Are you hungry?" He asked, not sure if that was the best opening.

"I was wondering when you were going to ask me that." Nomsa responded, with a smile; Walter was taken in by her openness and free-spiritedness. He found himself loosening up.

The two of them were busy talking they hardly noticed the waiter standing on the side, until he politely announced his presence by coughing slightly.

He ordered whilst looking at the menu with the seriousness of a seasoned dinner; picking the most sophisticated sounding dishes, for starters, main and dessert. Taking a deep breath, Walter looked up at the waiter and then at Nomsa, giving her cue to order whatever she felt like eating.

"I will have *nsima* with *chambo*." Nomsa said with simplicity; "and a glass of wine, white please."

Walter raised an eyebrow; he had expected her to order something sophisticated, something foreign. Her choice of Malawi's staple food and fish intrigued him, there is no way he would ever be seen in a public place, a restaurant, ordering what she had just ordered; a meal of *nsima* and fish was synonymous with poverty, his past. He wanted to ask why she had ordered such bland food; he decided against such a question.

He chose to talk about something different while waiting for their food. At first it was just small talk, with lots of laughter, jokes and more laughter. He could not believe that he actually lost track of time just sitting there listening to her talk. They talked through their meal and their waiter came to remove their plates, not that he remembered seeing him.

"Do you know what?" Nomsa said, leaning across the table looking him in the eye.

"What is it?" Walter responded, enjoying the closeness of their faces.

"I have been here so many times, funny enough I have never trekked outside the immediate compound."

"You mean like what the white tourists do, trekking around the forest, up and down the slopes?"

"Yes, let's give it a try. We don't have to go far." She said; sounding excited, her giggles sent goose bumps all over his skin, he was thankful that he had on a long sleeved shirt.

"Are you sure about that?" He quizzed, looking underneath the table at Nomsa's high heel shoes.

"Don't worry, I will take them off," she laughed; "It won't be the first time I have walked barefoot."

"Walked barefoot in a forest full of twigs and thorns?" He could not hide his amusement.

"Come on," Nomsa said getting up; "if my feet start bleeding from stepping on thorns, you will carry me won't you?"

"What?" Walter laughed, getting up from his chair. He couldn't believe how relaxed she was with him. Yes, they had interacted countless times over the internet; however, this was their first meeting and surely he hadn't expected her to be this free. He liked what he saw.

With both shoes in her hands, the two of them slowly walked in tandem with Nomsa in front, negotiating the narrow footpaths of Zomba Mountain.

"You could at least pretend to be a gentleman and carry my shoes." She said jokingly, turning around to look at him.

She caught him looking at her behind, and giggled at his futile attempt to look the other way. He quickly recovered, started smiling and reached for her shoes despite her protests that she was only joking.

She had an amazing sense of humour, but the more she talked about her past, a picture of a tough woman started to emerge in Walter's mind. If he thought his past was rough, hers sounded gruesome and unforgiving. Only a mentally strong female would have survived such a childhood with her sense of humour intact.

They were strolling purposefully slow, not going anywhere in particular and not wanting to get there, even though they had no idea where they were heading. She occasionally turned back to look at him; Walter noticed that she was trying hard to mask her pain with a smile. Her past, just like his, caused her pain; unlike him, she was not ashamed to talk about it. He had buried his past deep inside and did not like bringing it up.

After an hour of walking they chose a spot, a large greyish boulder which was sticking out of the green earth like an oversized wart, overlooking the town of Zomba below. They climbed on it; he went first and once on top, extended his hand, grabbing her small fingers. He heaved; pulling her up until they were both perched on its edge; their feet dangling on the side, much to the amusement of a few European tourists passing by, below. They waved up at them and Nomsa waved back.

He noticed that she looked happy; there was a free spiritedness about her. As soon as the tourists disappeared into the thick foliage, Nomsa turned to face him and carried on talking.

Two weeks after their first meeting, Walter and Nomsa decided to meet again.

"You still want to see me after I made you carry my shoes?" Nomsa joked over the phone.

"Yes, it's payback time; I want you to carry mine this time." Walter said softly.

He was sitting on the edge of his bed; his mobile phone on speaker mode on top of the bed, the portrait of his wife was flipped over flat on the bedside table. He couldn't bare her eyes looking at him while he was talking to Nomsa.

The following weekend the two of them drove in his Lexus, 15 km out of Blantyre, halfway down the slopes of the winding Chikwawa Escarpment Road. He found a secluded spot to park; a clearing along the edge of a cliff overlooking the scenic flood plains below.

"You enjoy looking at life from high above, don't you?" Nomsa asked as the two of them got out of the car.

"What do you mean?" He asked going round to meet her.

"You have a thing with heights." She said with a smile.

"Heights?" Walter laughed.

"Yes. First it was your choice of Zomba Mountain where we first met, and now here." She said gesturing to the breath-taking views of the meandering Shire River and the open valley which stretched as far as the eye could see; "it's almost like you want to be god."

"Maybe I try to make up for the things I missed out on during my childhood." He said without looking at her.

"By visiting places where you can view the world from a perched vantage point?" She said with a smile.

"No, that's not it." Walter shook his head, looking down as if trying to compose his next sentence.

"Sorry, then I don't follow." Nomsa frowned, turning around to look at him.

"My childhood . . . it . . . ahh . . . was a painful time, I was confined and . . . and . . ." Walter started, struggling for words, surprised that he wanted so much to open up to this woman.

She had told him so much about herself, it felt like they literally grew up next door to each other and shared the same suffering. The heavy lid that, for years, had covered the dark pit of his past was slowly opening up. He had forgotten how gloomy it was down there; things of nightmares and gruesome memories still existed on the other side of this heavy lid. He shut his eyes, not wanting to go on.

"You don't have to talk about it if you don't want to, Walter." She said gently.

"It's ok, I can manage." He said, opening his eyes slowly, letting the beautiful panoramic view in front dilute some of the images of his past; his bare buttocks being repeatedly lashed by a wooden stick.

Memories of cold nights spent on a cold floor; his father's way of punishing him for wetting his blanket the previous night. Excruciating stomach aches at school due to not having eaten breakfast or supper, another form of punishment by his constantly angry father. Then there were memories of his mother whimpering in the corner, trying not to cry in front of him, after sustaining cuts to her face from severe beatings by his angry father because he caught her trying to sneak in some food to him.

Walter found himself narrating his childhood to Nomsa, opening up to this woman who he had just met. He was eagerly digging up events he thought he had long cremated, some of which he hadn't even disclosed to his own wife; she wouldn't have understood. How could she? Things like these didn't happen in her world, Tamanda grew up in a world where parents didn't punish their children by punching them in the face with clenched fists. Nomsa, on the other hand, understood this world; like him she had once lived and suffered in such a world.

They stood there; two souls with identical pasts, talking and listening to each other as the sun slowly set in the distant mountains. The glow it cast over the valley below is what Walter was feeling inside; a strange glow, a different one.

It became obvious to him earlier on that Nomsa had built a high fortress around her heart to prevent her feelings being trampled on by men. Men had, for as long as she could remember, taken advantage of her body. That was as far as she would let them come; they used her as much as she used them. However, standing here, leaning against the bonnet of his car, listening to her; Walter started noticing that beyond that tough façade was a very fragile woman, someone who had endured things that would break an ox.

"We have been seeing each other for over a week now and yet it feels like I have known you longer." Nomsa went on, her voice pained.

She was stealing glances at him, her long eyelashes fluttering; she was shy. The realisation hit Walter, causing his lips to tremble slightly as he tried to suppress a smile. She was no longer the bubbly Nomsa or the strong Nomsa of the internet.

She kept on talking, confiding in him how she had been abused physically and emotionally by men. Her own uncle was the first man to abuse her; she had just turned thirteen then. The abuse from other men followed in form of rape, neglect and beatings; resulting in painful abortions, not once but three times. The fourth one she was told that if she went ahead with it, chances that she was going to make it alive were nonexistent. That's when Prince was born.

Nomsa's voice was soft and melodic, like that of someone recounting a folktale; in a way, she was trying to feel him and see if he was not like those men. She had a way of saying things that sounded poetic and it was causing him to like her more. She even confessed how illegal drugs had become her only source of refuge; drugs which triggered hallucinations, hallucinations that served as a form of escape from the cruel reality.

Walter listened as she tried to disguise the pain she felt by reliving her childhood all the way to adolescence. He watched the way her beautiful lips were moving; trembling as she spoke, he found himself nodding, smiling and at times getting angry with those who had abused her. She had been explicitly honest with him, something which surprised and shocked him.

"I don't know why I am telling you all this Walter." She said whilst sniffling; he noticed the tears coming down her cheeks.

The sight of the clear reddish skies, the exquisite view below and her crying culminated into something that was tugging at his heart. He found himself reaching over, gently wiping them off with his thumb.

"It's okay Nomsa . . . it is okay for you to cry." He said, almost stuttering as she reached for his hand which was still on her damp cheek, her fingers running along its length. He felt the tickling sensation of her long well-manicured nails spread throughout his entire hand to the rest of his body.

"I am sorry Walter . . . I . . . I didn't mean to offload so much on you. It's just that I have never shared my past with anyone." Nomsa said as she finally broke down, her sobs echoing against the cliff behind them.

"That makes two us Nomsa." He whispered, stepping around, pulling her closer to him into what was to be their second hug.

This one had warmth and something extra, he could feel her heart beat as she buried her head into his chest. Her tears seeped right through his shirt, they felt warm, they felt like some glue binding him to her.

~ BICYCLE & THRILLS ~

WALTER LOOKED AT his phone. There was disbelief etched all over his face; he had actually sent pictures of himself wearing nothing but tight fitting swimming Speedos. Since he got married to Tamanda, seven years ago, he has never sent his wife anything like what he had just sent to Nomsa.

There was nothing wrong posing in Speedos; it's not like he had sent nude pictures of himself. However, as much as Walter tried to convince himself otherwise, he knew that anyone seeing this picture would deem it inappropriate. It was provocative and suggestive.

What was happening to him; he wondered, feeling giddy and excited. The adrenalin gushing through his system was surreal, almost like the time he took his father's bicycle without his permission.

He was twelve years old and had only ridden at the rear of the bicycle, on the thick iron carrier, holding on to his father's waist. Sometimes when the elderly Lumbadzi got tired of pedalling, especially while negotiating the hilly roads of Blantyre, he would often commandeer his son to push the bicycle. Walter often looked forward to these moments; the only time his hands would hold the handlebars, his small frame heaving the cumbersome bicycle; always with a wide grin on his face.

It was during these moments that he would often ask his ever frowning and serious father for permission to ring the bicycle's big bell. Rarely would he allow him, on few occasions, especially when he was slightly drunk, permission would be granted; an excited Walter would ring the bell until he was told to stop. The command for him to cease toying with the bicycle's loud bell would often be delivered in his father's trademark yell.

"*Basi!*" His father's voice would crack like a horsewhip behind him.

It was enough to freeze Walter's playfulness; he knew that failure to do so would most likely result in serious consequences, either right by the roadside or the minute they arrived home.

Ringing the loud bell was as far as he got with the bicycle. When it came to riding it; his father had stressed to him that such an endeavour will only happen when he turned fifteen. However, as luck had it, one day his father had gone out of town.

"Behave yourself Walter!" His father had said in his usual threatening tone, just before he left.

He then bade farewell to his wife; it was more like informing his timid mother that he was going to his home village. It was one of his usual bogus trips to the village, often undertaken either on payday or the day after he got paid. Walter stood by the living room window, watching his father walk over to the bus stage. He held his breath until he saw his father's imposing frame get on a minibus. Even at twelve, he was old enough to know that his father was going on a drinking spree which would culminate in him spending the rest of the weekend with one of his many girlfriends.

He could not understand why his mother didn't protest, it was obvious she knew that her husband was lying, surely the stories going round about him impregnating other women must have gotten to her. However, his mother would politely bid her husband goodbye.

The minute the minibus carrying his father disappeared around the bend, his mother also left the house; she told him she was going to get her hair plaited at a friend's house on the other side of Ndirande.

Walter was left alone at home. The big black bicycle was perched against the wall of their dilapidated house, unchained; it was beckoning him to ride it.

"Wait until you are fifteen Walter!" His father's booming voice echoed at the back of his mind, he felt his presence even though he was alone.

A cold chill crawled up his spine, goose bumps spreading all over his skin at the mere thought of what he was contemplating on doing. He swallowed hard, trying to garner sufficient courage whilst suppressing the uncontrollable shaking of his limbs; a mixture of excitement and fear.

"When I'm fifteen? That's like three years away." Walter muttered.

His eyes were still fixated on the bicycle; the temptation was overwhelming and after much agonising he caved in. The shakes had subsided; it's not like he was going to go far with it, was he? He rationalised inside his adolescent mind.

After a few wobbles and near falls, he was surprised how natural riding came to him. Years riding behind, on the metal carrier, holding on to his father had extinguished the anxiety of being on a bike. Before long, he was able to venture beyond the small clearing in front of their house. The thrill of riding the big bicycle; the feel of the hard pedals against his bare feet and the scintillating cold breeze blowing against his face was surreal, nonetheless short-lived.

Two days later his father returned; broke, tired and angry. He was in a state which always culminated into physical violence, with his mother at the receiving end. Most of the times it was for frivolous reasons like there was not enough salt in the food, or the house didn't look clean. However, this day there was a slight change to the norm.

Walter saw his father coming down the road, towards their house. His mother, who had also seen her husband marching towards the house, was busy trying to fix the house. She was hastily putting things in the right places, then dashed to the kitchen to sample the cooked beans; making sure that the salt content was right, not to warrant a beating.

From the living room window he watched as his father stopped by the house, just before theirs. He was talking to their annoying neighbour; a big breasted woman who was known along this street and beyond as the neighbourhood BBC. Even though he was only aged twelve, he knew exactly what Lady BBC was narrating to his father, especially when he saw her making bicycle gestures with her big fat arms.

Then he watched in horror as his father stormed towards the house; Walter felt the dampness around his khakhi shorts as his bladder contracted in terror. He was so petrified, frozen to the spot, to even run to into the sanctuary of his small room.

The wooden front door swung open violently; he stood transfixed in a puddle of his own urine, staring at his father who looked like he hadn't shaved since the day he left.

"You filthy little bastard!" His father yelled, lunging at him.

The punishment that followed was longer than the bicycle thrill Walter had experienced. For four consecutive evenings, his father made him drop his shorts, barking at him to kneel on the hard floor of their tiny veranda which had purposely been sprinkled with dry grains of sand.

"You stupid, ungrateful little boy! Get down on your knees!" He yelled whilst severely spanking him with a wooden stick dipped in water.

The pain emanating from the sand against his knees and tender buttocks resonated up his spine before exploding inside his head like cacophony of fireworks. He only cried on that first day of punishment.

The following three days Walter simply knelt down on the sandy floor, occasionally tilting his head, looking at his father as he repeatedly swung the wet wooden stick. He did not let out a single sob. He simply winced every time the stick landed on his tender flesh with a cracking sound.

Walter wiggled in his plush leather chair, painful memories of those lashings danced inside his head; he could actually feel the tingling sensations down his buttocks. It was all in the past now, he had long forgiven his father's unnecessary brutality. What he had not forgotten was the thrill of that exhilarating ten minute ride on his father's big bicycle; the joy of seeing the faces of the little girls, who used to sell cooked maize on the side of the road, as he rode past them. He smiled as he remembered how the envious kids had chanted his name as he zoomed up and down the street, attempting to ride hands-free, almost falling off the big bicycle.

His eyes roved around his office, his brain filled with nostalgic thoughts of that particular sunny day; those were perhaps the best ten minutes of his life, an exciting ride which still lived with him to this very day. It was the thrill worth the spanking; Walter thought—the smile on his face widening—until he found himself laughing all alone.

Sending nude pictures of himself in Speedos to Nomsa's phone, somehow, accorded him the same thrill he got from that bicycle ride. It had that added element of danger; something exceeding the prospect his father's wooden stick making contact against his bare buttocks.

There was something about Nomsa that he couldn't shake off, from his system. The moment he sent the photos, his heart started beating frantically like an animal trapped inside his chest was trying to escape. His adrenalin was bubbling over the brim; just like he was back on his father's bicycle. It soon dawned on him that this is how he felt every time he was with Nomsa.

"Why do I care so much about you?" Walter's inner thoughts somehow managed to escape through his parted lips; he jumped from his seat, surprised he had spoken his mind out loud.

He looked around his expanse office, trying to make sure that he was alone and that no one overheard him. He felt like a young, mischievous boy. Nomsa had a chequered past and yet he found himself fiercely drawn to her, despite the fact that he loved his wife.

The sudden thoughts of his wife made him snap out of his trance.

"Tamanda!" Walter yelled his wife's, his eyes blinking profusely.

He looked at his expensive wristwatch, relieved that he still had ample time to drive to Lilongwe and welcome her wife at the airport. Then there was the impromptu meeting with his friend Graham, the British High Commissioner to Malawi.

Blantyre to Lilongwe is a gruelling 300km journey; he would have liked if she had connected with a flight coming to Blantyre. However, today was her parent's anniversary and she had to stop by at her parents' in Dedza. Walter knew that the whole family was going to be there; his father-in-law, his mother-in-law, all seven of Tamanda's siblings, most likely accompanied by their spouses and children, so too cousins and friends of the family.

They did this every year and Tamanda always made sure that she arrived there with her husband in tow.

The wedding anniversary of Tamanda's parents has always been a big family event. The first time Walter attended one, soon after marrying Tamanda, he was impressed at how close his in-laws were. It was something he never experienced and he began to understand what his wife had told him; that apart from Christmas, this was the biggest date on the family's calendar. It was and has always been a day of festivities of sorts; parents, children and grandchildren coming together as a unit.

However, three years ago, his retired father-in-law; Judge Mathews Sambani had been diagnosed with mild dementia and the wedding anniversary vibrant atmosphere has somehow been affected. Although Tamanda had long come to terms with her father's medical condition, Walter always wept inside every time he was in the company of the once fierce judge. He had come to regard his father-in-law as his own biological father; he was well aware of how his disease affected the whole family especially his wife. Lately Chief Justice Sambani was having problems differentiating his own daughter, Tamanda, from Mkiche, his wife. Because this was only happening with Tamanda and not with her two elder sisters; Flocy and Deliwe, it was affecting her more. She would break down every time her father addressed his wife, and vice versa. Sometimes he would playfully spank Tamanda on her buttocks thinking that he is being romantic to his wife. It was soul wrenching to watch; Walter knew that he had to accompany his wife to the anniversary, to be beside her.

She always needed some comforting after meeting her father; she would act brave right before meeting her parents and hold a straight face while with them. However, as soon as they were alone, walking around the sprawling fields at the back of the mansion, Tamanda would break down in tears, crying uncontrollably to the point of startling the herd of cattle grazing in the fields. He had a feeling that today it was going to be the same; he had no choice but to be there, offering her a shoulder to cry on.

He opened the top drawer of his expanse office desk, scooping up a set of car keys; the Toyota Land Cruiser VX was going to be his choice of transport to Lilongwe, then Dedza after that. It would cope with the long stretch of dirt road to his in-law's farm at their village. It wasn't a bad stretch; it's just that a small car with low suspension couldn't go as fast as a four wheel drive.

Since he married Tamanda, Dedza had become a second home for them. His father-in-law was a man of great vision; he had built such a big house in the village when he was still living in town, before his forced retirement. It was purposefully built to accommodate his large family; children and grandchildren alike; a house so big, it looked obnoxious and out of place surrounded by small village houses. However, it served its purpose; the first time Walter visited, he could not believe the amount of human beings the structure was able to swallow.

Walter envied his father-in-law and mother-in-law's relationship; it was something he constantly commented to his wife, falling short of saying; "how I wish my parents were like yours."

Walter had done well for himself, financially; yet every time he was in the presence of his in-laws, he still felt like the poor boy from Ndirande. His brothers-in-law; Kondwani, Brandon and Zachariah would always congratulate him every time he bought a new car, however he always felt that these congratulations sounded hollow; they didn't seem to be impressed with his material success. Only, Mathews Jnr, the last born was the one capable of showing genuine admiration, whereas Elijah, the eldest, never commented on Walter's expensive habit. It always happened that, as the others were busy admiring his new acquisition, Elijah, on the other hand, wouldn't even turn around to acknowledge his presence.

Walter swivelled back facing his desk; smiling at the thought of his eldest brother-in-law. He switched off his computer; reaching for the office phone.

"Hendrina!" He pressed a button on the phone's keypad, speaking in a flat voice.

"Yes sir?" Hendrina responded in a soft voice, smiling even though her boss couldn't see her.

"Tell Samson to come in here." He ordered her before dropping the handset back in its cradle.

He needed the driver to take the car to the filling station. Walter had to go over to the constituency before leaving for Lilongwe. Juggling politics and marriage was becoming second nature. The fact that the anniversary was taking place during the week didn't bother him. He was simply astounded that the Sambani's were that well respected, people were willing to flock to Dedza on a weekday to celebrate with them.

He would then leave for Lilongwe soon after visiting the site where he had been constructing a communal borehole, with his own money. They were unveiling it today; he had planned a brief visit, stand in the periphery of the crowd, just showing his face for ten minutes or so. He was not an MP yet and he did not want to be seen as overplaying his hand.

"People love modesty." Tamanda had once told him.

The place was in a very bad location as far as the logistics of getting there. Walter had chosen to sink a borehole in such a place on purpose; it was a calculated move. He made sure he whispered to the right people, promising them that he was going to construct a road, all the way to the borehole, once elected MP. The whispers had quickly made headlines and one of his newspapers, a subsidiary of *Lumbadzi Investments*, splashed the story on the front page for five consecutive days.

For now, the rugged Toyota four-wheel drive was ideal to take him there; from there he would have to drive straight to Lilongwe. There would be no time to go home afterwards. Last time he drove the car, there was hardly any fuel; he figured Samson would have to fill it up while he was ripping his accountants apart about the discrepancy on the abhorrent budget figures he had just seen.

"Sir, Samson is here." Hendrina's gentle voice crackled out of the office phone.

"That was quick." Walter mumbled, more to himself than to his secretary.

"Pardon sir?" Hendrina's asked with eagerness; her boss had already cut off the line.

For months now there have been acute fuel shortages throughout the country. However, the joys of owning a few filling stations and running his own fleet of tankers meant that he didn't have the same fuel problems other motorists were facing. He knew that there would be long queues at the filling station; it would be detrimental if he arrived there and jumped the queue. That would make him appear pompous and out of touch with the very same people who would, soon, be voting for him come election time. Yes it was his filling station; however it was better to send the driver.

He unlocked the bottom drawer where he kept petty cash and was about to reach inside when his mobile phone started ringing. He shut the drawer and reached for his mobile phone, frowning at the caller ID before answering.

"What now?" He grumbled because the number did not look familiar, it was a land line.

If this had been the days before he jumped into the political fray, Walter was certain that he would not have answered an unknown number. Not so the case anymore, nowadays a lot of well-wishers were calling him; to offer assistance, pledge their votes to him or simply to get to know him. The newspapers had already started speculating how Walter Lumbadzi was the future; the person likely to hold the highest office in the land.

The insinuation that one day there would be a President Lumbadzi always ignited a smile across his face. Maybe he would be able to stand tall amongst his in-laws, especially Elijah Sambani.

"Hello, this is Walter Lumbadzi." He answered politely into his mobile phone.

"Hello, Mr Lumbadzi?" An unfamiliar voice quizzed in response.

"Yes, this is Walter . . . may I know who is speaking?" He said calmly, trying to suppress his agitation that someone was asking if he was Walter Lumbadzi after he had just introduced himself.

"Oh! I am calling from Queen Elizabeth Hospital. We have a woman by the name of Nomsa Salala in critical condition. She says you are her next of kin." The female voice answered back in a calm voice.

"Hospital? What happened, is she ok?" He stuttered, a thousand pictures crisscrossing his mind, his strong hand squeezing the razor thin mobile phone.

"Sir, if you can, it would be best if you came to the hospital please." The woman said sounding calm and professional.

Walter immediately got up, calculating whether to rush to the hospital or start getting ready for the Lilongwe trip. He looked at his wristwatch, cursing at the awkwardness of the timing, there is no way he could accomplish both. Something had to give.

"I am on my way!" He yelled into the phone grabbing his jacket off the hook, bolting out of his office, startling Hendrina who was talking to Samson.

"Hendrina, call Maxwell, tell him to start off for Lilongwe. He needs to go and pick up madam at the airport. The keys to the white Benz are in the right drawer of my desk. Tell him to leave now!" Walter shouted, unnecessarily causing Hendrina to flinch and recoil in surprise.

"Yes Sir." Hendrina replied, her fingers fumbling with the keyboard to try and hide the solitaire screen she had been playing.

"Hendrina, I said now!" He yelled angrily after noticing his secretary's futile attempts to disguise what she had been doing.

"Yes Sir." The secretary responded, a slight tremor in her voice as her very long eyelashes fluttered with each blink.

"Samson, get the pickup and go to Limbe. You need to collect four bales of T-shirts at Tarmahomed Textiles." He yelled commands at the driver who was standing, frozen stiff like a statue.

"Yes Sir." Samson answered.

Walter was already barrelling down the stairs to hear him; walking with long strides, once outside, towards the parking lot. He pressed the small handheld immobiliser, unlocking his car, tossing his jacket on the passenger seat before speeding out of the office parking. The guards at the gate saluted as the Range Rover shot past them; Walter did not reciprocate the gesture. His mind was preoccupied with what could be wrong with Nomsa.

~ OBSESSIONS ~

Twenty-seven year old Hendrina Munthali opened the side drawer of her desk where she kept her mascara and makeup kit. She did not mind Samson, who was sitting on the other side of her desk waiting for Mr Lumbadzi; she struggled not to laugh at how nervous he looked. He was scared meeting the boss, but then so were most people.

Hendrina was the opposite; the prospect of meeting her boss always gave her a rash of excitement. She never got tired of hearing his voice in person or on the intercom. Whereas a lot of employees made sure to hide as soon as Mr Lumbadzi car pulled up the parking lot; Hendrina always looked forward to greeting him.

On the third floor; access to his office was via hers, and every morning she would ritualistically stand by the adjoining door, holding it open for him; inhaling the fresh clean aquatic whiff of his cologne as he walked past her. His expensive scent always did things to her she couldn't explain. A while back, she had been standing so close and his elbow brushed against her; Hendrina worked with a smile on her face the whole of that day.

With the pencil-like applicator she enhanced her long eyelashes; looking defiantly at the driver who uncomfortably looked away. Hendrina shoved the applicator back in the drawer. She grabbed the red lipstick pen and quickly applied some in modesty, then shoved the kit back into the drawer.

Hendrina stood up and tiptoed to the full-length mirror between the door and the filing cabinet. She could feel the driver's eyes boring into her; she wasn't bothered. She glanced at herself and was happy with what she saw; red high heel shoes matching her red blouse, red earrings, red butterfly brooch and her just-applied red lipstick. Everything contrasted well with her ivory white suit. The whiteness of her outfit extended to what she was wearing underneath the suit; she always wore her underwear with thoughts of her boss permeating her mind.

Satisfied with the conversation she just had with the mirror, Hendrina tiptoed back to her desk, making sure that the long sharp heels did not make too much noise against the floor. She knew that her boss would be coming out of his office anytime soon; she always liked looking her best whenever he was around. He never seemed to take any notice of her, nonetheless, Hendrina made it a habit to always dress smart.

Once, her boss made a compliment the day she wore a black suit with matching black high heels and a white blouse. Although he had complimented her in passing, the gesture had meant a lot to Hendrina. Eighteen months had passed, yet she vividly remembers the day; it was on a Thursday afternoon, just after lunch and it had been raining.

This particular Thursday was the same day her boss had an important meeting with a man by the name of Michael Chiluba Lata; Hendrina had spoken to him on several occasions before she met him on this day. Every time Mr Lata called for Mr Lumbadzi, Hendrina answered him with utmost reverence; she remembered Mr Lumbadzi's strict instructions.

"It doesn't matter whether I'm locked in a meeting!" He had said in a raised voice.

Since that day, every time Mr Lata called, she connected him straightaway. The fact that the man was in her office, on this particular Thursday, was enough to make Hendrina jump; she stopped what she was doing straightway.

"Right this way sir, Mr Lumbadzi is waiting for you." She said ushering him in.

For months, her boss and Mr Lata had exchanged countless phone calls; some of them were brief while others were lengthy. Hendrina had a feeling that the calls weren't entirely business, judging by the laughter coming from her boss's office, it was easy to assume that the two men were friends.

It wasn't until a week later, that Hendrina learnt that this man who had been calling from outside the country, the man she had ushered into her boss's office, was actually a prominent politician in Zambia; a leader of that country's biggest opposition party. It did not take Hendrina long to figure out what was going on between her boss and the Zambian politician.

He needed to print some campaign material; newsletters, fliers and posters. However, the government of Zambia would not let Mr Lata's political party to use any Zambian registered printing press for what they deemed to be propaganda material, spreading anti-regime rumours.

Hendrina was not sure how Mr Lata had heard that her boss owned a printing company; she was well aware of the massive order which had gone past her desk. It was addressed to the attention of the Chief Executive Officer of Lumbadzi Printers, one of *Lumbadzi Investments'* subsidiaries. It was an order well over US$900,000. Usually matters relating to Lumbadzi Printers were handled by Mr Mkorongo, the manager; Hendrina thought it odd that this one was handled by Mr Lumbadzi himself.

The day Mr Lumbadzi complimented her on the outfit, was the same day Mr Lata came to the office. It was her first time seeing the grey haired politician. She had debated whether to tell him to extinguish his cigarette before entering her boss's office, but decided against it. Mr Lumbadzi had told her beforehand that someone important was coming, the last thing she wanted to do was to agitate her boss's prominent visitor.

"Hendrina, once Mr Lata gets here, don't make him wait. Make sure he is ushered straight into my office." He had said with urgency in his voice, standing so close to her as she held the door open for him.

"Yes sir." She answered with a smile, the cologne and the closeness tickling her senses.

"You look professional and lovely Hendrina. I wish all the ladies here had your fashion sense." Walter had said to her, pausing as if inspecting her, then walked into his office.

Hendrina will never forget that day. Her boss must have paused for less than five seconds; that was enough. To her, those were precious seconds; for the first time her boss had looked at her as a woman, not as his employee.

Hendrina liked her boss, from the day she started working for *Lumbadzi Investments*, she always had a soft spot for him. She would always get fidgety when Mr Lumbadzi walked into the accounts department where she was the secretary to two of the company accountants. She envied Mrs Ndalama, the woman who used to be his secretary, and would often ask the older woman how it was like to be Mr Lumbadzi's personal secretary.

When Mrs Ndalama resigned, after her husband had found a job in South Africa, Hendrina couldn't believe it when the older lady told her that she had recommended her to the boss. The day she started working as Mr Lumbadzi's secretary was the day Hendrina realised that her wardrobe was not adequate for the new post. The following month end, she splashed a bigger chunk of her salary on clothes and not once did Mr Lumbadzi acknowledge her, until that day Mr Lata came to the office.

Hendrina was dedicated to her work. She did things to impress her boss, despite the fact that she was the most highly paid secretary, her salary did not bring her the same satisfaction she got when Mr Lumbadzi appreciated her efforts with a simple 'thank you.' He rarely made eye contact with her, which was just as well, because if he did, he might have noticed that she had a crush on him. Hendrina was so obsessed with her boss and she started using him as a yardstick for measuring how a man should be like. The first victim to fall short of this yardstick was her boyfriend Hetherwick.

Hetherwick was everything which Mr Lumbadzi was not; he looked older than his age; sadly, he was not serious about life and she found him to be too playful. He was too short, even shorter when she had her high heels on and had issues in the grooming department. Hetherwick always dressed casual seven days a week and used cheap deodorant, which often made her sneeze. He was not ambitious, he did not have a quarter of the money her boss had and most of all; he did not make her heart skip a beat every time he got near her.

One Sunday evening, while laying out—on her bed—what she was going to wear to work the following day, Hendrina looked at Hetherwick, who had come to visit her; he was lounging comfortably on her sofa with his shoes still on. He looked lazy and slouchy, the opposite of her boss, who was always upright, his shoulders straight and busy; Hendrina snapped.

"Hetherwick, I don't know how to put this in a nice way, I think we should stop seeing each other." She said without even looking at him.

"Excuse me? Where is all this coming from, darling?" Hetherwick was shocked, not by the words but by the tone in which those words had been delivered.

"I don't feel anything for you, Hetherwick. There is no point in dragging something if it makes us feel hollow inside."

"How . . . I mean what has changed, Hendrina?"

"I think I have, I have changed, Hetherwick. I have moved on."

"Hendrina, come on, you know I can change together with you, we can move on together babe."

"No Hetherwick, you are a nice guy and all, it's just that I need a man; a real man."

That was over a year ago, and Hendrina had not had a boyfriend ever since. She did not even look at any man with the same desire she showed for her boss; Walter Lumbadzi. Despite the fact that he never paid her much attention and that he was a happily married man, or that she could lose her job if the things swirling inside her mind became public; Hendrina still clung on to the slim hope that maybe one day he would acknowledge her as a woman.

The door to her boss's office flew open, startling her, it was Mr Lumbadzi, standing there looking agitated.

"Yes sir?" She said, a smile forming instinctively across her face. She could never get enough of her boss's handsome features; whether smiling or serious, he always looked stunning.

"Hendrina, call Maxwell, tell him to start off for Lilongwe. He needs to go and pick up madam at the airport. The keys to the white Benz are in the right drawer of my desk. Tell him to leave now!" Walter shouted, unnecessarily causing Hendrina to flinch and recoil in surprise, the smile on her face slowly fading.

She wondered what that was all about. Hendrina had expected her boss to leave his office any time to go pick up his wife at the airport. However, the sudden change of plans and tone of voice; all seemed a bit odd.

He had sounded fine earlier on, especially when his sample T-shirt had arrived; Hendrina mused. Then panic set in when she noticed that the computer screen was still showing the solitaire game she had been playing before Samson came in, before she had started applying her makeup. She fumbled with the mouse in a futile attempt to try and change the screen before he saw it; too late.

He yelled angrily at her before marching out.

Left alone, she sat there wondering if Walter had even noticed her prepped up eyelashes and glistening lips. She swivelled round on her office chair, getting up to look down at the parking lot, through the venetian blinds of her office window.

Her heart was beating fast, not from the angry rebuke she had just gotten, but from merely watching her boss as he walked towards the car park. She wondered which one of his four cars parked outside he was going to jump into.

Hendrina smiled as Walter jumped into his Range Rover; watching him reversing before speeding towards the gate. The guards had already opened it for him and were standing at attention; she liked the power he had over other men, from guards to important people.

She slowly sat down wondering how it would feel like to sit right next to Walter in his car; a man who was so sure of his destiny. Thinking of her boss on first name basis almost made her laugh; she mentioned his first name out loud, only when she was in the privacy of her own bedroom. Some nights she would be talking to an imaginary Walter, asking him what she should wear before going to bed. Hendrina didn't know whether she was losing her mind; could she be that much in love with her boss that she was now talking to him when he wasn't even in her bedroom?

The sound of her phone ringing brought her back to reality; she sat back down and reached for the phone. Maybe it was him calling her back to apologise for snapping at her; maybe he wanted to make up by inviting her for dinner at his mansion.

"Good morning. Mr Lumbadzi's office, Hendrina speaking." She answered; her mind still in fantasy land, she didn't even hear the faint beep, indicating that this was an international call.

"Hello. This is the State House secretary, calling on behalf of President Lata. Is Mr Lumbadzi available?" A female voice with a distinct Zambian accent said on the other end of the phone.

~ COUSIN ~

Nomsa could hear voices, unfamiliar female voices; talking to each other but making references to her. Was she dreaming? She wondered, struggling to open her eyes; there was a bright explosion of fluorescent light bulbs, the sheer whiteness felt like razor blades slicing across her retina. Nomsa clamped her eyelids shut, welcoming the darkness; trying to make sense of what had happened or where she was.

Her brain struggled to decipher the voices she was hearing. Then her nostrils twitched; the smell, she couldn't mistake that smell, it was familiar . . . almost like bleach. No, it was floor cleaning fluid like that used in hospitals; she thought. A hospital! The word ricocheted inside her head sending alarm bells.

"Where . . . where am I? Am I in a hospital?" Nomsa asked with a jolt, her body jerking up from the hospital bed.

"Yes you are at Queen Elizabeth Hospital, you are okay now." A young nurse, dressed in white uniform and a matching cap, said in a soothing voice.

The nurse's small rubber gloved hands were on Nomsa's left shoulder, gently forcing her upper body back down. She succumbed, letting her head sink into the fluffy hospital pillow; her partially open eyes watching curiously as another nurse, who looked much older, fumbled with her arm.

This one was attempting to insert a drip into her arm; how serious was her condition to the point of having medication administered intravenously? She wondered, her eyes darting from the younger nurse to the much older one, holding an IV needle.

"What happened to me?" She asked, barely wincing as the needle was inserted into her vein.

"You fell and banged your head on the floor madam." The elderly nurse answered, while adjusting the flow of Dihydrocodeine from the drip.

"How, where, when?" Nomsa was disoriented.

"Just over an hour ago, one of your neighbours rang for an ambulance."

"My son! Prince my . . ." She said, panic settling in.

"I'm sure your son is in safe hands madam." The older nurse reassured her.

"Walter, where is Walter?" Nomsa coughed, trying to get up again.

"You mean Mr Lumbadzi, your cousin? He just arrived and he is talking with the doctor." The nurse reassured Nomsa; her eyes still on the contents of the drip which was hanging from the metallic grey aluminium stand.

"My . . . my, who?" Nomsa asked; confusion all over her face. She sat up when a familiar booming voice from the door filled the room.

"Hello cousin!" He said warmly, approaching the bed.

"Walter?" Nomsa asked, still trying to make sense of why he was addressing her as his cousin.

"Nurses, can you excuse us please? I want to have a word with my cousin here." He said with a smile, looking at the two nurses.

Nomsa noticed the look on the faces of the two nurses; they had immediately recognised the man who was standing in front of them. As the older nurse politely left the room, the younger one appeared transfixed to the floor. She was smiling and appeared to be in awe at being in the same room with someone who has been making headlines lately in the papers.

"Nurse Patricia!" The older nurse, who had already made it to the door, chided her younger colleague.

The younger nurse was startled out of her stupor; walking out hastily, still smiling at Walter, who smiled back at her. She closed the door partly, almost running after her older colleague.

"I am so glad to see you darling." Nomsa winced, trying to force a smile through the pain.

"Listen Nomsa, while you are in here, please try and not to address me in any endearing terms. It is dangerous." He said; his voice on edge.

He walked the last couple steps until he was standing next to the hospital bed, his hand twitched; he wanted to reach out and touch her but was conscious of the surroundings.

"Anything you say sweet . . . I mean Walter." Nomsa said her voice drowsy, glad that he was here with her.

She understood that he was a prominent person and on top of that he was running for a political office. More significantly he was also married and had to play it safe in public. Nonetheless, months of seeing each other, sharing and being intimate with one another had changed everything. It had made other things easier while at the same time, highlighted some complications that came from having an affair with a married man.

There were times she looked at him as her man; her Walter. How could she not, when he treated her like his woman? He cared so much about her and showered her with respect in a way no man had ever done. Sometimes it felt wrong to hide what they had away from the public, she so much wanted to stand on top of a mountain and scream out his name in joy.

"Nomsa, be honest with me . . . were you doing drugs? Before you fell that is." His worried voice touched her.

There was a look of disappointment spread across his face.

"Yes I did darli . . . I mean . . . cousin."

"Why, why did you?"

"I had a relapse . . . I . . . I . . ." Nomsa failed to finish the sentence, she broke down crying. Ever since she met and fell for Walter, she noticed that she was finding it easy to cry and would often do so when rocked by emotions. He had successfully managed to peel off the hard layer that used to protect her from shedding tears unnecessarily, especially in the presence of men.

"You promised me Nomsa, you know you did." Walter said, slightly surprised with himself that he felt no anger; only concern.

He wanted to pick her up and hold her in his arms. He couldn't, not in here, not now.

"I know I did . . . I know I did . . ." She said, covering her eyes with both hands.

"Who is supplying you with these dangerous drugs?" He asked in a menacing tone.

Nomsa removed both hands from her face, startled by his change of tone; she looked at him. He was not smiling and she knew why.

They had talked about her drug problem before, but never had he asked her who her dealer was or what kind of drugs she was taking. This was the first time and she didn't feel like disclosing his name. Walter was a nice man and the last thing she wanted was for him to get tangled up in the murky world of drugs all in the name of protecting her.

"It's okay dear, I promise to stay clean, I promise." She whispered, averting her eyes from his piercing stare.

"Who is supplying you Nomsa? Is it the same Nigerian dealer?"

"How . . . how did you know it's a Nigerian?" Nomsa asked surprised by his accurate guess.

"So it's him, right?" He said, taking out the Mobile phone out of his pocket.

"Please Walter; just leave it alone, please." She pleaded with him, watching as he wrote a quick text message.

"Darl . . . sorry . . . I mean cousin, who are you texting?"

"Nomsa, the doctor said you could have died." He said, in a concerned tone, ignoring her question and shoving the phone back in his pocket.

"I am so sorry Walter . . . I get so lonely sometimes and memories of my past, they haunt me . . . I try to shut them out . . . they . . . they are like demons that won't leave me alone." Nomsa sobbed not being entirely honest with him; how could she tell him that she longed he was hers and hers alone?

She always looked forward to being with Walter, cherishing their time together when she would cook for him and talk with him. She hated the moments when he had to leave; she knew that with every 'goodbye' he was going back to his wife.

The thought of him with wife, the two of them alone in their bedroom felt like swords of jealousy slicing at her heart. Nonetheless, Nomsa could never bring herself to tell him this, not after everything he had done for her; the house she now lived in, her first meaningful employment—job which didn't pay much but had restored a sense of dignity in her life. She didn't really need her salary; Walter took care of all her financial needs.

"Nomsa, I know all about your past. We have talked about this, you need to start afresh and forget all the bad things that happened to you."

"Why are you always nice to me . . . you are the only man who has ever been like this with me, not even my father was . . ." Nomsa failed to finish the sentence, overcome with emotion she reached her arm out to touch the cuff of his jacket.

He flinched; a reflex reaction, then allowed her to touch him.

"Everything will be okay. I just need you to stay off the drugs please." He said in a soft voice, allowing himself to enjoy the feel of her touch.

He so much wanted to hug her and kiss her bruised face. The partly shut door of the ward, a reminder that theirs was not a relationship that could be flaunted openly; if someone were to walk in on them while in an embrace, they would make headline news nationwide.

"I will Walter, just promise to love me forever." Nomsa whispered.

Her voice was barely audible. She was squeezing his wrist with her left hand as tears cascaded down her cheeks onto the white hospital sheets.

"You will be fine Nomsa." Walter paused briefly, he could no longer hold himself back; he gently touched the bruise on her face, his fingers trembling and he noticed that she had closed her eyes, a smile spreading across her teary face.

"I have to go now Nomsa; is there anything you want me to bring for you tomorrow?" He asked, getting up ready to leave.

He was obviously upset, suppressing his simmering anger, hating whoever was responsible for supplying her with the drugs.

"Walter dear?" Nomsa voice snapped him out of his trance.

"Yes." He answered, forcing a smile.

"Can you stay just for a little while; there . . . there is something else I have been meaning to tell you."

"Come on, you need to get some rest, we have a lot of time to talk once you are discharged, which, according to Dr Bandawe, shouldn't be that long. Tomorrow, if the tests come back satisfactory."

"Darling . . . sorry I meant . . . cousin, this won't take long. I . . . I have already been putting this conversation off long enough, I think . . ."

"Shhhh . . . Nomsa, if it has waited all this time, surely another day won't do us harm, will it?" He said, gently running his hand along the length of her arm; a smile creasing his features.

"I guess you are right, we will talk tomorrow. I will miss you Walter." She said her fingers weakly holding on to his, reluctant to see him leave.

"I will miss you too Nomsa." He said, turned around and with six long strides he was out of the ward.

"I always miss you when you are not with me." Nomsa whispered at the closed door.

She gingerly turned onto her side, burying her face into the pillow and started sobbing.

"Dear God, of all men on this planet, why did you have to send me a married one, why?" She cried, her words muffled by the thick pillow.

Walter was different; the first time they met at Ku Chawe, he had told her how gorgeous she was repeatedly. She remembers giggling at how was saying it; he had a unique way of saying things. His words almost made her forget that he was just a client.

At first she didn't take his pronouncements about her looks very serious, after all she had heard this from hoards of other men. However, what separated Walter from these other men was the fact that he was more interested in knowing more about her; he was constantly asking her questions and actually paying attention to her responses.

On their second encounter, Nomsa started getting comfortable with him; she had never been with a man who was genuinely attentive to what she was saying. She realised that she was confiding so much to this man. After Walter dropped her off at her house, in Ndirande; Nomsa stood by the window, watching the red taillights of his car disappear into the dark. Her mind was struggling to understand why he seemed to be interested in the things she talked about, at times empathising over what she was saying. So, a week later, she told him that he didn't have to show compassion in order to sleep with her.

"Walter, as long as you are willing to pay for sex, that's all that matters." Nomsa said, expecting him to drive her to a hotel or somewhere secluded.

He briefly looked at her, Nomsa noticed that his face had changed; he was serious. She quickly checked inside her handbag to make sure she had enough condoms. However, he drove to a parking lot outside Shoprite Mall. She was slightly perturbed by his choice of spot.

"Is there something you want to buy first? I already have . . ." Nomsa asked, letting the sentence hang, the insinuation was obvious.

"I will pay you double or three times what you make a night, I just want us to sit here and talk." He said, slowly turning to look at her.

"You will pay me for talking?" Nomsa asked, not sure what kind of game he was playing.

"Yes, isn't that what you do or rather expect?"

The honesty of his question took her by surprise. He was right; hearing him say it like that, touched a nerve and she looked the other way.

"This is the third time we are meeting, it's all new to me . . . I don't like getting comfortable with my . . . my . . ." Nomsa was surprised she couldn't say the word, *clients*.

That night, parked outside Shoprite in his car, they talked; actually she is the one who did most of the talking, Walter simply sat there looking at her, listening. She had already seen the bright wedding band on his finger; she decided it was not up to her to ask if he was married, widowed or separated, she figured if he wanted her to know he was going to have to be the one initiating that topic.

That information he disclosed to her on their next meeting; the seventh one, on a Wednesday, after she had finished work. Nomsa was surprised that she was actually counting the number of times they went out. On most days their rendezvous place was outside Shoprite, she figured being a public busy place, he felt safe; his car one of many.

He opened up, telling her that his wife was some sort of a doctor and she was currently in Australia for a short course. Nomsa found herself fascinated with his personal stories; he was no longer just the politician on Facebook, he was human and she was starting to have feelings for this man.

She couldn't believe that Walter had managed to convince her to stop selling her body to men. On that particular day, whilst licking ice creams he had gone to buy; Nomsa remembers laughing sarcastically, looking at him straight in the eye.

"If I stop doing what I do, are you going to marry me and take care of my child and my financial needs?" She casually asked, not expecting a response from him and surprised when one was forthcoming.

"I cannot marry you, although I wouldn't mind taking care of your financial needs." He said, licking his vanilla ice cream.

His response was the most sincere voice Nomsa had ever heard. She abruptly stopped laughing, almost dropping her ice cream, looked into his eyes searchingly and was scared of what she saw in them. A frown creased her forehead. This man did not want her body; he was looking for something more. This was a strange and unfamiliar territory for her.

"Tell me something; you have been seeing me for quite some time now. You give me more money than I care to count, twice you have taken me to that nice cottage of yours, you promise me things and yet you have never asked for sex. Why?"

"What do you mean 'why'?" He countered with a question, a cheeky smile creasing his gorgeous features; "I thought we already had this conversation, I don't mind paying for the time we spend talking?"

"Yes, we did, but I am confused Walter, what is it you want from me?" Nomsa asked.

"So you rather I coaxed you into bed?"

"Yes, I mean no. Come on, which woman wouldn't want to jump into bed with you?" She said hitting him playfully on the shoulder, almost causing him to drop his ice cream cone.

"I wouldn't know Nomsa, I'm not a woman. Would you like to jump into bed with me?" He asked, knowing that such a question was bound to make her uncomfortable.

"Be serious . . . be honest with me, what is it you truly want?"

"Do you want to know the truth Nomsa?" He asked; his eyes were watery as they looked into hers.

"Yes, because most men don't waste time with small talk, they get straight to the point."

"They get straight to the point?" He quizzed playfully, breaking eye contact.

"I meant; they used to get straight to the point." She corrected her tense.

"They didn't waste time talking? They slept with you on the first date?"

"Exactly, and yet with you, the closest you have come, is a hug and a peck on the cheek." Nomsa responded, surprised that she felt a twinge of shyness.

"I don't know what I want, I enjoy being with you Nomsa, I know I shouldn't because I am married and I love my wife, that's what my mind tells me." He said turning around to look at Nomsa, their eyes locking.

"What does your heart tell you?" She asked in a soft voice, rolling closer to him, resting her head on his legs.

"I am confused Nomsa, I don't know any more what my heart wants."

"Tell you what dear, you have been nice to me, as a matter of fact you have been way too nice. I could make love to you in the middle of a market if you asked me to. Right now there is nothing I want more than to get stark naked for you, but I won't."

"Right here in the middle of a public parking place?" He teased lovingly.

"I think you are just missing your wife, let's wait until she comes back from Australia." Nomsa carried on, struggling not to laugh at what he had just said.

"I don't understand." He was slightly startled by what she had just said.

"I think you just want some female companion, but you don't want to jump over the cliff."

"I don't follow." He said, a slight smile forming across his mouth.

"Yes you do, Walter. You tell yourself that, for as long as we don't end up in bed together, you are not cheating. Isn't that what it is Walter?" Nomsa asked with a giggle, surprised that she felt a slight twinge of jealousness talking about his wife.

"And then what?" He asked, tilting her chin so that she was facing him.

"What do you mean; 'and then what'?"

"What happens when my wife gets back?"

"We shall see if you would want to continue seeing me."

"Oh!"

"You have my number, if you don't call, I will know what you have decided and I will respect that." Nomsa said with a heavy heart.

"Will you?" He asked; his voice so low she turned to face him.

"I have no choice, dear. Of course I will miss you dearly." Nomsa said softly surprised that she actually meant that; she then licked her ice cream which was slowly melting.

In the past she had told many men that she was going to miss them, that she loved them; all that had been cosmetic chatter. As far as she was concerned, that is what men wanted to hear. Not this time, not with Walter. Right now, talking to him, it all felt different.

She loathed talking about his wife and had problems saying her name. With the other men she never used to think or care about their wives. Yet this time, she found herself thinking about this lucky woman in Australia; an educated doctor and a wife.

The pillowcase was drenched with her tears. The flashbacks felt as if it all happened yesterday; her love for Walter had compressed time. She couldn't believe that over two years had gone by since they started seeing each other. Her son, Prince, was only five months old when Walter entered her life or when she entered his; she thought, gently touching her bruised forehead. She could hear the faint talk of nurses on the other side of the door.

~ FOR LOVE'S SAKE ~

THE IMAGE OF Nomsa lying in a hospital bed looking sickly was still haunting Walter. He left the hospital his head filled with rage. After seeing her, his intentions were to rush home for a change of clothes and pick up toiletries; he would then drive to Dedza to meet Tamanda at her parent's place. However, no matter how much he tried, he could not shake off the image of Nomsa limbs connected to a hospital drip; whoever was responsible for putting her in such a state had to pay.

Instead of Dedza he headed towards Ndirande, a fifteen minute drive from the hospital. He would have preferred to drive there in a less conspicuous car, but he didn't have the time to go home and switch cars; he thought as he approached the roundabout.

Where Mahatma Ghandi Road joins Kamuzu Highway, he indicated left merging into the roundabout and floored the accelerator; the powerful car surged forward with some urgency.

Ndirande Township has changed considerably; Walter thought, his fingers tapping on the wheel of his Range Rover. He had parked on the side of the busy road, overlooking the row of drinking houses on the other side of the street. Even the dim glow of dusk coupled with a light fog could not camouflage the fact that this was an expensive vehicle looking a bit out of place. His window was partly rolled down; a lot about this township had changed. Not the smell, a familiar unexplainable smell was still as he remembered.

With his fingers drumming on the thick steering wheel; Walter could hear the comments of praise and he was conscious of the looks of envy coming from the people passing by.

"Mr Lumbadzi, you are the man!" A man who was with a woman shouted from the other side of the road.

"You should be visiting us more often big man!" Another man loudly said, as he walked past, he was carrying a big baton stick; a security guard most likely going to a night shift, Walter surmised.

Ndirande has always been a human beehive of activity, more so around this particular area called Chinseu. It was a lively place; to an outsider it might appear as a breakdown of civility, however there was some order to this anarchy, it could almost be deemed premeditated chaos. The township thrived on this chaos which was the oil that lubricated the cogs of Ndirande's economy; bars selling alcohol to imbibers, prostitutes servicing patrons, vendors selling roasted meat, mechanics working on vehicles, pickpockets, drug dealers, roadside preachers and women selling traditionally made confectionaries.

Anyone would have been nervous parking where he did. Not Walter. Although he no longer lived here, he still regarded this as his backyard; he grew up here, played here and matured here. To outsiders, Ndirande is a high density residential area which they might find intimidating; however, to those living here, the place is a learning institution. An institution which teaches lessons not taught anywhere else and he was one of its graduates.

He did not choose to live here, Ndirande chose him; however, he learnt a lot during his childhood, vital lessons about life and survival. As much as he loathed the place with a passion, he was very grateful for having experienced what he did; it taught him how to appreciate certain things and how to take care of himself.

With his hands lazily resting on the steering wheel he slowly panned his eyes, taking in his surrounding, disgusted at how the Ndirande of today was far different from that of his time. Back then everyone knew everyone; drinking places like *Iponga* or *Flats* used to be places for fun. Now everything had changed; there was immerse overcrowding and proliferation of foreigners from Mozambique, scrupulous Nigerians even hardened refugees fleeing the war in Somalia. Foreigners had shifted the demographics of what used to be a strictly Malawian township. Although violence was the order of the day when he was growing up, now guns had been inserted into the equation; people were literally getting killed if they took a wrong step. He was glad that he had gotten out of this Wild West.

As if someone had just read his mind; at that exact moment a door to one of the bottle stores flew open and a man staggered backwards, tumbling over the steps and landing hard on his back. Even from where he was parked, he could clearly see that the man was badly bruised and bleeding. Three men, who looked like his friends, came to his aid; they lifted him up and started walking away with him. Whoever had beaten him did not even bother to follow up; he or they definitely must have been satisfied with the damage caused.

"Some things never change." Walter whispered; shaking his head as his thoughts went back in time.

Growing up, Walter had constantly been captivated by the big houses with their sprawling green manicured lawns in the neighbouring low density suburbs of Nyambadwe. Every time he went into the city centre or on his way back, he would always slow down as he passed these big houses, looking at gardeners tending flowers and was fascinated by water splashing out of sprinklers. The same precious water they had to queue and fight for on a single tap that serviced a dozen houses or so, was being wasted here by watering grass.

At the age of sixteen, he had made a silent vow that Ndirande might have been his birth place, no way was it going to be the place he would spend the rest of his life calling home. One day he would own a sprinkler and lawn full of green grass; Walter had written this in a small notebook which he kept under the straw mat in his tiny bedroom that served as a storeroom as well.

Through hard work, determination, a meagre education, hustling and self-made luck, by the age of thirty, Walter was renting a house in Nyambadwe. By thirty-five, he bought the house from his landlord. When he turned thirty-eight he owned several houses in low density areas; Namiwawa, Mandala and flats in the capital city of Lilongwe. He was letting them out to executive tenants; lawyers, managers or expatriates. How he rose so quickly from rags to riches, is a story he has never shared. He has never commented on persistent rumours that the source of his wealth could be traced back to the shady contracts he got from the United Democratic Front (UDF) government.

When father died from Aids, Walter went to live with his uncle on the other side of Ndirande, called Makhetha. At the age of eighteen he inherited an old 1975 Bedford TK 7.5-ton truck from his uncle after he passed away.

He started hauling anything from river sand, bricks, quarry stones and cement to various building sites. His break came when he hired out his truck to the UDF when it was just a pressure group. The UDF used his truck extensively, transporting supporters to various political party venues. It was a business decision which seemed ridiculous at the time; when he had told the UDF pressure group that they could use his truck free of charge.

When multiparty politics was legalised; the UDF, which had now registered as a political party, won the country's first general elections. Prominent individuals within the party remembered the young transporter who had offered his truck without charging. In a typical *scratch my back and I will scratch yours* scenario. Twenty year old Walter Lumbadzi found himself neck deep in lucrative contracts; the government was awarding tenders to those who had been loyal during its infancy.

From that single old truck, he built a business empire and managed to sustain it by publicly shunning politics. However, in private, Walter was paying and buying politicians who could be bought. The era of the UDF government spawned overnight millionaires and he was one of them. Whereas, over time, most fizzled out and ended up in jail after being prosecuted because of their ill-gotten wealth, young Walter became wealthier and untouchable.

His latest desire of wanting to join the political fray by contesting for the Blantyre Constituency seat came as a shock to those closest to him, especially his wife. Nonetheless, Tamanda had been with Walter for so long to know that her husband's every move, business or otherwise, were well thought through.

"It's not the MP thing you are aiming for is it?" Tamanda had asked him one night after he had just announced publicly about his political intentions.

"Come on darling, what else would it be?" He had laughed dismissively, hugging his wife and kissing her on the neck.

He knew how much that tickled her; she laughed so loud, gasping his name out and dropping the whole subject about his political aspirations.

Walter looked outside the Range Rover; he was smiling as he remembered how his wife had laughed so seductively that night, tilting her head sideways, exposing her slender neck to him. He gently kissed her, going up to her ears, sticking his tongue like a painter's brush, stroking her earlobes with it. He listened to the change in her breathing; her mouth open, searching for his . . . finding it, finding his tongue. Walter smiled as thoughts of that day played right in front of him.

The buzzing of his phone, on the console, jolted him back to reality. He glanced at the illuminated caller ID which was showing his secretary's name and number.

"Yes Hendrina, what is it?"

"Hello sir, I hope I am not interrupting you." Hendrina said, sounding friendlier and informal.

"What is it Hendrina?" He barked into the phone, his eyes looking at his expensive wristwatch. There was no way his secretary would be calling him from the office at this time.

"When you left, the Zambian State House rang and . . ." Hendrina stuttered regretting her idea of calling her boss while lying on her bed.

She had thought that he would be interested to hear what the message was all about. It was a short simple message;

'Tell Mr Lumbadzi his friend from Zambia called.'

Hendrina thought she could drag it out; maybe it could lead into a conversation with her boss. She was wearing her purple sexy lingerie, with a dim bedside light on; hoping that maybe he was going to ask her what she was wearing or what she was doing.

He always called her by her first name, how she would love do likewise; call him Walter. His was a name she had said so many times while taking a shower, while lying on her bed alone, while on the minibus to work. But never to him, never in public; maybe today would be the day, Hendrina thought while lying flat on her back, her left foot resting on top of her right knee.

If the tone of his voice was anything to go by, then she had gravely miscalculated.

"And you are telling me this now? Shouldn't you have called me before you left the office, instead of calling me from your house?" He said with a tone of annoyance.

"I'm sorry sir, it's just that you left so abrupt and . . . and . . ." Hendrina panicked, sitting upright as if he was standing right there in her bedroom, looking at her disapprovingly.

"It's okay." Walter snapped, cutting off his secretary when he saw another call trying to come through.

The caller ID was showing *Tosh*. He hung up on Hendrina and answered the call.

"Hello." He said in snappy voice; "I don't like waiting, you know how I hate waiting for people." He paused for the other person to respond.

"I thought I told you to be waiting for me by the time I get here?" He went on interrupting the speaker on the other end.

"You need to stop whatever you are doing and get here now! I mean now Tosh, not tomorrow!" Walter hissed, hanging up the phone.

His earlier smile was replaced with a serious frown. From where he was parked he could see people milling around the row of shabby looking bottle stores; drinking and eating roasted meat, most likely cow's intestines. The place was infested with prostitutes and bored men; mostly husbands seeking adult fun which they weren't getting at home. Each bottle store was blasting music different from the next bottle store. The result was a pollution of noise which, instead of putting people off, was like a magnet to the majority of those who frequented these joints.

There was a time he used to hang around this place, running errands for the men who would often send him to go inside the bottle stores to buy them beer while they stood outside chatting to friends or prostitutes. Sometimes he would buy them roasted meat and they would often let him keep the change, which he was depositing in a tin buried just behind their small house. Some men used to send him to go coax prostitutes for them; often a drunkard and a prostitute would disappear in the dark shadows of a bottle store or into a car, he would be commandeered to keep watch. These drunken men used to pay him handsomely, despite the fact that he used to get pleasure from the human sounds coming out of the shaking car. It was during this time that Walter managed to save up money to afford brand new pair of shoes.

He still remembers the day he walked into Bata Shoe shop and bought himself a pair of sports shoes. He regretted not wearing them straight away, instead opting to save the shoes for Sunday. His father was having none of that; he quizzed him where he had stolen the pair of shoes or the money to afford such a luxury. He remembers his father dousing paraffin inside the white box which contained his brand new shoes.

"Tell me where you stole these shoes!" His father who was drunk barked, a mist of saliva exploding from his mouth.

"I did not steal them, father . . . I didn't." Walter sobbed, his eyes looking helplessly at the flaming match that his father was holding over the paraffin soaked shoes.

"Aaah! Shut up! You . . . you lying little bastard!" His father yelled, dropping the match stick into the box.

"I did not steal them father . . . I did not steal them father . . ." He sobbed watching the box of shoes go up in an inferno.

"Poverty teaches humans lessons no school can impart . . . but I will not have my son lying to me . . . you hear me?" His drunken father mumbled things that did not make sense to young Walter.

Even though he grew up here, Walter didn't like coming back to his old township. Not out of fear, but what it reminded him of; a past he so much wanted to forget. He did everything in his power to distance himself from Ndirande. Even after he had moved into the posh residential area of Nyambadwe, the fact that he could see his old township from the balcony of his mansion was adequate reason to prompt a house move. How he wished his father was still alive to see how much he had achieved.

Walter built a seven bedroom behemoth on the foothills of Sanjika, just on the outskirts of Namiwawa residential area. It was a place far removed from his past; another premeditated move. From the moment he left Ndirande, everything he did in life, was aimed at distancing himself from his past; this was also true with his love life.

The large, sloping plot on which Walter constructed his dream home, first belonged to the most prominent and powerful Chief Justice in the country; Mathews Sambani.

Walter had seen the '*plot for sale*' advert in the classifieds section of the Daily newspaper. The plot had two things going for it; the size and the location, which was far away from Ndirande as one could possibly wish. The price, he thought, was ridiculously high; however, he considered himself a shrewd negotiator.

The first day he went to see the plot, the owner; Chief Justice Sambani, was accompanied by his youngest daughter; Tamanda. Walter saw the grey Mitsubishi Pajero already parked at the plot when he purposefully pulled up twenty minutes late. A faint smirk danced along his lips; the seller hadn't left, this meant that he was eager, maybe even desperate to sell—Walter thought as he jumped out of his Toyota Land Cruiser.

The minute they saw him, father and daughter got out of their car. She was the last one to come out; she appeared to be opening the door in slow motion, carefully setting both feet on the ground, her short skirt looking out of place in the field of nothing but overgrown vegetation. For Walter, the mere sight of her was awe-inspiring and for a split second nothing else mattered, not even the reason why he was here.

He was standing right in front of her when she straightened herself, running her hands over her black skirt; getting rid of wrinkles. She had on a white sleeveless blouse, the complexion of her skin shimmered as the sun kissed her. An exciting chill crawled up Walter's spine and his breath became shallow and measured. The first thought that crossed his mind was; I hope she is single.

"By the way Mr Lumbadzi, this is my daughter who answered the phone when you rang yesterday, she has just returned from UK where she was doing her PhD." Chief Justice Sambani spoke with pride, looking at his own daughter than he was looking at Walter.

Not once in his life did his father look at him like that, with pride and adoration; Walter thought enviously, his eyes fixated at the chemistry between father and daughter.

He was constantly looking at her and thinking how attractive she was. In the middle of the overgrown plot she was like a single rose flower in a garden of cactuses, a diamond in a field of rusting metal, a lone star in the middle of the night.

When she spoke to her father, the perfectly pronounced words tumbled out of her pretty mouth in flawless English. Surely she had to be an angel whose wings had been clipped; he thought, looking at how her smooth skin glowed in the afternoon sun. She had the most amazing eyelashes, they appeared to move in slow motion and he felt an exciting knot in the pits of his stomach. Walter decided right there and then that; despite the price of the plot being prohibitively high, he was going to buy it. The instincts of shrewd negotiator and strong believer that, 'you never pay the asking price of anything,' all went up in smoke. He surprised himself when agreed to what Chief Justice Sambani was asking; he didn't want to appear cheap, not in the eyes of his gorgeous daughter.

"Should we walk around the plot?" Chief Justice Sambani asked with a smile.

"That won't be necessary sir; I think you have found yourself a buyer." Walter extended his hand to a slightly surprised Chief Justice Sambani.

Although Walter was smiling and facing the Chief Justice, his eyes were focused over his shoulder, at his daughter. Their eyes met, she smiled and Walter's smile widened. A week later, the two of them went on their first date. He told her how he had fallen in love with her the moment their eyes met.

"The moment you stepped out of your father's Pajero, I couldn't stop stealing sideways glances at you."

"I noticed that, and realised that you weren't even listening to what my father was saying."

"Was I that obvious?"

"Yes. And I started wondering if you had really come over for the plot or other ulterior motives." Tamanda joked.

Walter started laughing, thinking back to that day on that barren plot; a plot which was later to become the resting place of their home

Tamanda was heaven sent. Despite her goddess-like beauty, she also possessed vast amounts of intelligence that left him gobsmacked. Walter soon learnt that her past and childhood were just the opposite of his. She could spell the word *poverty* backwards with ease, but had no idea what being poor meant. Here was someone who had everything that had nothing to do with his past. There was a certain aura about her, a mystique that oozed class, not the ghetto girls of his past.

Going out with her was exhilarating; her table etiquette was sophisticated, the way she addressed waiters and the articulate manner in which she dealt with the cutlery. Most girls he knew could not tackle a chicken drumstick with a knife and fork; they would resort to using their hands, even if they were in a posh restaurant. Such was not the case with Tamanda Sambani.

Indeed, during the early stages of their romantic relationship, Walter did all he could to impress Tamanda; trips to the lake, dinners at Ryalls Hotel, expensive jewellery from South Africa. However, he couldn't understand why material things didn't impress her one bit. Tamanda was born and bred in money. She grew up in a house of strict and loving parents; it became clear to him that she was not looking for financial security from a man. Love, companionship and sharing of emotions were the things she was seeking for; from the get-go, it was obvious that she was least impressed or fazed with his wealth.

Walter's thoughts were interrupted when Tosh emerged out of a bottle store. He was holding a bottle of Carlsberg beer; however he wasn't staggering like some of the other drunks around him.

Very few people knew that Tosh's real name was Peter Gwenembe; he had adopted the name Tosh way back in primary school because notions of Rastafarianism, reggae music and an addiction to marijuana.

Tosh was a very complex character; fiercely religious in his Rastafarianism, he also had a high propensity to violence. Back in primary school, out of five fights that broke out every week, chances were that Tosh was involved in four. He carried his battle scars like some sort of trophies and his body was riddled with these trophies.

Like many boys, Tosh went to school because his parents expected him to. Every morning he would walk to school while chatting with the girls; most of them had no choice but to let him accompany them along or risk being slapped if they refused.

Whilst the rest of the students went to their respective classrooms, Tosh would either go to the football pitch to roll some marijuana or go chatting with the girls who used to sell homemade confectionaries. Rarely did Tosh venture into the classroom, and if he did, it was left to the likes of Walter to do his work for him; arithmetic or spellings. Most of the boys who wrote down wrong answers got a severe beating after school.

Tosh had a very intimidating physic. He was built like a lion, a very humongous head that was supported by a thick neck which rested on an enormous muscular torso. He had massive arms; his weapons of choice. Tosh never used his legs in fights; his big fists and head were the only weapons he needed and he used to use them with devastating consequences. He still did up to now.

"Some things never change." He mumbled for the second time while turning off the in-car sound system.

His eyes were focused disapprovingly at the approaching mountain of a man dressed in a tight fitting T-shirt and faded blue jeans.

"Hello sir, I apologise I thought it was going to be Samson, your driver, meeting me as usual." Tosh said in a shaky voice as soon as he entered the passenger side.

"Tosh, please no beer bottles in my car." Walter snapped before Tosh could shut the door.

"Sorry big man." Tosh replied taking one long swing, emptying the contents of the beer bottle and tossing it into the nearby maize garden.

"Is that blood on your T-shirt?"

"It's nothing sir, someone was talking rubbish about me inside the bottle store."

"Is that the man who came out flying through the doors?"

"Yes sir, he was going on and on about how a forty-four year old man can still be living with his parents at home." Tosh said while looking outside the window, avoiding eye contact.

"Tosh, you are forty-four and you do live with your parents?"

"I know that sir, but he didn't have to say it in there, not in front of the bar girls and my friends."

"So you beat the daylights out of him, for saying the truth?" He looked at Tosh, shaking his head disapprovingly.

Both of them grew up in this neighbourhood. Back in the day, Tosh was a hustler. Being much older and of course, stronger, he took care of Walter by fighting his battles, making sure that no one bothered him. In return, Walter did Tosh's homework, running errands for him, delivering notes to girls.

Unlike the men who paid him while they did their shenanigans with prostitutes, Tosh offered him protection in the tough and rough neighbourhood. Looking back now,

Walter often wondered what was more important; the money he made or the protection he got from his muscular guardian angel.

Walter had moved on. However Tosh was still Tosh, sending notes to girls and still breaking bones of anyone who crossed his path, like he had just done ten minutes ago. It was because of this latter skill, why he had kept in touch with Tosh. The roles had now changed, Tosh was the one running errands for Walter; he was basically his bulldog. Walter had not gotten to where he was by being Mr Nice-guy and playing Pope.

"Any way, I guess you are what you are Tosh." He said, drumming his hands on the steering wheel; "Now, back to business."

"Yes Sir, what do you have for me?" Tosh said, smiling widely exposing a gap where two teeth used to be.

"That's for you my brother." Walter said, gesturing to a brown envelope perched on the middle console; "That's more than you make in six months working as a bouncer at these filthy bottle stores."

"Thanks big man." Tosh grabbed the thick envelope, not even bothering to open it, and looked at Walter expectantly.

"There is this scoundrel, a Nigerian who is supplying drugs and causing a lot of grief."

"Yes?"

"Tosh, I want you to put a stop to it."

"Big man, just give me some details about this Nigerian and I will do the rest."

"I hear he resides right here in Ndirande, I want him on the next flight to Abuja or wherever he came from. Is that clear Tosh?"

"Not a problem boss." Tosh said reassuringly.

Despite appearing confident, Tosh shifted uncomfortably in his seat. He was stealing sideways glances at this Walter.

There was a time when he was a skinny boy who used to run errands for him now the roles were reversed. The once scrawny boy was transformed into a giant, not physically but in stature, all thanks to money and power. He still couldn't figure out where exactly their paths had diverged, how Walter had become so prominent that people were bending over backwards to please him.

"I want him out of Malawi as soon as yesterday; I'm paying you a lot of money for this job."

"Consider it done Sir, I am sure this is priority because I must admit, it feels strange for you to come meet me in person." Tosh said stuffing the thick envelope inside his jeans. He jumped out of the Range Rover and melted into the noisy dusk.

As soon as Tosh disappeared, Walter reached for the ignition, paused; deciding whether to call Tamanda or wait until he got home. He looked at the time; 18:55, he turned the ignition on, the powerful V-8 engine coughed to life and he gently engaged into drive.

~ FROM DEDZA WITH LOVE ~

It was heart wrenching seeing her father wasting away right in before their eyes. The ongoing prognosis by the medical team revealed that Judge Sambani had not yet reached the advanced stages of Dementia. However, it was obvious that the disease was eating her father's mental faculties, in so doing, putting enormous stress on the rest of the family, especially their mother. She was being strong, albeit pretentious; always smiling when the children were around, however her shrinking body told a different story. Mrs Mkiche Sambani knew that her husband was dying; she had given up on herself, she was dying together with the man she had loved all her life.

In the early stages of his illness, when he was still in control of all his mental faculties, Chief Justice Sambani had summoned all his children; five sons and three daughters to his mansion in Dedza. Being a learned person, he knew what was happening to him, he was well aware that time would come when he was going to lose all his reasoning faculties; the disease he had been diagnosed with was irreversible. Someone else would have to be there to make decisions on his behalf; decisions pertaining to his estate.

He surprised the children by bestowing the power of attorney to Tamanda not Elijah; the first born son. It was a heated debate, whereby Elijah, made his feelings known.

Three weeks ago, before Tamanda left for South Africa, all eight children of Chief Justice Sambani had been locked up in another fierce meeting. The friction was on whether to go ahead with the annual event or abandon it altogether on medical grounds; their parents' 50th wedding anniversary, an event which four of her five brothers, especially the first born, Elijah, were vehemently opposed to.

During the fierce debate, her sisters had put up a good argument.

"For forty-nine years, our parents have always celebrated their wedding anniversary. Don't you think it would be absurd not to go ahead with the anniversary while both dad and mum are still alive?" Deliwe, the eldest of the girls, had argued.

"Yes, what message would that send to our mother?" Flocy Sambani had agreed with Deliwe.

"I think I will go with the girls on this one." Junior, the youngest of the boys chipped in, averting his eyes away from Elijah and his other three brothers; Brandon, Zachariah and Kondwani.

However, the four brothers opposed this vehemently, arguing that it was wrong to put their father through something he was not aware of; he was tired and should be left alone resting.

Tamanda understood where her brothers were coming from, they made a compelling case; however, she was inclined to go along Deliwe, Flocy and Junior. That would basically make it a tie and she could feel Elijah's penetrating gaze cutting through her. He was not going to capitulate that easily. It was very tense; they all looked at her for the final say.

Tamanda had agonised, weighing the arguments put forward by her siblings; finally she excused herself, tiptoeing to the master bedroom where her mother was feeding her ailing father.

"Mother I need your help." Tamanda had whispered into her mother's ear; averting her gaze away from her frail looking father who was drooling like a baby.

It was hard for Tamanda to come to terms with her father's condition. The heavily built man, the one whose presence used to be noticeable; a man who had a commanding aura whenever he walked in court or in church, was now an unrecognisable shadow of his former self.

As a young girl, her father used to take her to court every Wednesday afternoon. School used to finish at lunch time, leaving the afternoon for sports which she was bad at, and had long given up on. He would pick her up outside St Andrews; drive to court, where she would sit in his office, eating lunch which he always kept for her. She would watch him going over final touches for the afternoon proceedings.

Inside court, Tamanda used to sit in the gallery, still dressed in her primary school uniform, watching the organised chaos of court proceedings. Her tiny nostrils inhaling and enjoying the rustic smell of polished wood and old books, her eyes fixated at the judge; her father, presiding over the entire court. He was like an experienced conductor of a symphony orchestra.

He had always wanted her to become a lawyer, maybe a judge like him, but she had always known that this was not her path. As Tamanda grew older she started dropping hints to her father that law was not her calling; she found it to be too boring and not scientifically stimulating. These verbal hints were backed by the subjects she did extremely well on her A-Levels; maths, biology and chemistry, a tell-tale sign that her brain was more inclined towards science.

Even in church, she would sit on the front row, next to the towering figure of her father; watching him with fascination as he flipped through the bible; locating a particular verse or chapter the preacher had directed the congregation to. He seemed to know exactly where to go, his fingers arriving at the requested verse long before most people did.

The best moment, for young Tamanda, was when her father got up, walking to the front of the church to make that week's announcements. It was not the fact that he spoke with a deep, commanding and yet compassionate voice that fascinated her; unlike the readers who used to grace the front of the church, her father was the only one who never had notes to aid him through the tedious announcements. He would prepare himself before mass; slowly reading and storing all bits of information inside his head. Towards the end of the mass, after receiving Eucharist, he would stand in front of the church making announcements; reciting each and every name, time, location, with amazing accuracy.

Now she looked at her frail father; it was painful to watch him deteriorate. The once fierce judge couldn't even chew food; it had to be fed to him in puree form. Nomsa averted her eyes, looking down at the floor uncomfortably.

"Yes, what can I do for you my dear Tamanda?" Mrs Mkiche Sambani, spoon in hand, smiled at her youngest daughter.

"Mother, it's about you and daddy's upcoming wedding anniversary."

"Yes my dear, what about our anniversary." Her smiling mother asked in her usual soft voice.

"I mean . . . seeing that dad's condition has deteriorated and . . . and . . ."

"You want to know if it is okay with me, if you children can organise something for me and your father." Mrs Sambani jumped in, after noticing that her daughter was at pains how to frame the question.

"Yes mother, should we go ahead or would you rather we didn't?" Tamanda asked, relieved that her mother had rescued her.

"My dear daughter, why don't you decide?" Her mother returned in a gentle voice, whilst wiping the drool from her husband's mouth.

"But mother . . ."

"My child, when your father chose you to take care of his estate, it was for moments like these."

"It's just that the others seem to . . ."

"Disagree with you?" Mrs Sambani finished the sentence for her daughter.

"There seems to be a split."

"Of course there will be disagreements; you are all strong minded individuals who want the best for us."

"So what do I do mother?"

"Now, go out there and tell your brothers and sisters what you have decided. They will listen to you and most importantly, your father and I will go along with your decision Tamanda." Mrs Sambani said with a smile, setting the tablespoon in the bowl of porridge and rubbing her frail hand on her daughter's lap.

She then turned to face her husband who had started coughing, spitting the food that was in his mouth. The disease had spawned other ailments for her already asthmatic father; lately he had been rocked by serious bouts of breathing problems. Tamanda managed to order him a battery operated nebuliser machine from Europe.

She watched painfully as her mother filled the Salbutamol and Saline Nebules into the nebuliser mask; she then gently fastened the mask over her father's mouth and nose, before turning it on. After a few minutes her father was no longer gasping for air; he was actually smiling at her mother, his frail hand was rubbing against her cheek. Even in sickness, the love, affection and devotion between her parents was evident; looking at them made her miss and long for Walter even more.

In the end, Tamanda decided to go ahead with the anniversary.

The whole function had been a disaster from the start. It got worse when Chief Justice Sambani started hallucinating and calling his wife all sorts of derogatory names. It was complete shambles; despite the fact that their father had no idea to what he was saying, it still caused unease amongst the invited guests. Tamanda's five brothers descended on her accusingly, Elijah being the most vocal. Even Junior who had backed the sisters during the meeting—three weeks ago—now sided with the boys; both Deliwe and Flocy were nowhere to be seen.

The boys took turns ripping her decision to shreds.

"I knew dad shouldn't have entrusted such responsibility to someone so young." Elijah vented his anger in front of all the invited guests.

"Being the Deputy Inspector General of Police doesn't give you the airs to talk to me like a child Elijah!" A tired and angry Tamanda lashed back.

"I will sis, if you keep making these childish decisions, putting father's wellbeing at risk!" The towering Elijah shot back.

"Dad did not choose you Elijah, he chose me, the decision I made to go ahead with the anniversary was final." Tamanda yelled, wishing Walter had been there with her.

She did her best not to breakdown into tears, if only he was there, calming her with his reassuring voice and comforting presence. The fact that she was still exhausted from her trip from South Africa did not help matters.

Finally, after their mother came back from putting their father to bed; the argument tapered down, most of guests slowly slithered out of the mansion. Tamanda felt like she had just come to the end of a gruelling marathon. How she wished Walter had been there with her.

Before leaving Dedza for Blantyre, Tamanda instructed Maxwell, not to turn on the radio; she forced herself to sleep the rest of the journey. After a couple of hours, Tamanda blinked, thinking she was still on the flight from South Africa. It was dark outside; vegetation-trees and flowers—bathed under a glow of bright security lights, ruled out thoughts about being on a plane. She was inside a car; she thought, waking up and trying to get her bearings.

She smiled at the familiar surroundings; the white Mercedes had just entered their sprawling yard with its well-manicured green lawns. One of the security guards, standing next to well-trimmed bougainvillea shrub, waved at the passing car. Tamanda waved back as the car slowly approached their house.

She never got tired of its grandeur; splashed in imported white avocado paint, its reflection bounced against the blue surface of the rectangular shaped swimming pool, with its underwater lights. Her father's house in Dedza was enormous, with a conflicting shape that was at times painful to look at; hers and Walter's was much bigger but tight, the intelligently designed architectural lines accentuating its beauty. Of course, when her parents built their house in Dedza, they had in mind their eight children and grandchildren, on that end, theirs failed miserably; seven huge bedrooms upstairs and not even a single child to run through them, Tamanda thought while subconsciously massaging her belly.

Maxwell eased the car between two cars which were flanked by more cars.

"Walter and his toys." Tamanda whispered to herself, glad to be home finally; she was dying for a hot bath and a cuddle in her husband's arms, she didn't care in what order.

"Pardon madam?" Maxwell said, turning his head around, not too sure what Tamanda had just said.

"Nothing Maxwell, I was just mumbling to myself, I must be getting old." Tamanda said with a smile.

She could see the discomfort on the driver's face. He promptly looked back in front, avoiding her gaze. Tamanda could tell that Maxwell was torn between Malawian mannerisms and the urge to flatter her. Commenting that she looked like a twenty year old would come across as disrespectful; however, agreeing with her that she was getting old might bring about similar results, if not worse. Maxwell chose the third best option; he hastily jumped out of the car, going round to open the rear door for her.

Tamanda smiled at Maxwell who was holding the door open for her; she disliked these protocol-like gestures. She was able bodied and capable to open her own doors, but their staff still insisted on pampering them as if they were royalty. Most days she would beat the eager driver to the door, however, today she was exhausted from the trip and little family feud; so, she simply sat there waiting for Maxwell to have the pleasure of holding the door open for her.

She gingerly placed her both feet on the concrete driveway, wishing she was wearing flat shoes not these Proenza Schouler high heels; squinting her eyes at the bright lights. She knew how Walter loved seeing her in high heels; she had put them on after leaving Dedza, just for him.

Tamanda got up, holding on to the roof of the car to steady herself, still a bit woozy from the deep sleep. She managed to muster a smile at two workers, dressed in matching white outfits, who were approaching the Mercedes.

"*Mwaswela*." Tamanda greeted them both, her eyes scanning the parking lot; it was difficult to tell if her husband was home or not.

Her husband's expensive habit of collecting cars meant that the parking lot outside their mansion was always cluttered with vehicles; one would think there was a mini party going on. One of these days she needed to have a small chat with him about getting rid of some of these vehicles.

"Thank you Mr Maxwell." Tamanda said to the driver who closed the door as soon as she stepped clear.

"Welcome back madam." One of the workers clad in white cheerfully greeted her before dashing at the rear of the car to collect her luggage from the boot.

"Is everything okay as I left it?" Tamanda asked the other house worker who was walking slightly behind her, on her right side, carrying her black leather laptop case.

"Yes madam, just like you left it." The worker responded politely, holding the front door open for her.

He did not enter with her; gently closed it as soon as she was inside. He was going to enter the house using the back door instead; another frivolous protocol she just couldn't understand. Although to be fair on the workers, Walter did not encourage them using the front door.

Tamanda took five steps inside the foyer, her eyes adjusting from the brightness of the security lights outdoors, to the dim interior. She could smell his expensive cologne before she even saw him; she could smell that fresh clean aquatic scent from a million miles away. Her heart missed a beat; she smiled as her head slowly arched up, towards the staircase. He was standing there looking at her, at her shoes then her legs, like seeing her for the first time.

"There is my beautiful doctor of a wife." Walter's booming voice resonated from the top of the stairs; "I am so in love with those shoes and I'm doubly in love with the person inside them."

"Oh, darling, I will pay you anything if you promise to carry me up those stairs." Tamanda said with a smile, looking at her husband who was slowly coming down the stairs with his arms extended.

"So, what do you think?" Walter asked gesturing to the T-shirt he was wearing on top of his formal shirt.

"To start with, you look ridiculously funny with a T-shirt on top of a long-sleeved shirt." Tamanda said, her smile turning into a laboured laugh.

"I am glad that made you laugh. What else?" He asked standing three steps away from where she was.

"Walter, I am too tired." Tamanda groaned in protest.

"Come on tell me, what else my tired beautiful wife?"

"Well, you are wearing a T-shirt with my handsome husband's face on it and for that you deserve a kiss Mr MP-to-be." Tamanda said in a sensual tone, climbing the two steps until their bodies almost touched.

"Do I have your vote then doctor?" He asked taking a step down, their bodies now touching.

"It's going to take more than a T-shirt to squeeze a vote out of me, especially because you weren't there to protect me from my overbearing brother." Tamanda whispered, wrapping her arms around Walter.

"Who?"

"Who else? His Royal Highness King Elijah the Righteous." Tamanda sarcasm was coated with a thin layer of anger.

"Will this do?" He said, bending over to kiss his wife on the mouth.

Tamanda closed her eyes, enjoying the feel of his lips; she opened her mouth and felt his familiar tongue invade her insides. She felt lightheaded; goose bumps slowly spread throughout her arms like a bushfire.

"I missed you like crazy sweetheart." Tamanda struggled to speak with a mouth full of two tongues, hers and Walter's.

"Really? While in South Africa or while in Dedza?" He teased, trying to pull away but she pulled him closer; grabbing him right by his biceps and squeezing them tight, her well-manicured fingernails digging into his flesh.

"Where do you think you are going, Walter Lumbadzi?" She asked in a threatening albeit mocking tone.

"Mmmh, somebody is certainly hungry for someone." He teased.

"That's not funny Walter!" Tamanda said punching him in the chest.

"Ouch! Okay I missed you too my feisty doctor." He whispered, playfully clutching where her tiny fist had connected with his chest.

"Take me to bed honourable MP-to-be, earn your vote." Tamanda whispered, wrapping her arms around his neck.

Walter held on to the banister with one hand as the full weight of his slender wife almost knocked him off balance. He regained his composure, wrapped his arms around her bum, picked her and carried her upstairs, making funny sounds like he was carrying something prohibitively heavy. She wrapped her long legs around his waist as he staggered into their bedroom, gently setting Tamanda on the king-size bed.

"I missed you Walter." She said in a sensual voice, her big eyes looking up at him.

"I love it when you talk and look at me like that." He whispered, looking at her thighs which were exposed when he set her on the bed.

"Mmmh, really?" She purred.

"Yes, really. I find you very sexy sweetheart. I'm not just saying this to make you smile, sweetheart; you are way too beautiful in all departments." There was a slight tremor to Walter's voice, his eyes were watery.

"Wow darling, you sound as if I have been away for a hundred years." She said, cocking her head to one side.

"These days I never get to say these things as often as I used to, dear; it's just that looking at you now, I mean your face, your figure . . . then there is your voice; your accent, especially when you are talking in *chichewa*, the way you laugh, like you just did now, so lazy and so provocative . . . your tired eyes, how they correspond with your lazy voice . . . both of them doing things to me." His voice was so full of emotions; passion, love and some guilt too.

"Walter darling, are you trying to seduce me or what. Do you know how delicious that sounds to my ears, sweetheart?"

"I'm not trying to seduce you, darling. I guess you being away just made me realise and appreciate what I have."

"You are such a perfect husband, darling."

"No I am not, sweetheart; I am not as perfect as you are. How I wish I was like you . . . how . . ."

"Shhhh, you talk too much, Walter; you talk way too much." Tamanda whispered, cutting him off by placing her finger on his lips.

Walter stood looking down at her smiling face and her wet eyes; in them he could see the ocean of love his wife had for him. She was crying with happiness and he felt a tug of guilt. Not long ago he had been with another woman, Nomsa; she had also been crying.

What was happening to him? How could he fall for another woman when all his happiness was right here looking at him from their bed? His wife has always been there for him, through thick and thin. Her intelligence was an asset to him; there were times, in his business and more recently political dealings, when he wanted to take a left turn only at the last minute to be convinced by Tamanda to turn right. Not only this, she was the embodiment of beauty, brains and a sense of security; the woman he had said vows with, in front of family members, friends and the church.

"Are you okay?" Tamanda asked, noticing the distant look in Walter's eyes.

"I am fine sweetheart, I was just thinking about what you said."

"What's that?"

"About your brother, King Elijah; I can't believe that he was giving you tough time." Walter said jokingly, failing to disguise the underlying seriousness of his remark.

"Don't worry about my brother; he has never gotten over the fact that Dad did not choose him to be head of the family."

"Are you sure that's the reason? Sometimes I feel like your brother has never forgiven you for marrying me."

"What? Don't be ridiculous Walter. Now, are you going to stand there all night looking at a woman hungering for a man or are you going to jump in bed with me?" Tamanda teased, beckoning him with her finger.

Walter has never told Tamanda that the two of them had, for years, played a dangerous game of cat and mouse. He had always known that Detective Elijah was investigating and incarcerating a lot of corrupt businessmen. He was well aware that the rising detective star was sniffing him out. Nonetheless, Walter had always been one step ahead, outsmarting the policeman.

It took Walter months to realise that the girl he was dating was the youngest sister of his nemesis. He has never been able to figure out whether Elijah had finally backed off because they were now brothers or the fact that he had risen to the post of Deputy Inspector General of Police and was no longer dealing with detective work. There was a third option, more ominous which at times gave him nightmares; had Elijah retreated, changed his tactic to give him the impression that he was no longer pursuing him but waiting to pounce if and when he took a wrong step? Walter thought, and kept reminding himself to never let his guard down.

The fact that Elijah was his only brother in-law absent at their wedding was not lost on most people; the reason he gave that the wedding ceremony had coincided with the day the country's President had summoned police chiefs to his presidential palace, did not convince most of the family members.

Walter smiled as he slowly slid between the sheets; the soft and warm feeling of Tamanda's skin against his was enough to take his mind off his brother-in-law. He kissed her neck, it tasted salty and so did her cheeks. Tamanda reached up to him, her warm hands cupping his handsome face, her sensual lips millimetres from his. He clasped his strong arms around her tiny waist; their lips touched and he let out a muffled groan.

"Walter my sweetheart, are you okay?" She asked, her head snapping up from the pillow after noticing that a few drops had cascaded down his left cheek onto her breast.

"Yes sweetheart, I guess am just happy to see you." Walter lied, avoiding her eyes by sliding further down to kiss her belly button.

"I love you Walter."

"I love you too, Tamanda." He whispered, gently grabbing her silk skirt with both hands, he literally ripped it off her body.

"Oooh . . . Walter . . ." She gasped as he slowly and gently pressed his open palm on her bare breast; she folded her own arm, placing her hand over his, causing him to increase the scintillating pressure.

~ BLACKBERRY & HOSPITAL WARD ~

EITHER THE BRUISE on her forehead was getting better or the Dihydrocodeine oozing from the drip was doing what it was meant to do. Apart from the slight throbbing on the side of her head, Nomsa felt better than she had since regaining consciousness. Nurse Patricia had brought her handbag which contained her makeup, bank card and cash. Nomsa could tell the young nurse wanted to strike up a conversation about her make-believe cousin, Walter.

"I had no idea that you were cousins with Mr Lumbadzi." Nurse Patricia giggled.

Nomsa could see that the nurse was holding the handbag, slightly out of her reach, hoping that she would divulge more details about Walter.

"Nurse, he is married!" Nomsa snapped surprised by her response.

A jolt of pain exploded from the bruise on her forehead and the side of her face. Nomsa winced, snatching the handbag away from the disappointed looking nurse. The young nurse dejectedly walked back towards the door, closing it gently.

Nomsa was surprised by the sudden rush of jealousy, which erupted from deep inside her like an angry volcano the moment the nurse mentioned Walter's name.

"I am in love with him." She whispered.

This didn't come as a surprise; to say that she was just finding out would be a lie. The fact that she was coming to terms with this emotion state; the acceptance of it as normal, is what felt strange.

"He is married." She murmured whist staring upwards at the bright fluorescent tube.

Nomsa felt weak, not from the strong Dihydrocodeine in her system, but from the strange and exciting feelings bubbling up inside; emotions which were originating from the bottom of her heart.

With one hand, the one not connected to the drip, she rummaged through her bag, sifting through all sorts; searching, hunting. A faint smile danced across her lips when she felt the cold sleek gadget amidst all the clutter. Retrieving her Blackberry, Nomsa tossed the handbag on the floor. Memories of when Walter gave her this smartphone came flooding back. Nomsa's smile widened just thinking about that day.

It was the last week of January; five weeks after their first meeting in Zomba, six weeks after the two of them drove down the meandering Chikwawa escarpment M1 Road—they met again at Mount Soche Hotel, they sat by the pool. It was during this date that Walter asked her if she could move out of her small one bedroom house in Ndirande.

"Where else would I go?"

"Is that a yes?"

"What is this all about Walter? Ndirande is all I know, it's where I was born and raised."

"Let's go for a drive." He said, getting up whilst fishing his car keys from his trouser pocket.

They drove for fifteen minutes to the township of Chilomoni. He parked his Range Rover outside a two bedroom house; small but lovely, splashed in sky blue paint.

"Who lives here?" Nomsa asked with a slight frown.

"You, my dear Nomsa. If you want to, that is." He said in a husky voice, it was as if he was pleading with her.

Walter explained to her that he owned the house; an ex-employee of his had been residing there, until he got fired two months ago.

"Walter, no. I can't. Don't get me wrong it's a beautiful house, unfortunately I cannot afford to pay . . ."

"Shhhh, Nomsa, Nomsa, you don't have to pay rent." He cut her off, gently placing his hand over her mouth.

Nomsa was used to being given money, bought expensive clothes and taken to fancy hotels by men, but she had never been given a house to live in rent free.

"Walter, why . . . why are you doing this?" She choked the words as he handed her the keys.

"I don't want you living where you are now." The disapproving tone in his voice revealed that he didn't like the fact that she was living in Ndirande.

"Oooh Walter." She sobbed, leaning over to the driver's side, planting a gentle kiss on his left cheek.

It was on a rainy Valentine's evening, two weeks after she had moved into her Chilomoni home, when Walter visited her. It was actually his fourth visit and she was getting used to his unique knocking; a rapid succession drumming on using knuckles of both hands. Her heart missed a beat with excitement and she jumped up from the sofa to go open the door for him.

"Why do you always do that? You have a set of keys and yet you stand there knocking politely" As far as Nomsa was concerned it was his house, she couldn't understand why she always knocked and waited for her to let him in.

"Blame it on my mother, that's what she taught me." He answered standing by the door, his figure towering, filling up the frame.

Nomsa had been expecting him; she was dressed in her lacy white lingerie, whose flimsy material did little to conceal her full nipples. She looked at his face and smiled; her sexy outfit had achieved its desired effect.

"Mmmh." He said, giving her a seductive look.

"Mmmh, what? She teased, getting so close to him their bodies were almost touching.

"Mmmh where is the Prince of the house?" Walter asked, referring to her son.

She noticed that he was holding a thick bar of chocolate, expensive looking chocolate.

"Playing with his toys in his bedroom, we should be safe." Nomsa answered, looking at him provocatively.

She found him irresistibly handsome, in a black pinstriped suit, his silk tie partly loosened and the top button of his white shirt undone; Nomsa was fighting the urge to throw herself in his arms.

"What makes you think I came here for you?" He teased, sidestepping her, walking towards her son's bedroom.

She laughed; staggered towards the sofa and slumped in it. Nomsa stopped laughing when she heard his voice; he was making some baby sounds and her son was giggling loudly. She didn't know whether to cry or laugh, she was overcome with emotions, so she did both.

Moments later, Walter emerged from the bedroom without the chocolate. He stood looking at her; chocolate stains all over his silk tie. Nomsa stared at him, she was no longer laughing; tears were still pouring out of her eyes. He walked to the edge of the sofa and pulled her up, holding her.

"What's wrong? Are you crying because I gave the chocolate to Prince and not you?" He teased, wiping tears off her cheeks with his thumb.

"Walter, you are my guardian angel." Nomsa sobbed, snuggling closer to him, his expensive cologne doing things to her she couldn't even explain.

"Your tie . . . it's . . . it's all messed up." She said, looking up at him.

There was so much she wanted to tell him, but didn't know how; how could she tell him that no man has ever developed a close relationship with her son? Every time he visited her, she sat watching him play with her son on the floor, like he was his father. The two of them, pushing plastic toy cars while making the most terrible and funny noises.

Nomsa always wondered how it would be like if he didn't have to leave, if this were their home, the three of them. How could she tell him that just last night her son was pointing at the portrait of his, the one on her bedside table and was mouthing the word; *Dada* none stop?

"It's ok, I have got something for you, something better than chocolate." He said, smiling cheekily and going back outside.

She heard the car door open and close; he emerged, hands held behind his back, concealing something.

"What is it Walter?"

"Close your eyes Nomsa dear." He said shutting the door with the back of his foot.

Walter walked over to where she was waiting expectantly; he knew she was dying with anticipation.

"More chocolate?"

"Let me see your hand, keep your eyes closed." He said grabbing her right hand and placing a box wrapped in pink gift wrap, nicely tied with a purple ribbon.

"Wow, it's heavy. It's definitely not chocolate."

"You can open your eyes now." He spoke like a magician prolonging a climatic finale.

"What is it dear?" She asked expectantly.

"Happy Valentine's my dear Nomsa. Open it." He said in a deep husky voice.

She did just that, not sure what to expect. The wrappings fell to the ground; inside the box was a very sleek looking Blackberry phone.

"Oooh Walter baby, why do you keep doing these nice things for me? I don't deserve you." Nomsa tiptoed, kissing him on the cheek, leaving a smudge of red lipstick which she gently wiped with her palm.

"Look at us; first, Prince smears chocolate all over your tie and then I am sharing my lipstick with you. What will your wife think?" Nomsa regretted saying the last bit.

It came out before she could stop herself. She felt him flinch but didn't say a word; he just kissed her gently on the lips and her neck. She arched her body to him, wanting him to kiss her more, to go lower, to do more to her.

"Happy Valentine's Nomsa." He said, again, almost as if he was leaving.

"Happy Valentine's to you too, Walter." She spoke softly as if pleading with him not to go; she wrapped her arms around him.

Walter, still smiling, gently tapped her on the nose with his index finger, wiggled out of her grasp and left.

She sat back on the sofa, looking at the expensive Blackberry, thinking of this wonderful man; when she first met him, he was simply a client, a job which had to be executed. Now, he was much more, she had allowed him to enter areas of her heart no man had been before.

Now lying in a hospital bed she looked at the Blackberry, a wide smile spreading across her face. That's when it hit her; before she fainted she had texted Walter to send her a naughty picture. She fumbled with the keypad; there was unopened mail from him with an attachment; it contained photos. She started laughing, pain shooting from the side of her face every time her jaws moved.

"Walter, Walter, Walter . . . I thought you promised to delete these pictures." She shook her head from side to side, staring at the photos.

Nomsa remembered the day these photos had been taken, how could she forget? One of the photos caused her to raise her eyebrows; it showed the two of them lying side-by-side. He must have taken this one by holding the camera phone with his right arm. She didn't know he had taken this photo; he must have taken it while she was fast asleep on his chest, both of them sprawled on the bed at his Salima cottage.

Nomsa smiled, this was the first day they actually made love; it was the first time she had made love at all. Before, with other men, it had been sex . . . a job she was expected to do in order to get paid. She always looked at other men as clients, what transpired between them didn't involve emotions. Of course there were times when, with her clients, she felt hatred. She always wondered if these men would let their daughter go through the things they were forcing her to endure.

With Walter, it was different.

They had spent months just talking, either while driving or at her house in Chilomoni. Kissing was far as they went. Nomsa even started thinking that he didn't find her sexy enough; she couldn't understand why he hadn't taken the extra step.

But the day she thought would never arrive, finally did. It was well worth the wait; going to bed with him for the first time made her feel like a virgin. If he was gentle and caring with his words and deeds, he was even gentler in bed. Nomsa remembers screaming his name over and over again, almost choking with a passion she didn't know existed. He had paused briefly, looking at her then gently wiping the tear that had escaped from the corner of her eye.

Now, lying in the hospital bed she looked at the photo on the Blackberry. She felt tears welling up again. She was missing Walter; to think that he was just here not so long ago and yet she was already missing him.

Nomsa took out her Blackberry from her bag; holding it with both hands, she started typing a text message;

"*How I long to be in your arms Walter, sometimes I get so scared that you are just a dream and I will wake up. I love you Walter, if only this was another time another place, I would die to have you all to myself.*"

She had just pressed send when she heard a commotion outside her ward, she could hear Nurse Patricia's voice, she was arguing with someone. It was a familiar voice with a very distinctive accent, a foreign accent. It dawned on Nomsa who that was and she panicked, fumbling with her Blackberry to call Walter. The door flew open; her nightmare was staring at her.

"Please . . . please don't hurt me." Nomsa pleaded, pulling the hospital sheets all the way up to her neck.

The small figure was standing still, sneering at her; displaying yellowish teeth, resembling that of a vampire. Closing the door, she watched as her nightmare took deliberate slow steps, approaching her bed.

"Please don't hurt me . . ." Nomsa trembled with fear and nausea; her eyes were dilated as a feeling of hopelessness enveloped her.

~ DISTURBING PHONE CALL ~

WALTER HAD DOZED off whilst Tamanda was taking a shower, after their passionate lovemaking. He opened his eyes, smiling at her, standing with just a cream towel wrapped around her waist. Water was still dripping from her breasts, cascading down her abdomen before being absorbed by the towel. She was looking at him mischievously and yet shy.

Over the years, she had decorated the master bedroom tastefully; with local ornaments and expensive imported ones. His wife had an eye for attractive items and a knack of placing them at the right place to achieve a classy result. She was a perfectionist when it came to beautifying their home. Walter always said that; if she hadn't been a doctor she would have made a wonderful interior designer.

However, every time she went abroad, the bedroom felt different; the surroundings became bland, like someone had plucked the sun off the universe, plunging the planets into a dark abyss. That's how the bedroom had felt, until now.

Watching her standing in front of him, glowing and radiating sunshine throughout the room, it hit Walter just like it did the first time he saw her getting out of her father's car.

"Tamanda, you are very beautiful." He said for the second time since she arrived from Dedza.

"You seem to be repeating that sweetheart and I'm starting to believe you." She teased.

"You didn't dry yourself on purpose, right?" His voice was croaky, her beauty so alluring.

"I didn't?" She said, laughing teasingly.

"Gosh, you are so beautiful sweetheart."

"And it's all yours." She playfully said spinning around on her wet feet like a ballet dancer. She stopped and struck a pose, like a model.

"You are posing without a bra, are you trying to get me arrested for making passionate love to my wife twice in the same night?" He said lazily, sitting up on his elbows.

"Ha! I doubt if you still have it in you." Tamanda teased, shaking the top part of her body at him.

Walter groaned as her firm wet breasts teased him, mocking him; there was a tug coming from his lower abdomen. The excitement from watching her was causing his bladder to contract. He jumped out of bed, planted a quick kiss on his wife's cheek as he dashed past her for the master bedroom's en-suite toilet.

"Don't move until I get back!" He shouted from the toilet.

"After all that sweet sex, you mean to tell me that you are still hungry for more of me?" Tamanda teased from the bedroom.

She was challenging and goading him on; she wanted to have him again. She had missed him, missed his manliness. The first time, last night, had been too quick; they were two hungry beasts devouring each other. Now Tamanda wanted him to take her slowly, gently all the way to the top of the mountain and stay with her there.

"You bet I do, especially after seeing you looking like that." Walter yelled, flexing his lower muscles, hurrying himself up. He almost flushed the toilet before finishing.

"Really?"

"Yes, and you also smell delicious. Did you buy a different perfume to the usual one?"

"Yes, sweetheart, I got this one from the duty free shop at the airport."

"I love it, what is it?" He asked surprised how full his bladder had been.

"It's called Bright Crystal by Versace." She said, forcing her voice to sound posh.

"Uuuh! Versace, mmhhh? He teased.

"Sweetheart, you have a text here from someone called *Land-Lord*." Tamanda's voice hit Walter like a ton of bricks. He painfully tried to halt the urinating process, partially succeeding, pulling his boxers up despite the fact that he was still dripping. He didn't care, dashing back into the bedroom with a concerned look.

Tamanda was sprawled naked on the bed, her back to him, holding his mobile phone.

"Who is *Land-Lord* Sweetheart?" She asked in a flat tone, without turning around to face him.

"Are you reading my text message?" He asked, struggling to inject some blame-tone into his scared voice. The excitement he felt moments ago replaced by a sense of trepidation.

"You are not serious, are you? All these years that we have been married, have I ever read your text messages?" She asked, turning around with a smile on her face. She stopped smiling when their eyes locked.

"Sorry, I don't know why I said that." He said, recovering from the shock.

"Should I be reading your texts? Who is *Land-Lord* by the way?" She asked while handing out the phone out to him.

"It's someone helping me with the whole political campaign process." He said, forcing a smile and grabbing the phone from her extended hand.

"Why save his name as *Land-Lord* and why is he texting you this late darling, it's almost midnight?"

"*Land-Lord*, err . . . he owns several shanty homes and people call him Land-Lord, I guess I just thought of saving him in my phone by that name." He said; his voice slightly croaky.

Walter was surprised by his flawless lie; the words caused a pang of guilt they tumbled out of his mouth. At the same time, he breathed a sigh of relief; Tamanda had just seen who sent the text, she hadn't opened it. Not only did his wife love him, but she trusted him and she believed each word he was telling her. What was he doing to her, to their marriage? What was it about Nomsa that he couldn't resist? Walter grappled with these questions, still holding the phone in his hand.

"Well, it must be something urgent, aren't you going to open it?"

"Oh yes, I guess." He mumbled opening the text, thankful that he was standing up.

"*How I long to be in your arms Walter, sometimes I get so scared that you are just a dream and I will wake up. I love you Walter, if only this was another time another place, I would die to have you all to myself.*"

He quickly read the romantic text and immediately pressed delete, then jumped in bed next to his wife.

"Whatever *Land-Lord* wrote must be good news." Tamanda said, wrapping her arms around him.

"What do you mean?"

"Well, you are smiling again. You weren't a short while ago."

"Oh is that so? Maybe because next to me is the most beautiful and the sexiest woman on the planet." He said in a lazy husky voice.

"Is that the best you can do?" She said teasingly.

"I can also do this." He said bending over, kissing his wife passionately.

"Mmhhh . . . now that's more like it." Tamanda purred like a cat whose fur was being stroked the right way; "did you just wet your boxer's darling?"

"I was rushing for you."

"Yeah right, you are such a lousy liar Walter, sometimes I wonder if you will make it as a politician."

"Who are you calling a liar you little ungrateful doctor?" He said in a soft romantic voice, his finger zigzagging down Tamanda's belly.

"Mmmh, who are you calling ungrateful? Don't stop what you are doing with that finger, keep going . . . down . . . mmhhh"

Then Walter's phone rang, causing him to jump. He angrily grabbed it from the side table.

"Hello! Who is this?" He yelled so loud; Tamanda, who had been purring to the feel of his finger, froze.

"Hello, Mr Lumbadzi, it's me Nurse Patricia, from the hospital, do you remember me?"

"Yes? What is it?" Walter asked his anger morphing into worry and he bolted upright from the bed.

"Sorry to disturb you at this time of the night, but there has been an incident at the hospital. You need to come straight away." Nurse Patricia said on the other end of the line.

A chill crawled up his spine. With Tamanda lying right next to him, there was no way he could start asking questions to the nurse over the phone. What could it be? He wondered. Nomsa looked fine when he left the hospital, before meeting Tosh. He hung up the phone, aware that his wife was looking at him, surely she would want to know who or what was that all about. He would if the roles were reversed.

"I have to go to the hospital sweetheart."

"Hospital? At midnight? What's wrong?" Tamanda asked, alarmed and sitting up next to him.

"One of the trucks coming from Mozambique has been involved in a bad accident and the driver is in critical condition."

"Another tanker?" Tamanda asked as her mind went back to the last fatal accident involving another one of their tanker trucks; which, two months ago had caught fire, killing the driver and some passengers of the bus it had collided with.

"I believe so, yes." Walter lied.

"And you are going to the hospital to see him?" Tamanda asked, surprised.

"Yes darling, I am going to visit an employee of mine who has been badly injured, is that okay with you?" Walter snapped as he jumped out of bed, avoiding eye contact with his highly perceptive wife, scared she might see the lie in his eyes.

"I am sorry sweetheart, I didn't mean to sound so inconsiderate, it's just that it's very late and I have never known you to go visit employees at the hospital. It's usually Mr Daudi who does that." Tamanda said, sounding apologetic and standing behind him, wrapping her arms around his waist.

"I am sorry too for snapping at you sweetheart, you are right, it's just that with this whole political campaign, I want to be seen doing the right thing." Walter said, gently wriggling out of Tamanda's hug and pacing towards their walk-in closet.

"Do you want me to come with you?"

"No! I mean . . . I would love you to, but no sweetheart, try and get some rest. You just got back today remember?" He yelled, grabbing a pair of trousers and a shirt.

"Call me when you get there darling." She said, sounding concerned.

She hated the fact that he had to leave this late in the night; she thought they would spend the rest of the night together after missing him considerably while in South Africa.

"I will sweetheart." He said walking back into the bedroom, fully dressed.

He learnt over the bed, warmly kissing her on the cheek. A small voice was telling him how wrong this was, one part of him wanted to stay . . . just to cuddle next to his wife and confess everything to her. He hugged Tamanda tighter than normal; he was going to see what was wrong with Nomsa and tell her he could no longer go on with the affair. It was time to be honest with her as well; he was married, he loved his wife, the woman he had said vows with. He had to do what was right and tell her that what the two of them were doing was wrong on so many levels; it could ruin not just his life but of those he cared for.

"Wait for me sweetheart; I want us to have a little chat when I get back." He whispered into Tamanda's ears.

"Okay? That sounds ominously intriguing." She said, looking at her husband with a smile; "I am dead beat from the duel I had with my brother, so I can't promise that you will find me alive when you get back."

"I will pour cold water on you." He said jokingly, not fully managing to inject the right amount of humour, failing to achieve the intended reaction.

Tamanda looked at him blankly and he turned around, pulled the bedside side drawer, sifting through a plethora of car keys. He grabbed the one he was looking for and dashed out of the bedroom, down the stairs and out the front door.

The night security guards were surprised to see him emerge from the house; all four of them stood at attention as he walked towards the parking lot. Walter was oblivious to their salutations; jumping in his Toyota Land Cruiser, he sat behind the wheel, not moving.

With both hands on the steering wheel, he took a deep breath then inserted the key in the ignition. He looked up at the bedroom window upstairs; the curtains were drawn. He could just make out the dim yellowish glow; she still had the bedside light on. Walter banged his hands repeatedly on the steering wheel; confused and wondering how it had gotten this far. Here he was, leaving his wife, a woman who loved him dearly lying in bed to go see another woman; a girlfriend, who loved him dearly as well.

"What a mess." Walter whispered to himself, fishing out his mobile phone; he dialled Nomsa's number.

Her phone was switched off.

~ DON'T DO THIS TO ME ~

THERE WAS FEAR all over Nomsa's face. She couldn't believe Obafeni had tracked her down all the way to the hospital. There was a tight feeling at the pit of her stomach; she regretted the day this dangerous man entered her life.

Obafeni was a notorious Nigerian, a street drug dealer, who lived in Ndirande. He arrived in Malawi and started frequenting a Pentecostal church near Ndirande Market. Obafeni knew his bible very well and his conversations were always spiced with biblical verses; he soon became the darling of the church. His generous tithes during service and his eloquent speaking, every time he was asked to read the bible, caught the eyes of single women in church. It was not long before he got engaged to a local Malawian lady; a born again Christian, called Delilah.

Soon after his wedding to Delilah, the cunning Obafeni managed to get a Malawian passport; he revoked his Nigerian nationality and became a Malawian naturalised citizen. Fourteen months later, Obafeni and Delilah divorced. Nonetheless, he still ingratiated himself deeper into the Malawian society; donating considerably to the church.

Despite his religiousness and the revoking of his Nigerian nationality; Obafeni had a darker ominous side. He was a gangster and he still maintained his contacts to the Nigerian underworld. He was smart and very cunning, always one step ahead of the Malawian law; smuggling in drugs and smuggling out cash. Illegal drugs were entering the country concealed in bibles, whereas cash, in dollars, was leaving the country concealed in coffins or inside dead bodies of Nigerians who had died mysteriously while in Malawi.

Obafeni managed to stay under the radar of the law by living a simple life. He had more than enough money to live in a more expensive low density suburb, but he chose Ndirande. It is here where he terrorised and instilled fear in anyone who ended up crossing his path. Obafeni, on the most part, worked alone; a wolf prowling the dense juggle of Ndirande at night and a committed born again Christian by day.

Not only did he supply drugs to students, from wealthy families, who went to the nearby St Andrews private school, Obafeni also cast his net far and wide. He was selling to young executives, who used drugs for recreational purposes and prostitutes who took drugs to numb them of the realities of their trade.

Nomsa, a sophisticated call girl, was one of his loyal clients.

However, since moving to Chilomoni, Nomsa hadn't seen much of Obafeni; it was a blessing having to escape from his vicious clutches. He had made drugs so readily available at a time when she needed them. She had Walter now, she had a new life and she felt clean.

A few days ago, Nomsa and Obafeni bumped into each other while on a queue inside one of the banks in downtown Blantyre. He wanted so much to know where she was living, but the last thing Nomsa wanted was for him to re-enter her life; she resisted his veiled threats and did not disclose her current address.

"I understand your reluctance Nomsa, but you can have this." He said with a smile, dropping some drugs in her handbag.

"Obi, no. I am clean now, I no longer . . ."

"It's okay Nomsa; you don't have to pay me now." He simply said before exiting the bank.

She watched him jump into his BMW, reversing out of the parking lot before speeding off. Only then did Nomsa breathe a sigh of relief. She peeped into her handbag, nervously looking at the drugs, then around her; just to make sure that no one saw what had just taken place. Nomsa shook her head; telling herself that she was going to dispose of them once she got home.

Lately she had been spending amazing time with Walter; he had become her drug—a life giving drug. However, every time he was not with her she felt like she was dying inside. Walter had grown inside her like a wart that oozed life; he had become part of her. She needed him like she had never needed any man before. It was all this missing and longing that led to the relapse she had. She needed an escape and the drugs Obafeni had placed in her bag started beckoning to her.

Now, lying on the hospital bed; looking up at Obafeni who was sneering down at her like a vampire thirsting for blood, Nomsa regretted her relapse. Why did she inject those drugs? She agonised and loathed the day her life crossed paths with this Nigerian leach.

"Where is my money?" Obafeni said in a heavy Nigerian accent.

"Ob, I was going to pay you tomorrow, I swear." Nomsa whimpered, holding the hospital sheet up until it covered her chin.

"How come your phone is constantly switched off then?"

"I am sorry Ob, I changed my number, I have a different phone but I swear I was going to pay you."

"Do you know what I had to go through just to find you?" Obafeni said looking at her handbag which was on the floor.

"I am sorry, but like I said, I will pay you." Nomsa sobbed.

"You are lucky that I'm a God fearing man Nomsa, I am worried about you." He said coldly, his reference to God so out of context in the current situation.

"I swear Ob, I will pay, as soon as I get out of here, I will Ob, I will." Nomsa pleaded.

"I know you will pay me back Nomsa, that's not what worries me." Obafeni said with a smile that did not reach his eyes.

"I . . . I . . . don't follow you Ob." Nomsa quizzed, scared to look at his smile which made him look like a rat—a sewer rodent—bent on making people miserable.

"Since you abruptly moved out of Ndirande, I have noticed some changes in you Nomsa." He said, running his hand along her lower arm.

"Change? Me? No I haven't changed Ob." Nomsa coughed, forcing herself not to flinch from his repulsive touch. His hand felt cold, the same coldness that was radiating from his eyes. It felt like someone was rubbing frozen human faeces along her arm; she summoned all her energy not to shake his hand away, she did not want to inflame his short temper.

"Well, for starters; you are not buying as much as you used to and for a moment there I thought you have found another supplier."

"That's ridiculous Ob; you know I will never abandon you." Nomsa said, fear in her voice, wishing someone could just walk in.

She wished Walter hadn't left her alone in this hospital ward. If he was here, she knows he would have taken care of Obafeni. She should have given him his name when he asked her; Nomsa thought as Obafeni stopped stroking her arm; he took a step towards the drip which was hanging on the side of the bed.

"I know you wouldn't Nomsa, but word on the street is that you are trying to quit." He said without looking at her.

Obafeni was now standing right next to the head of the bed, the rat sneer on his face exposing his yellowish fang-like teeth. His red eyes were looking up at the drip of Dihydrocodeine; then down at Nomsa. She averted her eyes and looked towards the door.

"I . . . I . . . I have been thinking about it, but . . ."

"Have you been thinking about it or is it that rich boyfriend of yours who is instilling these crazy ideas in you?" Obafeni said, his hand squeezing on the clear bag of Dihydrocodeine solution hanging on the end of the metallic hospital stand.

"Please Ob, who told you that?" Nomsa stuttered, her eyes darting from Obafeni to the door and back at him.

"Don't worry about who told me and don't worry about the night nurse coming in here, I told her I am your brother, that just heard about your nasty fall." Obafeni said, dipping his hand into his leather jacket; it came out holding onto a brown leather pouch.

"Please Ob, don't squeeze the drip, it's . . . it's hurting me." Nomsa pleaded, but he ignored her and carried on squeezing. She could see her vein, where the needle for the drip was inserted, bulge out as the liquid medicine was being forced into her body.

"Are you in pain Nomsa?"

"Yes Ob, please stop. It hurts, it . . . it is so painful." Nomsa winced, her free hand clamped her mouth; her eyes squeezed shut supressing a scream, her whole body quivered.

"Why didn't you say so then? I have got something for you Nomsa that might take care of that pain." He said, letting go of the drip.

She watched him as he slowly unzipped a small leather pouch; he took out a medical syringe with a hypodermic needle at its end. It was similar to the one she had at home, it had to be similar, after all, it was him who supplied it to her; Nomsa thought, dreading of what he was contemplating on doing next with that ominous looking contraption.

"Ob, please don't do this, please I am begging you." Nomsa pleaded, tears pouring out of her eyes.

"Don't worry; it will be like old times. I am just trying to help you Nomsa. Look on the bright side, this one is on me, free of charge." Obafeni said biting the safety cap with his yellow teeth, exposing the sharp needle.

Then with his left hand he held and squeezed tightly on Nomsa's biceps, close to the elbow causing the veins to pop out. In one fluid motion, his right hand deftly inserted the hypodermic needle, squeezing it with thumb; injecting the rest of the whitish contents into her blood stream.

"Please Ob; please . . . I beg you . . . don't do this to me please." Nomsa sobbed silently as Obafeni retracted the now empty syringe; he covered the needle with the safety cap and tossed it back into the leather pouch. His hawkish eyes looked at her, the smile gone from his face, only loathing.

"For the money you owe me, I think I will keep this nice looking Blackberry phone." Obafeni sneered, pocketing her phone; her valentines present from Walter.

"Why Ob, why are you doing this to me?"

"Just have my money ready when you get out of the hospital, I now know where you live. I see your neighbours are taking good care of that little bastard son of yours." Obafeni chided her; he turned around and walked out of the private ward.

"Please, Ob . . . please . . . don't hurt my son . . . please don't . . ." Nomsa coughed, raising her hand weakly towards the door; trying to stop him but he was gone.

She tried to get up but couldn't; the room was spinning and she started feeling hot and nauseated. The mixture of the drug he had just pumped into her system, mixed with the Dihydrocodeine from the syringe, was lethal. She yanked the syringe of the drip out of her arm, tearing her skin in the process.

Nomsa's chest was now on fire, she urged herself to vomit but nothing happened, she stuck two of her fingers down her throat; trying to heave. Still nothing; the best she could do was to induce a cough and a spasm of chokes.

Her eyes were rolling in their sockets; her heart began to race and she was sweating profusely. Breathing was becoming difficult, despite opening her mouth wide she felt like someone had covered her head inside a plastic bag.

The lower part of her body felt cold, she felt like her legs were immersed in ice, whereas the fire raging throughout her upper body was increasing in temperature.

"Walter . . . Walter my darling . . . Walter." She gasped his name; her head slumped back into the pillow, it felt heavy.

She heard screams and shouts, it was the night nurses trying to summon for help. In her dazed stupor she must have managed to set off the call-light.

"We are losing her! She is flat-lining, call Dr Bandawe from the theatre!" A female voice was yelling frantically.

It sounded like the nurse who had been asking her about Walter, the young looking nurse, she tried to remember her name but couldn't.

"Nurse . . . nurse . . ." Nomsa mumbled, her words slurred.

"Yes this is Nurse Patricia, stay with me madam!"

"Pat . . . Patricia . . . call him, call my Walter."

"Call the Doctor!" Nurse Patricia yelled at a medical assistant who had just walked into the commotion.

"Please, it's important . . . call him, get Walter here fast." Nomsa's voice was coming out laboriously; she had no idea where she was.

"I said get the doctor in here!" Nurse Patricia yelled again, fumbling to feel her pulse.

"I did, he . . . he is on his way." The male medical assistant responded, looking confused.

"Okay, go back to the nurse's station, on the yellow pad there is a phone number. That's the patient's cousin, Mr Lumbadzi; call and tell him to come to the hospital quick!" The nurse yelled while the other nurse was flashing a tiny torch into Nomsa's eyes.

"Walter . . . is he here? Walter . . ." Nomsa mumbled, her speech getting worse, her eyes not reacting to the flashing of the torch light.

"No, Nomsa this is Dr Bandawe." A young doctor said running into the ward, armed with a stethoscope.

"Walter . . . I'm glad you came, my love." Nomsa whispered, sounding delusional and croaky; her arm was stretched, weakly tugging on the doctor's green surgery scrubs.

"Nurse, I can't find the number!" The male medical assistant said, barely sticking his head inside the ward.

"Ok, come help the doctor, just come!" Nurse Patricia bolted out of the ward. She had memorised Walter's number, she was going to call him herself.

"Stay with me Nomsa! Do not close your eyes, stay with me!" Dr Bandawe said loudly, pressing his stethoscope on Nomsa's chest; "pass me my bag, quick!" He yelled at the spellbound male assistant.

"Walter . . . I love you Walter . . . thank you for everything."

"He loves you too Nomsa, hang in there now!" The doctor said, trying to keep Nomsa's mind busy whilst gesturing to another nurse, who had just walked in.

"Walter . . . sweetheart, can you hear me Walter?"

"Nomsa! Stay with me, Walter is on his way!"

"Walter . . . take care of my son . . . take . . . take care of our son . . . please Walter . . ."

Nomsa! Stay with me, okay?" The doctor pleaded with her, turning to the nurse and shouting; "where is the oxygen I asked for?"

"Walter, you are a good man . . . I will . . . I will always lo . . ." Nomsa whispered unable to finish the sentence, her eyes closed and all was still.

"We lost her, she is gone." The deflated doctor said to the distraught looking nurse.

"Oh Lord no, she was just okay before that man, her brother, came in." The nurse said, more to herself than to the doctor.

"You mean her cousin?"

"No, another man was here, he told Nurse Patricia that he was her brother." The nurse said, as she slowly covered Nomsa's face with the white hospital linen.

"Time of death: twenty past midnight." Doctor Bandawe said in a sombre tone. He took a deep breath and let it out slowly.

"He is on his way, her cousin is on . . ." Nurse Patricia said entering the ward; she stopped in her tracks the minute her eyes fell on the covered up body of Nomsa.

~ KILLING FOR LOVE ~

FOG ROLLED IN from Ndirande Mountain, cascading down the slopes, curling through the yellowish beam of the only street lamp along this street. It was a nameless street, littered with plastic bags, empty bottles and dry leaves. The road sign that once bore the street's name had long been stolen, not that people cared about names of streets around here. However, they cared about eating. It was a season of flying grasshoppers, called *abwanoni*, a local delicacy which tends to be attracted to light at night. Stripped of their wings and fried or roasted, these *abwanoni* are consumed as a relish with *nsima* or gobbled up by the handful and washed down with beer, in bars.

On this particular evening, a lot of them were flying around the yellowish glare of the streetlight. Being the only working light along this dark street meant that the concentration of the flying grasshoppers was more than usual.

Since 18:30, over twenty people; mostly women and children had converged under the yellow glow of the streetlight since; there was an excited commotion of people running back and forth. They were chatting, laughing and yelling whilst busy scooping up the tiny grasshoppers into plastic bags, ready for roasting and drying up the following day.

By midnight, the women and children had long dispersed. Only a handful of men, about six, remained; quietly picking up the few *abwanoni* which were still fluttering around the yellow glow of the streetlight.

Beyond the periphery of the yellowish glow, deep in the pitch black darkness, a figure of a man shifted. Knowing that he could not be seen, Tosh breathed into his hands, rubbing them together to generate warmth. For hours he had remained still, watching the excitement around the streetlight with some concealed amusement and a bit of anger. Tosh felt that eating *abwanoni* was synonymous with poverty. He was certain that people, like Walter Lumbadzi, who lived in the posh low density areas of Namiwawa or Nyambadwe were not chasing grasshoppers as tomorrow's relish.

At forty-four, Tosh had reached that age in his life whereby he had stopped believing he will ever escape the poverty of his immediate surroundings; there was no way he will ever live Walter's life. Neither would these people chasing the *abwanoni*, they would probably be doing the same thing years from now, that is if they lived that long; Tosh thought as he gazed towards the streetlight.

He hated his life and was always angry because he didn't have a lot of options left to make things better. His parents had stopped asking long time ago if he will ever find a proper job. They hadn't gotten tired of asking, but they were scared of his outburst at being asked what he considered to be a frivolous question.

"Find work as what father? As a garden boy?" He would lash out at his petrified parents.

The poverty here didn't leave one with that many options to start with; stealing, prostitution or the last resort—suicide. As far as Tosh was concerned suicide was for cowards and he was not a coward, so he sought another option; violence.

Tosh was attracted to violence from a very young age; he still remembers stabbing a fellow student when he was only nine. Over the years he had perfected violence into a trade. There were people out there, mostly prominent people;

politicians or businessmen who needed muscles for hire, someone who could do their dirty work, deeds that on some occasions involved the spilling of blood.

Walter Lumbadzi was one such man who always needed the services Tosh offered. Tosh knew a side of Walter not many people were aware of; not the politician who was constantly praised and lauded as a role model, golden boy and the future of Malawi by the media. Walter was a violent man; only that he hired the likes of him to coordinate and carry out that violence.

In his crouched kneeling position, Tosh's right hand was gently caressing the ivory grip-handle of the long knife inside his jacket. His bloodshot eyes were fixated on the jubilant chaos ensuing around the streetlight.

This was just a sideshow; Tosh's main focus was the nondescript house not far from the street lamp. He was certain about the house; he had visited the street the day before, asking clandestinely about its occupant. A few kids confirmed that a Nigerian man lived there alone. Some women even voiced their suspicions about their strange neighbour, who rarely spoke to them and appeared to be shady, coming or going only in the cover of darkness.

The fat woman who lived across the house was forthcoming with information about the Nigerian; he claimed that he was Malawian and that his wife had divorced him because he was spending too much time at church.

There were no lights inside the Nigerian's house and the black BMW which Tosh had seen the day before parked outside the house was not there. This meant that he was not home.

When Tosh arrived at his hiding place, the neighbourhood dogs started barking loudly at his unfamiliar scent. He had come prepared; taking out a plastic bag full of chicken bones, he slowly tossed them, one by one, on the ground whilst whistling a calming tune. Before long, the dogs ceased barking; they were wagging their tails while gnawing at the chicken bones. The plastic bag was now empty; it didn't matter though because he was now friends with the dogs.

"Where are you, you Nigerian parasite?" Tosh whispered, rubbing his hands together for warmth.

The fog had thickened a bit, it was difficult to ascertain if there was any movement inside the house or not. Did someone else drive the BMW? Was the Nigerian still inside the house? Tosh wondered, debating whether to remain hidden in the shadows or wander closer. He didn't want to expose himself, but then he couldn't stay crouched in the shadows forever. Dawn would break in a few hours.

The dogs looked up at Tosh as he got up and walked towards the street lamp. The six men who were still busy picking up the grasshoppers looked at the approaching large figure of a man briefly; they smiled then carried on with their task. Tosh smiled, joining them, blending in and becoming part of the grasshopper picking crew. From this new vantage point, he had a better view of the Nigerian's house. There was no sign of life, no lights and all curtains were drawn.

He was about to call it a night when he saw the car. At first he thought it was a motor bike, because only one headlight was on. As the bright beam drew closer, Tosh realised that it was the black BMW. From the corner of his eye, he watched as it slowed down, turning into the short driveway which was as long as the car itself. Tosh tried not to freeze; instead he bent over, his movements so fluid, pretending to be picking up the *abwanoni* from the ground. He crouched lower to disguise his huge frame, wondering why the occupant of the car was not stepping out. He could see the silhouette of a man inside the car but he couldn't make out the features.

Obafeni sat there looking at the rear view mirror. Years in this trade had taught him one thing; never fear that which is in front of you, it's what you can't see that should arouse concern. He was watching to make sure that he hadn't been followed home. He looked at the houses of his nosey neighbours on either side of his and across the street. Everything looked normal.

"Lazy stupid Malawians, already in bed; no wonder they are born poor and die poor." He murmured to himself while craning his neck sideways; he was observing the group of seven men who were picking grasshoppers under the glow of the street light.

"Disgusting . . . simply disgusting human beings; look at them, eating insects." Obafeni murmured while leaning over the passenger seat to open the glove box.

It was full of cash; US dollars which he had exchanged during the day. He always exchanged the local Kwacha currency for dollars or Pound Sterling at the curios market, downtown Blantyre, where he was a regular. Sometimes he would exchange his Kwachas at a particular forex bureau run by a fellow Nigerian.

Unlike the banks, there were no questions asked at these places. Despite the dangers of dealing with the black market forex dealers at the wooden curios market, their rates were far much better than that offered by the banks. The only Malawians he respected for the ingenuity were those dealing in black market forex; the stupid Fiscal Police were always ten steps behind these dealers.

Inside the glove compartment, behind the wads of cash, were two bibles which Obafeni carried at all times. Inside one of the Bible, whose pages were deliberately gauged to create a cavity, was a handgun: a small Glock 9mm pistol. He opened the bible and took the handgun out. He scooped the cash into a plastic bag while shoving the small pistol into his leather jacket.

Since coming to Malawi he has never had to use his firearm; this was a sleepy country as far as violence was concerned. He had heard a lot about Malawi when he was still in Nigeria; how backward its people were, a country full of potential which its own citizens couldn't see. He was surprised how true that was when he first arrived; he was even more surprised that he didn't even have to show his gun to scare these backward people. They were scared of him just by hearing his Nigerian accent.

"Lazy grasshopper eating cowards." He chuckled to himself as he opened his door; cursing as his shiny polished shoe stepped on fresh dog faeces.

"*Mmxiiiii!*" He seethed, closing the door lightly so as not to make any noise that late in the night.

Obafeni despised the fat lady who lived in the house across; she was one nosey hippo, always peeping through her curtains to see what time he came home. She reminded him of Delilah's mother.

Even though he never felt any love for Delilah, she was just a gullible and the right person he could use to get his Malawian citizenship; she was a nice person. He actually liked her and if she had been Nigerian, Obafeni thought he would probably have grown to love her. However, for the whole time he was married to Delilah, he hated her mother; he couldn't even bring himself to calling her 'mother-in-law' or *Apongozi*, as was the custom here in Malawi.

The fat woman from across the road reminded him so much of Delilah's mother and if there was a Malawian he so much wanted to shoot, it was this fat hippo neighbour of his.

Maybe a bullet hole would deflate some of that fat out of her mass and turn her into a normal size woman; Obafeni thought as he inserted the key to lock his car.

Something was not right; Obafeni thought and his muscles instinctively tensed. It took him a few seconds to realise what it was. Every time he gets out of his car, he would be greeted by the neighbourhood dogs, pissing on the tyres of his car or barking excitedly at his arrival. There was none of that. The dogs were absent.

Inside Obafeni's brain, a scene he had just seen, before getting out of the car, replayed itself like a movie. The seven men picking up the flying insects from the ground, one of them had been crouching too low to the ground, why? Obafeni wondered and immediately saw the answer in flash in front of him like a Eureka moment.

The man didn't want to be seen. Unlike the other men, this one was not holding a plastic bag; he was only pretending to pick the flying grasshoppers. Obafeni hated himself for not noticing this before exiting the safety of his car. That man was not here to pick insects, he was here for him; Obafeni concluded and immediately started to pivot on the heels of his shoes like a dancer.

That's when he sensed a movement before he saw it. A shadow was moving fast in the shadows; way too fast, like a ghost. Obafeni immediately knew that the shadow was the seventh man, and he was not advancing towards his direction to offer him edible insects.

Living in Malawi had made him rusty; Obafeni realised. He could not believe that he had stupidly held on the plastic bag of money with his right hand; his gun hand. He dropped it to free his hand, fumbled with his jacket until he could feel the familiar handle of his Glock.

It was too late.

The big shadowy figure of the seventh man was up on him. The impact was surreal as it was violent.

Tosh had done his homework. He had heard that the Nigerian was always armed. He saw the small Nigerian drop a plastic bag to the ground, his hand swiftly sliding inside his leather jacket. Tosh could not afford to let that hand reappear or that would be the last thing he will ever see. There was no point in moving stealthily; they had made each other out and both knew that only one of them was going to see the break of dawn. Tosh was determined to be that person; he had two prostitutes waiting for him in his bedroom, at his parent's house.

With adrenalin pumping, Tosh's powerful legs propelled him towards the Nigerian; his big knife glittered in the moonlight, expertly held in an arched position, for a frontal assault.

Putting all his weight behind the right shoulder, Tosh crashed into the surprised Nigerian, simultaneously clasping his left hand on the little man's mouth and nose. He managed to pin him against his own car; Tosh's right hand swung in five swift successive thrusts. Each blow was precisely administered, the big knife slicing the Nigerian's belly and the side of his neck.

Tosh heard the muffled screams against his big palm which was still around the Nigerian's mouth. He felt the little man's body go limp; he slowly released his hold, stepping back and watched as the Nigerian slowly slid to the ground. He was looking at him with wide dying eyes, a frozen look of horror.

Tosh's intentions had been to scare the Nigerian, maybe break his fingers or knees and tell him to leave Malawi and go back to Abuja or wherever he came from. However the little man had gone for his gun, leaving him with no choice; Tosh thought wiping the smudge of bloody saliva on his palm by using the man's jacket.

A smile crossed his face but immediately disappeared when a movement caught the corner of his eye; a curtain from one of the houses across was moving, a light had just come on and there was a huge figure of a woman.

Tosh spun around and started running away from the scene, his mind already on the two prostitutes waiting for him.

Obafeni was shocked, almost in awe, at how his assailant had swiftly closed the gap and overpowered him. He knew he was dying, there was excruciating pain from around his neck; with the last ounce of energy left in him, he held the gun steady with both hands, aiming it at the escaping figure of his assailant. He held his breath and squeezed the trigger six times in sporadic succession. It was the last activity Obafeni conducted.

The gun fell from his hand, his head slowly slumped forward.

Tosh was just about to run past the six men who were still busy picking grasshoppers when something hot and heavy hit him at the back of the neck. He saw a mist of blood in front of him as his neck exploded from the existing bullet. His mouth was contorted into a scream; he wanted to curse obscenities at Walter so bad, but no sound came, only air rushed out of his punctured neck in some horrible gurgling sound. His massive frame tumbled forward uselessly and he landed with a thud, face down. Darkness quickly enveloped him. The last image

Tosh had was that of a grasshopper hopping on the ground next to his cheek.

He thought of the two prostitutes, then thought of Walter and finally, he thought of nothing.

~ SIBLINGS & DETECTIVES ~

THE BLUE LAND Rover was parked between the two houses; its dark colour completely camouflaging it from curious eyes. At this time of the night, the occupants of the houses on either side of the police car; were fast asleep or not at home. The two men sitting inside were Detectives Aubrey Zeneya and Ezekiel Gunda. For months, they had been following Tosh's movements on orders from their Detective Chief Inspector—DCI.

"He is to be kept under surveillance for as long as it takes." The DCI had stressed to the two detectives.

The only details furnished to them were that; Tosh was a suspect of arson; a vehicle belonging to the incumbent Member of Parliament for Blantyre Constituency had been torched. Even though he was the main suspect, the two detectives were told not to bring him in.

"Do not alert him, just watch him and report straight to me." Their DCI had ordered.

And watch him, they did. Following him at a discreet distance to filthy drinking places, observing him flirting with prostitutes, groping young girls and occasionally getting involved in nasty fights around the bottle stores.

"This guy is a thug, why can't we just arrest him?" Detective Gunda remarked to his colleague as they observed Tosh from a safe distance.

"Reminds me of what my trainer once told me . . ." Detective Zeneya said, pausing to light a cigarette.

"That in this line of work, nothing extraordinary happens. It's often long boring hours spent watching shadows moving within shadows." Detective Gunda finished the sentence which he had heard a countless of times from his colleague.

"Yep! And staying awake is the hardest part of this job, especially when the suspect is in a brothel with a prostitute, as is often the case with our guy here." Detective Zeneya groaned, gesturing to a small door in which Tosh had just entered with a scantily dressed woman.

He emerged half an hour later and re-entered the bottle store next to the brothel. The two detectives sat there, watching the door and looking at the time. Their break came two hours later, when Tosh emerged out of a bottle store.

"Finally, our Mr Tosh is now making a move. My buttocks were starting to itch." Detective Gunda sighed, shifting uncomfortably in behind the wheel.

"I wonder where he is going." Detective Zeneya mumbled, tossing the cigarette out of the open window.

Bottle in hand, Tosh looked left then right before crossing the road towards a parked black Range Rover. The detectives had been so engrossed at watching the bottle store they hadn't seen the expensive 4x4 pull up on the other side of the road, next to the maize garden.

"Hello, what do we have here?" Detective Gunda's eyes popped out their sockets.

They both knew whose car that was, the personalised number plates, *Lumbadzi 3* gave it away. Everyone in Blantyre knew the name Lumbadzi.

"Isn't that the car of the same Lumbadzi who is trying to unseat the incumbent Member of Parliament . . ." Detective Zeneya was cut off in midsentence by his colleague.

"Yes, the MP whose car the suspect is alleged to have burnt to crisp." Detective Gunda said out loud.

They looked at each other, baffled with what they were seeing; Tosh getting into the Range Rover.

"We have to call this one in." Detective Zeneya said, fumbling for his phone.

A phone call was hastily made to their Detective Chief Inspector reporting on the status of their operation. Twelve minutes later a call came back, not from their DCI but from high above, so high it was the pinnacle of the police pyramid.

"Hello." Detective Zeneya, who had gotten out of the car to stretch his legs whilst satisfying his nicotine cravings, answered in a bored voice.

"Hello?"

"Hello! Is this Detective Zeneya?" A commanding, but polite and a bit familiar voice resonated on the phone.

"Yes, speaking?" Detective Zeneya continued in his bored tone, his detective brain trying to discern the voice.

The familiar voice did not match anyone's at the station; nonetheless, Detective Zeneya knew that he had heard that voice before. He did not have to wait long to find out.

"This is Deputy Inspector General Sambani." The commanding and polite voice said and paused, fully aware that a particular reaction was going to be forthcoming on the other end. It did.

"Yes Sir!" Detective Zeneya who had been leaning on the Land Rover lazily when he answered the phone snapped to attention; his relaxed pose gone, instead he was standing straight like a plank. He dropped his cigarette as if the Deputy Inspector General was right there in front of him; in the police force hierarchy, the man on the other end of the line was the summit. There were only two other people above him; the Inspector General and the country's president. This was a good enough reason to cause Detective Zeneya snap to a standstill, his ears listening attentively and every fibre of his body tense.

"Yes Sir," he saluted with his right hand; "Not a problem sir!" Detective Zeneya barked obediently before hanging up the phone, after his Deputy IG.

He jumped back on the passenger seat of the Land Rover, looking at his colleague who was also looking at him.

"You look like you just got off the phone with devil Lucifer himself. Who was that?" Detective Gunda teased his rather shaken colleague; "was that the DCI?"

"No, that was the Deputy Inspector General." Detective Zeneya said in a low shaky voice.

"You mean Deputy Inspector General as in DIG Sambani?" Detective Gunda asked in disbelief.

"Yes, it was the big Kahuna himself and he says we are not to lose sight of this Tosh character and we are to report directly to him."

"Report to the Deputy IG! That's odd isn't it? What about headquarters? What about chain of command?" Detective Gunda mouthed a staccato of questions, his hand on the ignition, confusion on his face.

"Do you want to call him and offload those questions yourself?" Detective Zeneya said, mockingly handing the phone to his colleague.

Detective Gunda looked at the phone like it was a hand grenade with the safety pin removed; his right hand trembling on the keys in the ignition and so was his left firmly on the steering. He shook his head and turned the keys clockwise. The Land Rover coughed to life.

That was over six hours ago when the two detectives had watched Tosh get into the parked Range Rover. He got out and jumped into a packed minibus. They discretely followed it, stopping at each stage the minibus stopped. Five stops later, Tosh got out, walking along a dark street; from their parked Land Rover, they watched him as he entered a dark alley; between two houses.

"Is he relieving his bladder right between those houses?" Detective Zeneya scoffed.

"That is just disgusting." His colleague Detective Gunda said with a smirk.

"I feel like entering that dark alley and cuffing his hand to his manly extension and parading him all the way to the station." Detective Zeneya scoffed.

"Mmhhh . . . he is taking longer than usual." Detective Gunda quizzed, frowning and leaning over the steering wheel, not sure if Tosh had just given them a slip.

"Do you think he noticed us and managed to elude . . . no, wait a minute. Look carefully, can you see?" Detective Zeneya whispered, a faint smile looking out of place on his rather serious facial features.

The two detectives concentrated their focus right where Tosh had disappeared. He hadn't eluded them; careful scrutiny revealed that he was concealing himself; a predator waiting to ambush someone. Then after several agonising hours the shadowy figure of Tosh slowly emerged, joined the grasshopper picking men by the street lamp. The two detectives looked at each other in bewilderment;

"Why would a thug like Tosh wait for hours only to emerge and start picking *abwanoni* from the ground?" Detective Zeneya whispered.

The answer came soon after; an approaching vehicle with one headlamp pulled into a house across from the streetlamp. That's when all hell broke loose. As soon as the door of the parked car swung open, Tosh took off sprinting like a panther towards the unsuspecting driver. Everything happened so fast, they watched him confront or rather attack the driver of the parked car, he was brandishing a knife. In less than two minutes he started fleeing the scene. Both of them were caught off guard; not sure whether to go and assist the fallen man or pursue the fleeing Tosh.

Then four, five, six shots rang out . . . successive cracks in the middle of the night. They watched as Tosh fell hard to the ground.

"Were those gunshots?" It was more of a statement than a question coming out of a shocked Detective Gunda.

"He has been hit, the suspect has been hit! Call it in!" Detective Gunda yelled, reaching for the door handle.

His colleague did not respond; he was already on the phone; dialling Deputy Inspector General Sambani's number.

Deputy Inspector General Elijah Sambani was still seething from the little exchange he had with his youngest sister, Tamanda. He loved his sister with all his heart and was fiercely overprotective of her. Ever since she was a baby, all the way to her teenage years, he had been the big brother. Somehow along the way, Tamanda changed, especially after coming back from America; there was some arrogance about her.

The fact that she had turned her back on Catholicism—and on God altogether—was something he could not stomach; this was something Elijah constantly said to his wife Nambewe, every time Tamanda's name came up.

Of course, when his youngest sister started dating Walter Lumbadzi; a man who he viewed to be a crook, Elijah regarded this as the final straw.

"You see that, you see that Nambewe! She is doing things to spite me!" He yelled, pacing the length of their bedroom.

"Just come to bed dear, don't stress yourself." Nambewe had tried to calm him down in her usual mellow diplomatic tone.

Still, Elijah couldn't understand why his sister had stopped seeing the decent Accountant, Anton Banda; a man she had been dating before going to the States.

Unlike Walter, Anton was a God fearing man, who also happened to be his best friend. As a brother, he had high hopes for his youngest sister, thinking that on her return the two would rekindle their affair and tie the knot. She, however, did the opposite; breaking off with Anton placed enormous strain on Elijah's friendship with his Accountant friend.

He remembers looking disgustingly at the *wedding invitation card* of Tamanda to Walter. Despite Nambewe's attempts to coax him into attending, Elijah could not bring himself to go to their wedding. How could he bring himself to witness his baby sister marrying a man he had investigated for years, a man he had vowed to expose?

Long before the Public Accounts Committee of Parliament released an audit report which exposed that about K187 million, an amount equivalent to $1.8 million, had gone missing, Elijah was already on Walter's tail. This money was meant for constructing schools and other developmental infrastructures. Reliable sources had told him that, Walter's budding business enterprise was dubiously winning tenders and had taking a huge slice of this pie.

Detective Elijah Sambani was extremely tenacious; he always chased his prey to the very end. Long before the formation of the Anti-Corruption Bureau, he had, singlehandedly, managed to expose a lot of corrupt politicians. However, one prey—Walter Lumbadzi—had constantly eluded him; not just on one occasion, but on so many.

In his eyes, Walter epitomised the very essence of corruption and greed within the Malawian society. Men like him had no morals or qualms in stepping over other people's toes in order to maximise their wealth, just so that they could be seen driving around town in flashy cars or live in dubiously acquired houses in expensive neighbourhoods. Elijah had vowed to bring down men like Walter; men who brought misery to the majority within the society.

The day he found out that his nemesis was dating his youngest sister, Elijah felt physically sick. As far as he was concerned, Tamanda's marriage to Walter was as distasteful as it was abhorrent.

Then one day their father called for a family meeting where he chose Tamanda, a last born and a girl, to be the administrator of his estate. Elijah felt like he had just been violently kicked between the legs. He couldn't hide his shock, that his father, a man he had idolised from childhood, had overlooked him.

"I can't believe father has chosen the last born instead of the first born, and worse still; a female instead of a male." An enraged Elijah hissed to Brandon; his immediate younger brother who had been sitting next to him during the meeting.

"Why don't you raise your voice and speak to father." Brandon said fully aware that his elder brother was hurting.

Elijah did; getting up from his chair whilst his father was still talking. Everyone looked at him as soon as the chair made a scraping noise.

"Father! How I mean why? Why when I have done everything you had expected of me? Not only that father . . . I . . . I am the first born son." Elijah's voice was coarse, he ignored the fact that all his siblings were staring at him strangely.

"It doesn't mean that I love you less my son; nevertheless, it's my decision that it has to be your sister." His father had said with a smile, and that was that.

Elijah could not understand why his father was trying to turn the Sambani family into a matriarchy. Why not him? Especially that he was a church going person and a man of the law; someone who enforced it and had risen from a mere detective to the post of Deputy Inspector General of Police.

Even after years had gone by, Elijah never stopped agonising over this betrayal; on the other hand, he knew that it was too late to confront his father about it. The man was sick, his once intelligent mind, now reduced to that of an infant; Elijah felt robbed. He still respected his father, but—since that day of Tamanda's anointing as the family's head—he has never forgiven her.

He held his breath; his sharp police ears sifting through the familiar sounds of Dedza night. He could hear the loud crickets and beating of drums in the distant, most likely people drinking beer at the nearby village, just on the other side of the valley. He could also hear the distinct humming of the medical device; his father's nebuliser machine, coming from the master bedroom, on the other side of the sprawling house.

"Darling, are you going to go to lie down?" Nambewe asked as she rolled over in the bed, looking at the silhouette of her husband sitting on the edge of the bed.

"I will in a minute, am just worried about father, he has been coughing for over an hour now." Elijah responded, leaning over to touch his wife tenderly on the shoulder.

"Is he coughing? I can't hear him."

"It's because of the crickets, they are too noisy tonight."

"Yes they are, but it is past *one* in the morning darling, don't forget we have a long drive home tomorrow, try to get some sleep." His concerned wife whispered, running her hand on Elijah's thigh.

"Yes, you are right dear . . . it's just that his nebuliser has been humming for ages and his coughing is not subsiding that's all." Elijah said, easing his body next to his wife.

"He will be alright."

"It's all Tamanda fault, I told her we shouldn't hold the anniversary party. I'm sure it's what has . . ."

"Shhhh, come on now dear, we don't know that, do we?" Nambewe whispered; opening her arms, cuddling herself into her husband's chest, wrapping them around his frame.

Elijah snuggled closer to his wife, stretching his arm to switch off the side-lamp when his phone started vibrating. He paused, reaching out for the phone on the side table, almost knocking it to the floor.

"Hello!" He answered, a bit annoyed considering the time.

"Sir! This is Detective Aubrey Zeneya, sir! I apologise for calling you at this hour Sir! The . . . the gentleman we were following has just been shot Sir!"

"Shot? Where?" Elijah asked, bolting straight up, almost knocking his wife out of the bed.

"We followed him somewhere in Ndirande Sir; my colleague has just rushed down to the scene."

"Whatever you find, keep it off the record, you hear me? Gather as much evidence as you can and keep me updated Detective."

"Off the record, sir?" The detective hesitated, not sure if his boss had just ordered him to keep a gruesome homicide off the record.

"That is exactly what I said." Elijah snapped; he couldn't tell the detective his reasons for issuing such a command.

He wasn't sure himself if this wasn't going to backfire on him. Elijah was following instincts, he had a feeling Walter had an informant or more, working for him in the police force. His brother-in-law always seemed to be one step ahead of him; surely someone from the inside had to be tipping him. With the current meagre salaries police officers were on, people like Walter were utilising this to their advantage. He knew Walter had infiltrated Customs, what would stop him for doing the same with the Police?

He wanted his brother-in-law to be kept in the dark about the death of Tosh, even if it was only for twenty-four hours.

"Yes sir, we will do that; my apologies again for waking you up sir."

"Secure the scene detective and find out everything that you can." Elijah said, hanging up the phone and looking at his wife.

He was smiling, a strange smile; his wife looked at him with a frown.

"Is everything okay dear?" Nambewe asked, scrutinising her husband's face.

"Everything is just fine Nambewe, everything is just fine." Elijah said, sliding back into bed and running his hands all over his rather perturbed wife.

He lifted his head slightly, reaching over her shoulder for the paraffin lantern; he turned the knob anticlockwise. The room was plunged into darkness.

This part of Ndirande might be rough and renowned for muggings and other criminal activities; however gunshots are not the norm. No sooner had the six shots rang out into the quietness of the night, did people start pouring out of the surrounding houses. Some of them emerged still half asleep, converging on the fallen body of Tosh. The six men, who had been picking up *abwanoni* just moments ago, were trying to narrate what had happened.

"His body was flung ten metres in the air before landing over there!" One of the men explained, in an animated voice.

"Yes, there were bullet flying everywhere, it sounded like an AK 47 we had to dive for cover." Another man cut in.

"I am a security guard, we are trained for this. I think fifteen bullets whizzed over my head, if I hadn't ducked in time, I would be dead too." A third man chipped in, stretching the truth as much as he could

Detective Gunda shook his head, he wasn't bothered with the men's narration of what had just happened; his priority was to try and secure the perimeter. While the men were still talking he was cordoning the area; he grabbed a piece of rock and, with it, he drew a circle.

"No one should cross over this line, okay?" He yelled to the men, noticing people were starting to converge on the scene.

"I have called it in." Detective Zeneya said, running towards his colleague.

"You need to check the other guy!" Detective Gunda yelled at his approaching colleague.

"Oh my God!" Detective Zeneya yelled; "What are they doing?"

He was pointing at a group of people, on the second scene, where the driver of the BMW, had fallen. They had started fighting over a bulging plastic bag; he dashed over only to find a lot of cash scattered all over the ground and around the fallen man. People were arguing as they tried to scoop up as much money as they could. Half naked women, their breasts flapping about, were tussling with men wearing only boxers. Some of the men only had a cloth wrap around their waists.

"All of you back to your houses, now!" Detective Zeneya yelled as loud as he could.

No one heard him or chose to ignore him. Most of them were down on their knees, picking up the bank notes which were scattered all over the ground.

"It's not every day someone drops a bag full of money in the middle of Ndirande!" A woman yelled without even bothering to look up.

"Who are you to tell us to go back to our houses?" A male voice, within the commotion, yelled out loud.

"I am only going to say this once then I will start arresting people, and shoot some if I have to." Detective Zeneya warned.

His booming voice reverberated menacingly, slicing through the chaos like a knife on butter. Everyone froze; they looked up and started backing away slowly after noticing the black metallic contraption the detective was holding in his hand. Detective Zeneya slowly approached the stabbed man whose hand was still clutching his gun; the murder weapon. The gruesome slash along the fallen man's neck was enough to tell the detective he was dead, he was sitting grotesquely in his own pool of blood.

The detective glanced at his wrist watch; taking mental note of the time. He shook his head in anger; he had told Mebo—his wife—that tonight he was going to come home early. He even pleaded with her to wait up for him. He had missed four suppers in a row and tonight was supposed to be the night he was going to make up; apologise to her, how this job was tearing their marriage apart. Supper had been five hours ago and she hadn't even bothered calling him; he mused.

He was going to face his wife later, Detective Zeneya thought whilst looking over at how his colleague was coping with his own crowd control, just where Tosh had fallen. He knew that Mebo was breathing fire. Even if he tried calling Mebo now, it wouldn't extinguish the flames. Knowing his feisty wife, she would probably tell him not to bother coming home.

"Why tonight?" Detective Zeneya mumbled, leaning over at the fallen body of Obafeni; "of all nights, why did you two choose tonight to slaughter each other?"

~ OVERDOSE ~

WALTER SLAMMED HIS feet on the brakes and clutch simultaneously. The Land Cruiser swerved, its tyres struggling bite into the asphalt road, the night dew causing it to skid precariously. The front Michelins smashed hard into the kerb, bouncing up then onto the pavement; the vehicle came to a juddering stop. A white G4S (Group 4 Security) pickup which had been coming just behind him, along the Highway, swerved to the right narrowly missing the rear of the Land Cruiser. The G4S personnel, who were sitting in the back of the pickup, swore obscenities for the near miss. He hardly heard the foul names being levelled at him as their pickup shot past him.

Walter was staring in horror at the phone which had just fallen out of his grasp. It had bounced off his lap then landed down the foot-well, next to the clutch pedal. He could still hear the crackling voice of Nurse Patricia.

"Hello! Hello! Are you still there?"

Walter slowly picked up the phone, disconnecting the call. He had heard enough, the nurse's words were still echoing inside his head, causing a sharp pain deep inside his chest. Tears slowly formed in his eyes. For the second time that night he banged his hands violently on the steering wheel, breaking the indicator knob. He was overcome by hysterical rage, disbelief and small hope that this was all a bad dream; surely he was going to wake up sweating and Nomsa will be there right next to him.

"No! No! Nooo! Nomsa! No!!!" A mist of saliva exploded out of his mouth as he violently and continuously pounded on the steering wheel.

He was in shock and could not remember starting the car nor making a u-turn, in the middle of the dual carriageway. His eyes were hazy; he didn't bother wiping off the tears, letting them cascade down to his chin, mixing with drool from his mouth. Walter was absentminded to the cars coming towards him, flashing their headlights to warn him that he was driving the wrong way. His mind was on Nomsa; he couldn't understand how she could have overdosed within the safe confines of a hospital.

He was driving erratically, weaving all over the road forcing approaching cars to swerve out of his way. Walter couldn't even hear his phone beeping, he didn't know where he was going and he didn't care where he was heading to.

Walter could not recall how he arrived in Chilomoni; he pulled outside Nomsa's house and killed the engine. The whole neighbourhood was quiet, an eerily silence that was occasionally punctuated by barking dogs. He switched off the headlights, plunging the immediate surroundings into pitch darkness.

Like a zombie, he slowly got out of his Land Cruiser, unaware that his front bumper was dragging on the road, after hitting the high kerb as he drove past the roundabout at Clock Tower. He dragged his feet towards the house, fumbled for his spare keys. He hesitated by the door; maybe if he knocked like he always did, Nomsa would come and open it. Yes she would, that stupid nurse was crazy, telling him crazy things. He was certain Nomsa was on the other side of the door, waiting for him.

"Nomsa! Nomsa, it's me darling! Open up!" He yelled, banging loudly on the door. The noise carried out in the still night rousing wolf like barks from the neighbourhood dogs.

"Nomsa! I am home Nomsa! Open up!" Walter sobbed loudly.

His human sorrowful cries conjoined with the loud barking prompted a few lights to come on from the neighbouring houses. Without turning his heard, Walter heard a door creak open from the house on the left.

"I don't think she is home, an ambulance came this afternoon and took her to hospital." An elderly lady spoke in a low tone. She expected him to turn around, to at least acknowledge her presence; however, Walter stood stern faced, staring at Nomsa's door.

"Nooo! She is inside, I know she is I know she is I know she is . . ." He screamed as tears poured out of his eyes.

Looking wary, the elderly lady slowly backed away into her house, closing the door and turning off the lights. From a slit between her curtains, she watched his disturbing behaviour.

"Nomsa why . . . why . . . why?" He was now crying loudly while fumbling for his set of keys.

He opened the front door and staggered inside, slumping on the sofa face down with his knees on the floor. As his sobbing slowly subsided, Walter no longer had the energy to keep his eye lids apart. Sleep finally took over and all was quiet.

Tamanda popped one of her eyes, the right one and immediately clamped it shut. She groaned lazily, stretching her legs under the silk sheets; arching her back like some sort of a feline waking up from a long nap. Sunlight was trying to steal its way through a narrow gap between the heavy velvet drapes. It was morning; she wasn't looking forward to getting up, not just yet.

Without opening her eyes, she reached her right arm over to the other side of the bed; to Walter's side. She must have been tired; a combination of jet lag, the chaos at Dedza and last night's explosive lovemaking, because she couldn't recall the exact moment that she passed out. A smile creased her face as her arm continued to move around, searching for her husband's body. Nothing! His side was empty.

Tamanda sat up right, both eyes wide open, the brightness of the room shocking; she suppressed the urge to clamp her eyelids shut. Memories of last night came flooding back; the accident, the injured driver at the hospital.

"Walter?" She gasped, recalling how she had tried to call him on his phone.

He hadn't answered. Or had he? She was trying to re-live last night. It dawned on her that she had actually passed out while the phone was ringing.

Tamanda jumped out of bed, searching for her phone between the folds of the silk beddings. She found it, looked at the time; it was almost 06:00am. She speed-dialled his number again whilst sitting on the edge of the bed, tapping both feet on the warm rug. The call went to his voice messaging.

"Hey sweetheart, call me back as soon as you get this. I love you." She said while getting up slowly.

She started pacing the length of the room and hating herself for not asking him which hospital the injured driver had been taken to. She hadn't even asked him the driver's name.

Walter had never spent a whole night out without telling her; surely he should have called her back. Tamanda looked at the time; it was still too early to call the office. She dragged herself into the bathroom, setting her phone on top of the towel; she filled up the tub.

Forty minutes later, Tamanda rang his office; she was certain that Mr Daudi, the Operations Manager, would be in and be in a position to know about the accident. Some of the staff worked half day on a Saturday, and Tamanda was hoping that the Operations Manager was in.

"Hello Lumbadzi Investments, Hendrina speaking, how can I help you?"

"Good morning Hendrina, this is Mrs Lumbadzi, does Mr Daudi come in on Saturday's?"

"He does, sometimes. I think he is in today, I saw his car outside."

"Can you put me through to his office please?"

"Yes I can, madam. Just hold on madam." Hendrina said in her usual low shy voice. In less than a minute, there was a faint beep followed by a gruff voice.

"Good morning madam, Daudi speaking." The Operations Manager greeted her politely.

"Good morning Mr Daudi. I am calling about the accident yesterday, do you know which hospital the injured driver was rushed to and if you do, can also furnish me with his name please?"

"Excuse me madam, which . . . what accident are you talking about?" Mr Daudi quizzed, sounding surprised from the other end of the line.

"The tanker the one coming from . . . from . . . Mozambique?" Tamanda asked.

She was annoyed that a whole Operations Manager wasn't even aware that one of the trucks had been involved in a bad accident and that the driver was in critical condition.

"Madam all thirty tanker trucks are parked in the yard as we speak. The five which were in Mozambique just arrived just before I got here." Mr Daudi said, sounding confused.

If Mr Daudi was confused, Tamanda was disturbed. Could she be losing the plot? She wondered, trying to re-live the conversation she had with Walter.

"I am sure my husband said it was a tanker, Mr Daudi."

"Like I said madam, all the tankers are here at the workshop."

"Ok, do you have any trucks currently in Mozambique?"

"We have twelve outside the country; ten of those are in Durban waiting to load and two are in Tanzania, they just arrived at the port of Dar-es-salaam this morning . . ."

"Do you have trucks in Mozambique?" Tamanda cut him off.

"No madam, none in Mozambique." Mr Daudi said, still not making sense what his boss's wife was on about.

"So you don't have any member of staff currently in the hospital?"

"Not in the logistics department, no madam. Maybe warehousing department, I could have checked with their Supervisor, unfortunately he doesn't work on Saturdays."

"Thank you Mr Daudi, you have been very helpful." She said, hanging up the phone, despair creeping up her spine.

Tamanda looked at the phone with a sense of trepidation and slowly dialled Walter's number again. She was afraid he wouldn't answer; on the other hand, she was also petrified that he might. She didn't know why she felt sharp fingers of premonition clawing on the insides of her stomach; Tamanda subconsciously reached for her belly, massaging gently. She still couldn't make the ghastly feeling go away.

There was a loud knock on the bedroom door. Tamanda's head snapped up, she almost let out a scream; she didn't realise she was tense. She cancelled her call to Walter; taking a deep breath, she slowly walked to the big oak door, a slight frown creasing her face.

"Who is it?" She asked, refraining from opening, she was still in her see-through lingerie and was wearing nothing inside.

"It's me madam, Stella." The maid answered in a polite voice, from the other side of the door.

"What is it Stella?"

"There are two gentlemen here to see Mr Lumbadzi."

"Tell them that he is not home!" She snapped, turning around to walk back to bed.

"They say they are police officers." Stella's small voice sliced right through the thick oak door, exploding inside Tamanda's head. She froze, turned back around and yanked the door open, disregarding her half naked appearance.

"What did you say?" She asked, startling the heavyset maid who didn't expect to see her boss coming out of the bedroom barely dressed.

"There are two men downstairs who say that they are police officers, but they are not wearing uniforms."

"How do you know they are police officers?"

"The security guards at the gate authenticated their ID badges, madam. They are the ones who let them through." Stella answered, looking sideways, avoiding to look at Tamanda's revealing bedroom outfit.

"Ok, tell them am coming." Tamanda said, closing the door to put on appropriate clothes.

As she sifted through her wardrobe, gruesome images of her husband's smashed-up car resting on its roof in a ditch kept clawing at her brain. She could see him lying helpless in a ditch, bleeding profusely and gasping for air. No matter how much she tried to shake these images off, they persisted; it had to be something serious, how else would the police want from her this early in the morning? Tamanda thought, her whole body shaking like a leaf.

"Please Walter baby, don't you leave me." Tamanda said repeatedly.

The two detectives sat there in silence looking around at the opulent surroundings. By the number of vehicles parked outside, they had expected to find a small gathering of people inside the house. There was no one, just soft instrumental music that appeared to be wafting from unseen speakers. Detective Zeneya's mesmerised eyes were glued on the large plasma TV on the other end of the expanse living room. It was not even switched on, however he was gawking at the sheer size of it, he figured it had to be a couple centimetres taller than him and he wasn't a short man.

"If that television set was in my house it would probably be touching the roof" He whispered to his colleague.

Detective Gunda did not respond. His attention was preoccupied with the imposing aquarium, the size of his freezer. He was fascinated by the blue and yellow African Cichlids which were swimming around gracefully in a synchronised fashion.

"This is . . ." Detective Gunda was about to make a comment about their exquisite surroundings when Dr Tamanda Lumbadzi walked into the living room, announcing her entrance with a slight cough.

Both detectives stood up immediately, bowing their heads slightly in courtesy.

"Please officers, please sit down." She said in a gentle voice.

"Thank you Dr Lumbadzi." Detective Zeneya said, slowly sitting back in the plush sofa, which seemed to breathe gently; "I am Detective Zeneya and this is Detective Gunda." He carried on, gesturing to his heavyset colleague.

"I hope I didn't keep you waiting for long, what can I help you with detectives?"

"Dr Lumbadzi, we were expecting to have a word with your husband, Mr Lumbadzi." Detective Zeneya said, his alert eyes holding those of Tamanda; trying to read her.

"I am sorry my husband is not home detective." She said politely, maintaining eye contact with the detective. She had a feeling the detective was looking at her suspiciously.

"Oh! Is there a way we can reach him, either by phone or other means?" Detective Zeneya asked.

He glanced at his wristwatch; Tamanda did not miss the insinuation of that gesture. He slowly looked up, analysing Tamanda's facial expressions. He could see that she was telling the truth about her husband not being home, although she appeared to be slightly uncomfortable. Many people tend to be when talking to police officials.

"I am afraid I can't tell you detective."

"Excuse me?"

"I don't know where my husband is detective."

"Oh, I see."

"If you don't mind me asking, what is this all about?"

"It would be better if we spoke to your husband first Dr Lumbadzi."

"Detective Zeneya, I don't mean to be rude . . . what is it you want to talk to my husband about?" She asked in a firm controlled voice.

"Dr Lumbadzi, like I said; its better if your husband was . . ." Detective Zeneya sentence was abruptly cut short by Tamanda's raised left palm.

She didn't want him to waste her time by finishing what he was saying. Breaking eye contact with the detective for the first time, she reached for her mobile phone, scrolling down for a name in her phone register, to dial.

"Detective Zeneya, I am assuming you know who my brother is? Should I call him and ask him to ask you to tell me what you want with my husband?" Tamanda said in an icy tone, holding the phone firmly, her eyes holding the detective's defiantly.

"That won't be necessary Dr Lumbadzi." Detective Gunda spoke for the first time, holding his hand in a gesture of peace.

"Thank you." She said, placing the phone on her lap and looking at heavyset Detective Gunda.

"There was an incident last night. As a matter of fact it was very early this morning and we have reasons to believe your husband is somehow involved." Detective Gunda spoke slowly.

"Incident, what do you mean incident?"

"There has been a double homicide, Dr Lumbadzi." The heavyset detective said, putting much emphasis on the word *homicide.*

"Oh no! Is it Walter? Is my husband okay, detective?" She exclaimed, losing her iron composure she had a few seconds prior.

She got up quickly, the phone—which had been resting on her lap—clattering uselessly on the polished parquet tiles. Her earlier images, of Walter badly hurt, were true after all; she thought.

"We don't believe your husband was injured or harmed in any way."

"Oh! He wasn't?" She breathed a sigh of relief; "Then why are you here?"

"It concerns the evidence which we found on the scene, which implicates your husband, Dr Lumbadzi." Detective Gunda said, picking up Tamanda's phone from the floor and placing it on the heavy glass table.

"Evidence? Wha . . . what is he talking about?" She stuttered, switching her gaze from Detective Gunda to his colleague.

"Dr Lumbadzi, I don't think we should be talking about this without your husband being . . ." Detective Zeneya said; his eyes unblinking.

"What evidence detective!" Tamanda yelled. She was getting annoyed with Detective Zeneya's condescending attitude; she switched her attention back to the heavyset one.

"We found a Blackberry phone in the possession of one of the deceased men and we have reasons to believe that the other deceased gentleman was an acquaintance of your husband's." Detective Gunda said in a drawl voice.

"My husband doesn't own a Blackberry phone, Detective." Tamanda shot back, surprised that her voice sounded hollow. Where are you Walter; she despaired inside, feeling her resolve starting to wane.

"So, you have never seen this Blackberry in the possession of your husband?" Detective Gunda asked, fishing out the sleek looking gadget from a brown manila envelope.

"No, that thing doesn't belong to my husband. Walter owns a Samsung . . . why I'm I even telling you this? Have you found any fingerprints that match my husband's?" She asked her eyes holding the detective's.

"I am afraid we haven't."

"Did you even dust for fingerprints?" Tamanda's sarcasm was obvious.

"We found something else though." The detective responded, avoiding Tamanda's question.

"You found something more incriminating than fingerprints?" She asked, leaning back into the sofa.

"Yes, we did."

"Seeing that this homicide happened just hours ago, even the police from the most advanced countries wouldn't come up with DNA evidence that quick, and I know for a fact that DNA technology in this country, is still stuff of the future."

"I beg your pardon?" Detective Zeneya asked, trying to keep his attitude in check.

"Detectives, what is it that has brought you to my house? If it is not fingerprints or a DNA match, then what is it?" Tamanda spoke in a lets-wrap-this-up tone, still looking at Detective Gunda and ignoring his colleague.

"We don't have fingerprints; however, this Blackberry contains a photo, rather, photos of your husband."

"Excuse me?" She sat back up; "let me see them?"

"I am sorry, that is not how it works . . . we cannot show you evidence to a crime, especially if you are not a suspect." Detective Gunda said; raising his chubby hand, trying to halt Tamanda's advances.

"A few minutes ago you showed me the Blackberry, didn't you?"

"No, I mean yes." The detective stuttered; "that . . . that was just so that you can ascertain if it belonged to your husband or not."

"Detective, I understand what you are saying, but it's important that I see those photos."

"I am sorry Dr Lumbadzi. That is not going to happen, especially without your husband being here." Detective Zeneya spoke; Tamanda ignored him.

"Detective Gunda, you look like a reasonable man and I know you have your police protocols to follow. Surely showing me the photos wouldn't interfere with your investigation would it?"

"Like I said, Dr Lumbadzi, that's not going to happen." Detective Zeneya said in a firm police tone.

He was losing his patience, there was something about Dr Tamanda Lumbadzi reminiscent of his wife Mebo; a feminine stubbornness.

"What did you just say?" Tamanda stared at Detective Zeneya.

"I think we are done here." Detective Zeneya said, getting up and looking at his colleague who was still sitting down, looking indecisive.

"Detective Gunda, please." She pleaded in a silky tone; her eyelashes fluttering at the heavyset detective, the nice one.

"Detective Gunda! I said we are done here!" Detective Zeneya yelled at his colleague who appeared sympathetic to Dr Lumbadzi's femininity.

"I am sorry Dr Lumbadzi, my colleague is right, showing you the evidence is against protocol; we could get in serious trouble with our superiors." Detective Gunda apologised, getting up to his feet.

The two policemen started heading for the front door; Tamanda abruptly got up, yelling. She had one card to play; the Deputy Inspector General card.

"Should I call my brother to order you that you should show me the photos?"

Both detectives stopped in their tracks, turning around, facing Dr Lumbadzi who was holding her mobile phone; she was about to start dialling. They looked at her then at each other. Detective Zeneya smiled sarcastically.

"Dr Lumbadzi, with all due respect, the Deputy Inspector General would not condone what you are asking us to do."

"So, you don't mind if I call him?"

"With no disrespect, you seem to have this habit of using the Deputy Inspector General to instil worry in us. Go ahead, make the call." Detective Zeneya said in an unwavering tone.

Tamanda ignored Detective Zeneya, instead concentrated on the fat one, the softer one.

"Are you of the same view, Detective Gunda? Should I call my brother?" Tamanda asked, hoping that she hadn't overplayed her hand.

The first time round she had sounded convincing, but this time the mean looking detective didn't fall for it; her hopes rested on the friendlier one. She fluttered her eyelashes in his direction, hoping that he was going to fall for her charm. He did.

"Detective Zeneya, maybe if we just show her the photo, surely it can't be that . . ."

"I can't believe I am hearing you right Detective Gunda, I will not be part of this." Detective Zeneya hissed, marching out of the house.

"Dr Lumbadzi, this is not right." Detective Gunda started as soon as his colleague left; "I am only doing this because the Deputy Inspector General is a relation of yours otherwise . . ."

"I truly appreciate this kind gesture; I will make sure my brother considers you detective." Tamanda lied, the words coming out all wrong, she didn't even convince herself. However, the detective was hooked, either by her threat to call Elijah or her pleading tone from before.

Detective Gunda switched the Blackberry on. His chubby fingers struggled with the small keypad; he clumsily flicked through the album and finally got to the particular photo he was searching for. The detective slowly set the Blackberry on the glass table, the small illuminated screen facing Tamanda who wasn't sure whether to remain standing or take a seat. She decided to sit.

"Oh my . . . Walter . . . oh no!" She gasped at the picture of a naked woman lying on her husband's shirtless chest. The background looked familiar.

It was their Salima cottage; suddenly then the image of a female's lacy underwear she saw in the boot of the Mercedes Benz at the airport when Maxwell came to pick her up, came back to mind. Tamanda got up and raced out of the living room, almost tripping over as she galloped up the stairs for the sanctuary of her bedroom. Once inside, she sat on the edge of her bed and went numb inside; it was all too much—her husband was having an affair, her Walter.

Downstairs, in the expanse sitting room, Detectives Gunda looked at the exit Dr Tamanda had just taken. He wasn't sure what to do next, wait for her to return, follow her or leave the house altogether? He licked his lips, a twinge of distress tugging at the back of his head. He was not sure if his actions—of showing her the photos—would endear him to the Deputy Inspector General or signal the end of his career in the police. He picked up the Blackberry and deposited it back in the brown manila envelope. He took one last look at the large fresh water aquarium with the blue and yellow African Cichlids; sighing in resignation he walked towards the front door to his waiting colleague. He knew that Zeneya was most likely waiting for him, to annoy and give him grief about breaking protocols.

Detective Gunda jumped in the driver's seat of the Land Rover and was shocked to find his colleague on the phone; he appeared to be talking to the Deputy Inspector General.

"Yes Sir, understood Sir. We will do just that Sir! Thank you Sir!" Detective Zeneya was saying respectfully into the phone before hanging up and turning to look at his colleague.

"That was the Deputy IG."

"What did he say?" Detective Gunda asked, nervously licking his thick lips.

"Start the car and I will tell you."

~ A NEW DAY ~

WALTER WAS WOKEN up by an unfamiliar cacophony of morning life; loud human noises, mechanical engines revving, blaring of minibus horns and an odd shrieking morning rooster; nature's morning wakeup alarm, even though more than half the population was already awake. Typical Ndirande noises; he thought to himself, he would have to get up before his father found him still sleeping on his straw mat. His father equated sleeping past a certain time to laziness; a punishable offense, which was delivered via a wooden stick, dipped in water. He had to get up.

Walter sat up so fast, heavily disoriented; he was not in Ndirande and he was not twelve years old. He looked around, cogs slowly falling into place inside his head; he was in Chilomoni at his . . . at Nomsa's house.

"Ten to six!" He exclaimed the moment he glanced at his wrist watch; was his phone ringing just now? He wondered, trying to make sense of everything.

Walter had been having the most terrible nightmare that Nomsa had died.

Click!

The last cog slotted into place and Walter felt a big chill ripple across his entire body like a tidal wave . . . he hadn't been dreaming. Last night had been real despite there being no recollection of how he got here. He gingerly got to his feet, looking around the small living room then noticing (for the first time) his blood stained hand. It felt numb. He couldn't remember how he ended up cutting himself.

Then he heard the beeping of his phone. His heart missed a beat; he hadn't communicated with his wife since he left the house last night. He looked at his phone; over ten missed calls from Tamanda and from some unknown numbers.

He had to call her; she definitely must be worried sick. As a matter of fact, he needed to see her and come clean—Walter told himself. It was going to be tough, complicated and perhaps messy; he had no idea how she was going to take it, nonetheless he owed her an explanation, he owed her much more. An honest confession would be a good place to start.

He was about to dial Tamanda's number when he heard a gentle knock on the door. Walter paused, tiptoeing towards the window. He peeped through the slit in the curtains, there was a woman standing by the veranda. He could just barely make out her enormous behind, clad in cloth wrap. It had to be one of the neighbours; he thought, walking over to the door. He opened it, his eyes staring at a heavyset woman with an ample bosom that matched her behind.

"Oh, I am sorry sir, I saw the car parked outside and thought that Prince's mother was home." The woman said.

She was clearly startled to see a man standing by the door; she had expected Nomsa to open the door. She was carrying Prince; the little boy was still asleep.

"I am afraid she is not." Walter said, his gaze switching from the woman to the little boy.

"Oh, I have a vegetable stall at the market; I can't take Prince with me."

"Yes?" He retorted, dreading where the conversation was heading.

"I was wondering if I could just leave him here until his mother comes back." The woman spoke softly and it was at that moment that Prince opened his big baby eyes. He looked at Walter, a baby smile creasing him face.

"Dada!" Prince bubbled joyfully.

Walter looked at the woman and she looked back at him. The words she had just said echoing inside his head; *I was wondering if I could just leave him here until his mother comes back.*

"It's ok; you can leave him with me." Walter mumbled and couldn't believe he had just said that.

What was he doing, what was he getting himself into? He wondered as the woman handed him the child. He watched her disappear behind the house, perhaps back where she had come from.

Looking from left to right, he shut the door and walked back into the house. Making up his mind on what to do next; Walter walked into the child's bedroom, grabbed whatever clothes he could, stuffing them into a bag and then gently closed the door. He was about to walk past the closed door of Nomsa's bedroom, hesitated then slowly opened it.

The curtains were drawn and it was still dark inside; Walter flicked the light switch on. He gasped; right there on the bedside table was a black and white picture of the two of them in a silver frame. Memories of the day this was taken, still vivid on his mind.

Still carrying Prince, Walter took several steps into the bedroom; he sat on the bed, setting the boy down. With a trembling hand, he picked up the frame; he couldn't just leave it here neither could he take it with him.

Walter opened the side drawer to hide the portrait; he got another surprise. The small box like drawer was full of A4 size ruled papers; they had Nomsa's scrawny handwriting—romantic poems and love letters she had drafted but never showed him. Most of it had to do with her thoughts about him. One paper had a hideous drawing of what appeared to be a man and a woman holding hands, underneath it she had written; *Nomsa loves Walter*.

He smiled, angrily shoving the thick stack of papers back into the drawer, slamming it shut. Picking up Prince from the bed, Walter marched towards the door, he paused; looked back at the bed, his eyes coming to rest on the pine side-drawer. He doubled back into the room, went straight for the drawer and scooped out all the papers inside. Without looking back, he stormed out of the house.

"Oh bloody hell! What now?" Walter yelled, expiration when he saw the front bumper hanging loosely.

He gently placed Prince in the backseat, walked back to the front and violently kicked the remaining side of the bumper, still attached to the vehicle. The chrome bumper fell to the ground with a loud clattering sound.

He jumped in the car, dialling Tamanda's number; he had to prepare her for what was about to happen. Walking into the house and explaining to her that he was having an affair with another woman was hard enough. Entering the door while carrying a child of a woman he had been having an affair with; explaining that to an angry and surprised wife would simply be pushing the envelope.

Walter contemplated taking the child elsewhere; he knew people who would be willing to raise Prince on his behalf. However, he felt as if that would be wrong; not only had he gotten attached to the adorable boy, but he also felt like Nomsa was calling out and begging him to look after Prince.

He looked at his phone with a frown, thinking that he had dialled the wrong number; Tamanda's phone could not be reached. It had been switched off. He tried the house's land line, no one was picking up. With a house full of workers, Walter knew that something was wrong. Someone, if not his wife, should have picked it up. The only reason the workers wouldn't pick up the house phone is if they had been told not to.

A chill snaked up Walter's spine; his hand was trembling as he reached for the keys in the ignition.

Tamanda had lost track of how long she had been sobbing, the silk sheets were damp with tears. She slowly turned her head to glance at the antique clock on the far end of the bedroom; 09:05, groaning before burying her face in the pillow.

She didn't feel like talking to anyone else; she had locked herself in the master bedroom, switched off her mobile phone and told Stella that no one should answer the house phones, no matter what. And they had been ringing soon after the detectives left.

Tamanda raised her head when she heard a gentle knock on the bedroom door, her eyes fluttered open.

"Go away Stella, I told you, I don't want to be disturbed!"

"But madam, it's . . ." The petrified housemaid struggled to explain herself; she was cut off in midsentence.

"Stella! I said go away!" She yelled furiously, grabbing one of the pillows and tossing it towards the door. It sailed through space like projectile, hitting the wall with a soft thud.

She could hear Stella's footsteps fading down the hallway; she grabbed another pillow and buried her head underneath it. There was a loud banging on the door, the sound of someone using their fists.

"Leave me alone, I said!" She yelled, pressing both palms against her ears.

"Tamanda open this door before I break it down!" It was Elijah's booming voice.

"Elijah? Elijah, what are you doing here?"

"Tamanda! Open this door!"

"Oh! Go away, just leave me alone . . . I am not in the mood; I know why you are here. Walter is not home, I don't know where he is ok?" She yelled then reburied her head back under the pillow.

"Tamanda, will you open this door, now!"

"You can stand there all you want Elijah, I don't care!"

"Tamanda, stop being a child and open the door."

"Elijah, didn't you hear what I said? I don't . . ."

"Tamanda, I have been trying to get hold of you; it's about father."

"What? What about father?" She sat upright in a flash.

"He passed away early this morning. I tried to reach you but your phone is or was switched off and no one was answering the ground line."

It felt like someone had kicked her hard on the face, not once but twice. Tamanda got up from the bed, dashed to the door. Surely she didn't hear what she just heard.

"What . . . what are you talking about?" She stammered as soon as she opened her bedroom door.

Her older brother didn't have to respond, his sombre look said it all; he looked haggard, his shoulders sagging.

"Father is gone, he is gone." Elijah's soft voice was almost a whisper.

"No, no, no, nooo, please nooo!" Tamanda croaked, she had been crying all morning, now her throat felt like someone was scrapping it with sharp razorblades; dry coughs rocked her entire body, she bent over, supporting herself against the doorframe.

For some reason her mind went back to the Pastor she had sat with on the flight back from South Africa yesterday, his words reverberated inside her brain; "*God always takes away from us those people we so dearly love . . .*"

Tamanda was surprised that she was even thinking about God. So much had happened in such a short period of time she didn't know where else to turn to. Walter's infidelity, the fact that he was a suspect in a double homicide and the fact that; for the first time in their marriage she had no knowledge of her husband's whereabouts—most likely he was with the scanty woman on that photo—and now this dreadful news about her father.

For so many years her father had been the main man in her life, a pillar of strength. Then Walter came along and took over that mantle. Her husband had provided her with security; emotional security. However, in a space of a day she had lost both men; through infidelity and death. How could so much grief, pain and loss be compressed into a short space of time for one person to deal with; Tamanda thought. Could it be that her atheism had angered the powers that be? Was there a God out there who had decided to take so much away from her to make her change her ways? There were so many questions and no answers. This left her weak, distraught and inattentive to what her brother was saying.

"Did you hear what I just said?" Elijah asked looking at her younger sister.

"I . . . I am sorry, can you repeat that." She said, trying to focus on her brother.

"I was saying that am going back to Dedza and I thought it better if you come along with me."

"I should, shouldn't I?" She asked; confusion apparent in her facial expressions and her responses.

"Yes Tamanda, you should. Remember you have the power of attorney, unless you feel that I should take charge of all proceedings?

"Sorry, what did you say?"

"Are you sure you are okay Tamanda? I thought it would be helpful if you came along, especially for mother's sake, she could sure use your company." Elijah said, deciding against bringing up *the power of attorney* subject up.

"Okay brother, you are right . . . let me just pack a few things." She said, closing the door.

She walked back into the bedroom like a zombie, almost tripping on the pillow she had tossed earlier on, all the way to the foot of her bed. She dropped heavily onto her knees and for the first time in many years, Doctor Tamanda Lumbadzi started mumbling a prayer as tears gushed down her cheeks.

"Lord Jesus Christ, have mercy on me . . ."

~ THE FUNERAL ~

IN MALAWI, IT is easy to discern a person's social standing by observing who attends their funeral. Even though Chief Justice Sambani had spent six years in retirement, living a life of a recluse at his village mansion, his prominence had not faded. The fact that a few of his children were also of high standing in society meant that the crème de la crème of Malawi's elite were present at his funeral. On top of the president of the country sending his personal condolences; lawyers, politicians from—both—the ruling and opposition parties, the clergy, the police and the whole village community and chiefs from surrounding villages, all came to pay their last respects.

It was a very hot and cloudless day. Dr Tamanda Lumbadzi and her siblings were watching the procession of mourners queuing up to go and view their father's body inside the large sitting room.

Despite the fact that her father had been sick, she couldn't believe that he was gone. The youngest of the boys, Junior, did not take the news well. Sobbing uncontrollably, she had to pull him aside in her bedroom to console him.

"Why sister, what happened to Daddy?" Junior gagged the question, blowing his nose constantly.

"The doctor said father had a stroke." Tamanda, who was trying to be the stronger of the two, said to her sobbing brother.

"But . . . but how, sis?"

"Father was very sick Junior, and according to Elijah, he said he had a prolonged coughing bout."

"Yes, that's what he told me as well."

"I wish I had stayed instead of returning to Blantyre, if only Walter had been here, I would have been by daddy's side when he passed away." She sobbed, talking more to herself than to her brother, who was now patting her on the back.

The family's youngest girl and the youngest boy, stood in the middle of the bedroom, grieving and consoling each other, as sounds of funeral music and cries of mourners could be heard from outside.

A familiar smell of cooked beans, roasting goat meat and *nsima*, wafted from the back of the house; the women were busy preparing lunch for the mourners. In front of the house, the whole family was sitting on chairs set out on the large veranda.

It was not lost on Tamanda that all of her siblings were flanked by their spouses, her in-laws. All the Sambani children were sitting facing the crowd of mourners. Her elder brother Elijah was sat next to his wife Nambewe, on the far end of the veranda. Flocy was next to her husband; Dr Rodney Jumani. Then her brother Kondwani was sitting next to her other brother, Brandon; together with his fiancée Tatiana. Zachariah, who they called the family's prodigal son, was sitting next to his wife, Nandiwe. Her sister Deliwe, the eldest of the girls, was next to her husband Kennedy. Tamanda, herself, was next to crying Mathews, the youngest boy in the family who everyone referred to as Junior. To her left was Cynthia her sister-in-law, wife to Kondwani.

Behind the black laced veil, she was looking at her stern faced brother Elijah who was dressed in his uniform like he was at a police function; she noticed that he kept glancing at his wrist watch. Tamanda wondered if her brother knew that two detectives had been to see her at her house, earlier this morning, asking about Walter.

As the soft sorrowful funeral hymns wafted from where the church choir was, tears slowly started to drip from her chin onto her lap. Tamanda wasn't sure whether that was a result of losing her father or losing Walter. It surprised her that she was thinking that she had lost him. As much as she wanted to ask him so many questions, she didn't think she had the energy to face him. Since she arrived, people had been coming to her offering their condolences. Almost all of them never failed to ask where her husband was; "We haven't seen our future honourable MP," they would say, all futile attempts to cheer her up.

There was no avoiding the fact that her husband was regarded by many as the youngest and brightest mind to have joined politics. It was obvious that even some of the reporters present at her father's funeral had come hoping to meet and perhaps take pictures of Walter Lumbadzi. While in the toilet, she had overheard two reporters complaining how it was going to be a wasted journey if the future MP and perhaps President of Malawi was not going to show up for the funeral. She wanted to march outside and confront them, but thought it was best not to.

"Where are you Walter?" She whispered to herself subconsciously, surprised that her thoughts had actually come out via her mouth.

"What was that sister?" Cynthia, her sister-in-law who was sitting next to her, asked in a low voice.

"Nothing sister, I was just thinking out loud." Tamanda whispered back.

"Oh! I thought I heard you mentioning your husband."

"What?" Tamanda asked turning round to look at her sister-in-law.

"I said, I thought you had mentioned your husband, because I think his car just pulled up. That's his car isn't it?" Cynthia gestured with her head to where cars were parked.

Tamanda's heart missed a beat. She looked up, across the sea of mourners, just beyond the mango trees where cars glittered under the afternoon sun. Walter's black Range Rover was reversing into a space between two other cars. For some reason it was like she hadn't seen him for months. She was now sitting upright; watching and not sure what to do next. She didn't want to be near her husband, at least not yet. She only hoped that he was going to sit with the ordinary mourners and not walk all the way to the veranda where she was.

Tamanda watched as the driver's side door opened and Walter; dressed in a black shirt and black trousers stepped out. He appeared to be taking off his sunglasses before shutting the door. Then she saw the rear door opening; Tamanda tensed, her fingers gripping the sides of the dining chair, her long nails digging into the soft cushioning, piercing it.

It was exactly at 13:30 when Walter got out of the car. He gently closed the door and slowly looked over the other side of the mango trees; where the mourners had gathered. He had expected to find the whole place choke-a-block with people, but hadn't expected to be confronted with an enormous sea of mourners. There were so many cars littering the surrounding open space. He noticed that where he had parked used to be a maize garden which had been flattened out to create more room for cars. Walter could only wonder where Maxwell had parked his brand new Mercedes; he wished he had let driver use a different car—he groaned for a split second before casting his gaze back towards the crowd of mourners. He couldn't make out the faces, he was still too far.

The sprawling house, splashed in white paint, stood out against the brownish vegetation all around. He had a feeling that Tamanda was amongst the mourners in black sitting in a row of chairs along the veranda, however, he was a bit far and the sun was in his face for him to ascertain if she was there. He stopped trying to find her, turning around when he heard the rear door of the car open. Stella, who was carrying Prince in her arms, slowly got out.

"Go with him to the small house, where children always gather during funerals." Walter said to Stella, noticing that the boy had slept during the long drive.

"Okay Sir." Stella answered politely and started heading in the other direction of the mansion, towards the house which Walter had referred to as *the small house*.

The brick house used to be the main house at the village before his father-in-law built the mansion. It was surrounded by other smaller mud huts; belonging to other relatives and workers. Behind the houses were three long stalls containing cattle, goats and pigs. There was a small brook separating the small brick house and the mansion. Walter had fondest memories of the small brick house; it was the house where they had held their two-day wedding reception. He remembers taking a stroll with his father-in-law from the brick house, stepping on stones to cross the small flowing brook and climbing up the gentle slope to where the big mansion now stands when it was just at foundation level.

The Chief Justice's eyes came alive when they arrived at the site. He kept bubbling with excitement on how he wanted to have a bedroom for each of his children, their spouses and a playroom for his grandchildren. Walter found himself warming up and bonding with his father-in-law more than he had done with his own father.

"Walter, between you and me, Tamanda is my baby."

"I know, sir." Walter emphasised on the word, sir; his way of showing respect to his father-in-law.

"She might be a doctor and, yes she is your wife, but in my heart she still is my little baby and I love her in a unique way."

"I have noticed that, sir."

"Did she ever tell you that her mother almost died while giving birth to her?" The Chief Justice asked, standing in a partition which, once finished, was going to be Tamanda's bedroom. It was right next to the master bedroom and strangely enough, bigger than all the other bedrooms.

"No Sir, she has never mentioned that detail to me." Walter had simply said, looking at his father-in-law who was looking towards the horizon.

He expected the Chief Justice to elaborate further, he did not. His next words were on a different tangent altogether, catching him slightly off guard.

"Are you a praying man Walter?" His father-in-law had surprised him with the change of subject. He was looking at him intently.

"I . . . I . . . it's been a while, sir."

"Mmhhh . . . I will take that is your diplomatic way of saying *no*."

"I have been meaning to go, but . . ." Walter, who over the years had come to regard church to be inconsequential, started answering but stopped.

"You are two of a kind, my daughter and you. When Tamanda was young, she used to go to church every Sunday."

"She did tell me that." Walter responded, not wanting to tell his father-in-law that what he had just said wasn't entirely correct. Walter had stopped going to church because of life's trappings; business, politics. His wife's case was entirely different; Tamanda was an atheist, he was not.

"My daughter would excitedly jump in the family car while I was still getting dressed." Judge Sambani was still going on; it was obvious to see that he was on cloud nostalgia.

"That part she left out." Walter said jokingly; smiling.

"I'm sure she did. However, something happened to her while in America." Chief Justice Sambani said with a frown.

"Mmmh." Walter mumbled, avoiding his father-in-law's eyes.

"According to my wife, our daughter started losing faith long before she went abroad for her studies. Nonetheless, I still lay the blame on America's doorstep."

"Oh!" Walter mumbled again, not sure what else to say.

"She returned to Malawi claiming to be an atheist." His father-in-law said in a pained voice; his attempts to coat it with laughter not succeeding.

"Yes, I know that Sir."

"You know what? That it is America's fault?"

"No, I mean; that my wife doesn't believe in the existence of God."

"Do you hold the same views?"

"Me, sir? I believe that there is a higher being, I . . . I . . . just don't believe that praying to this higher being, this God brings about success or whatever it is people pray for." Walter said, his voice trembling a bit.

"Is that so? So you think your financial success are down to your hardworking alone and not due to some divine blessings?"

"Yes sir, everything I have is down to my own sweat and self-made luck."

"Are you certain about that?"

"Sir, our country is a praying nation and yet, how many Malawians are doing well in life?"

"My son, I see you don't equate God to financial rewards."

"Not just that sir, even if we talk about health, people in this country die needlessly with diseases that are easily curable in other countries."

"True."

"Okay, I will admit my father precipitated his own death by his womanising, however all of his brothers; eleven of them died while in their prime. There was so much death in my clan we didn't feel grief anymore."

"Mmmh?"

"Yes sir, it became the norm hearing that, this uncle or that uncle has passed away." Walter said, slightly averting his eyes from the Chief Justice.

"You are talking like a politician, one day you should run for a political office."

"Me? I don't know about that sir. I am just talking like someone who feels as if we were abandoned by God at a time when He should have been there."

"Walter my son, the way you extrapolate our daily woes to formulate a conclusion that God is impotent, is crafty and typical of a politician, albeit not convincing. I still believe that God works in mysterious ways." His father-in-law said in a mellow voice.

"Maybe his ways are so mysterious that we never saw them."

"I beg your pardon?" Chief Justice Sambani raised his eyebrows quizzically.

"When I was growing up, my mother used to make me pray with her every night and she used to drag me to church every Sunday and yet we lived in grinding poverty." Walter said, his voice trembling.

"Sir, I never tasted rice until I was a teenager, we didn't even have a radio in our house and I used to sleep naked because my mother used to wash my clothes at night and I would pray that they would be dry by morning so that I could have an outfit to wear." He paused, staring in the distance.

The Chief Justice looked at him, not interrupting; waiting to hear more.

"Yes, I believe there is a God out there, but one would be stupid to think that their life will be made better if they kneel down and pray." Walter's voice was full of pain; surprised that he had said things which he has never disclosed to anyone, not even Tamanda.

"You kids of today," his father-in-law said, bending over to pull out a weed that had sprouted out of the ground, along the foundation wall; "the good thing is that my daughter can't stop talking about you. You seem to make her very happy and I have a feeling that you two will bless me with happy grandchildren." The Chief Justice said, tossing the weed into the bushes.

"It will be such an honour, sir." He answered, the prospect of one day becoming a father himself made him smile.

"Children and grandchildren, that's the essence of it all, it's the reason we acquire things, they are our extension and a guarantee that our name lives on. Do you understand what I mean Walter?"

"Yes, I believe I do, sir."

"I know your own father passed away, except that I didn't know that you lost all of your uncles. I am truly sorry to hear that. However, you come across like you don't like your father's name being brought up." The Chief Justice probed, sounding diplomatic.

"Sir, like I have said, my father was very poor; as a result we were poor also. There is nothing to talk about Sir."

"Walter my son," His father-in-law paused, sifting through his mind for appropriate words; "in life it is not a man's wealth that matters, rather his deeds."

"I understand that Sir, however, when you are poor such a statement rings hollow."

"Did you love your father Walter?"

"Sir, with all due respect, love is not a word which existed in our house when I was growing up."

"I am sorry, I don't follow." His father-in-law asked jumping from the outline of Tamanda's bedroom to what appeared to be a long corridor.

"Let's just say my father wasn't around much for a father-son union to foster, I was petrified of my father."

"What about your siblings? Surely you must have loved your siblings."

"My father had a very strong and true love for alcohol."

"Oh!"

"Yes. He also had a fondness for women, a lot of women. I was their only child, something you might have noticed from the wedding guest list."

"I did notice." The Chief Justice said, noticing the pain in Walter's eyes.

"I have a lot of brothers and sisters from his various women; siblings who I have never met and probably never will."

"Would you like to meet them?"

"No! I hope I don't meet them; they would simply remind me of the infidelities my father indulged in, and worse, how my own mother suffered as a consequence of that." Walter said, struggling to suppress the anger simmering from the depths of his soul.

"Nicely put my son, what you have said brings me to the crux of this conversation. Will my daughter ever experience what your own mother went through?" The Chief Justice calmly asked, his alert eyes looking straight into Walter's eyes. It felt like he was physically holding his head, urging him not to break contact until he answered him.

Walter was looking at his father-in-law and admiring the deftness of how he had articulated the question. Any other father would have simply asked him; *will you ever cheat on my daughter?*

"Sir, your daughter means the world to me, I would be a fool to ever look at another woman and feel the things I feel when I am with Tamanda." He responded, meaning each and every word that tumbled out of his mouth.

"You sound so sincere and as a father, I like to hear such words, Walter. Do you know why? I will tell you why." The Chief Justice looked towards the sky, as if what he wanted to say was hanging somewhere in the clouds, he then looked back at Walter's eyes.

"I'm listening, sir."

"Men, we are fools; you, me and the rest of them. All too often the passage of time makes us forget the promises and commitments we made yesterday." Chief Justice Sambani took a deliberate pause.

"Most of us forget that marriage is a fragile home, susceptible to crumble if we let Satan in. I know you are not a very religious person my son, nonetheless, I will still say this to you; if you don't let God be the guardian of your marriage, Satan will come knocking at your door in so many forms and shapes."

"I . . . I don't follow sir."

"Walter my son, you are a very young and good looking man. On top of that, you are fiercely ambitious, a go-getter. A lot of women out there hunger for a man of your calibre. Keep your guard up, for Satan will come in their shape; people think that Satan is ugly and abhorrent. Wrong. Satan is charming and alluring. Do not let Satan come between you and my daughter. Promise me that my son."

"I promise you father." He said, surprised how normal and right it felt calling the Chief Justice, *father*.

"Walter my son, I know I said this already, but I will say it again," the Chief Justice extended his hand; "I welcome you to the Sambani family."

Walter blinked as the funeral song wafted to where he was standing near the flowing brook. He actually felt a sense of loss, something he didn't feel when his own father had died. He had bonded with his father-in-law more than he had with Tamanda's brothers. The man had earnestly taken him into his fold like his own son, something which his oldest son frowned upon.

His brother-in-law, despite being the Deputy Inspector General, didn't bother him that much. The other reason he was joining politics was, so that he could be above the likes of Elijah; Walter thought.

He sighed then looked at the big house; the idea was to approach the front of the house from the south side. He would then sit together with the crowd of mourners on the lawn, facing the veranda. He figured, if he buried himself within the crowd, he could compose himself and what he was going to say to Tamanda later on.

He locked the car and was about to start toss the keys in his pocket when he noticed that Stella had forgotten Prince's bag on the backseat. Being a funeral, Walter decided against shouting for the maid who had already crossed the small stream. He grabbed the bag and hastily followed her towards the small brick house.

Walter was oblivious to the number of eyes watching him as he made his way down the small path.

~ THE ARREST ~

Elijah watched as the black Range Rover pulled up on the other side of the mango trees. He was seething inside; he couldn't believe that his brother-in-law had the nerve to show up at his father's funeral. He had specifically told the detectives to arrest Walter as soon as he showed up at the house, especially after he learned that one of the deceased men might be responsible for the mysterious death of a woman at the hospital. He bit his lower lip; he couldn't believe it had gotten this far.

Elijah was disgusted that his brother-in-law's corruption had culminated in deaths. He always wondered if his naïve little sister knew how her husband got all his wealth; the fleecing of taxpayer's and donor money during the UDF years, his recent dealings with Michael Lata and the multimillion printing deal on which Walter did not pay taxes.

Elijah was well aware that the day Mr Lata was deported—from Malawi—Walter Lumbadzi was the last person the Zambian had seen. Any attempts to squeeze this information from him proved futile. Elijah instructed the officers who drove the Zambia opposition leader to the border not to give him any cigarettes for the whole six-hour journey. He reckoned that when his nicotine cravings reached unbearable levels the old politician would fold and start singing about the real motive of his visit to Malawi, most importantly; what he had discussed with Walter. The Zambian prominent politician refused to deny or agree to any knowledge pertaining to Walter Lumbadzi.

Even after the infamous deportation of Mr Lata, sources were still informing Elijah that Walter was getting assistance from the neighbouring country to advance his political aspirations. He was informed that a fleet of twenty trucks belonging to Lumbadzi were now permanently based inside Zambia; he had secured a very lucrative contract with the new government.

Inquires with the operations manager at Lumbadzi were frustrating.

"Yes we sent some trucks to Zambia for repairs." Mr Daudi, the operations manager, had said dismissively.

Since Lata was elected president, Elijah knew that Walter had made nine trips to Zambia. Forex was scarce in Malawi; somehow his brother-in-law seemed to be able to import expensive campaign material from abroad.

Elijah was also aware of the two hundred metric tonnes of fertilizer which had somehow entered the country. His efforts to impound the ten '40-foot' containers had been frustrated by corrupt officials within customs. The documentation showed that the load was in transit from Durban for Zambia, not Malawi. The drivers concurred; they were simply making a routine stop by the workshop before continuing to their destination.

The trucks carrying the containers belonged to Lumbadzi Haulage and the load was intended for a Zambian customer. Police and customs had no choice but to allow the fertiliser to enter Malawi; however, like magic the trucks disappeared. His trusted informant told him Walter's trucks had not physically exited the country; strange enough, related documentation at the border post of Chipata was showing that they had. Despite arresting the customs officer-in-charge at the border, Elijah had again outsmarted him. However, the triple murder was something he was not going to evade; today the long arm of the law was going to touch Walter's shoulder. Deputy IG Elijah Sambani did not care for Walter's political shady dealings, but corruption and homicide is where he drew the line.

The heat from the sun was unbearable; Elijah shifted in the wooden chair, refraining from wiping off the beads of sweat from his forehead. He was police-trained and could not appear uncomfortable, especially at his own father's funeral. His unblinking eyes were still staring at the parked cars. Then he tensed at the sight of a woman getting out of Walter's car; it was too far to see who she was, but he could tell she was carrying a child. From the corner of his eye, he noticed that his sister, Tamanda, was also intrigued if not baffled by the same scene unfolding by the parked cars.

"Is everything okay dear?" Nambewe whispered to her husband without looking at him. She hadn't noticed what he was looking at, otherwise she wouldn't have asked; he thought.

"Yes, what do you mean?" Elijah responded; his eyes trained straight, ahead over the heads of the mourners.

"Because you are hurting me, the way you are squeezing my hand dear."

"Oh! Sorry dear, I am just a bit tense, I can't believe he is gone." Elijah said sombrely, moving his hand from Nambewe's and placing his own over his lap.

He noticed it was shaking. His hands always did, when he was angry. He clenched them into fists, to try and stop the shaking, looking up abruptly when a figure loomed over his right shoulder. It was Village Headman Bembeke, from the neighbouring village.

"Deputy Inspector General, I just want you to know how sorry I am at the loss of Chief Justice. Your father was . . ."

Village Headman Bembeke was going on and on with his words of condolences. Elijah had switched off.

His attention was on his sister Tamanda, she had just gotten up from her seat and quietly entered the house through the door adjacent the main door. Their father had redesigned that door long after the mansion had been built. It was to be used if one wanted to cut straight to the kitchen, bypassing the living room altogether.

There was an army of women in the kitchen, busy cooking; aunties, friends of the family and workers. There is no way Tamanda was going there to join them, Elijah thought. He had a feeling his sister was going to emerge through the back door and walk across the lawn, to where the cars were parked so as to confront her husband. He could not let that happen, as far as he was concerned, his brother-in-law was a suspect in a double homicide and he did not want his sister to complicate the arrest. As much as he hated Walter appearing at his father's funeral, maybe this was a blessing in disguise. It would even be better for the arrest to be made public.

"Thank you for those kind words Village Headman Bembeke, now will you excuse me for a minute?" Elijah said getting up, "I will be right back dear." He whispered to his wife.

"Okay dear." Nambewe responded, but Elijah was already by the small door, he hadn't heard her.

He took out his phone the minute he entered the house, switched it on and dialled. There were a few people on this part of the house, mostly grieving relatives; they looked at him with teary eyes. Elijah ignored them and walked hastily towards the kitchen and made his way out into the backyard.

"Hello!" He barked into the phone.

Detective Zeneya frowned when he heard the familiar beeping coming from his pocket.

"Not again." He mumbled; annoyance plastered all over his face.

He had just gotten off the phone five minutes ago, trying to explain himself to his angry wife; Mrs Zeneya had told him in the clearest language that it was either their marriage or his job. She even yelled at him that her friends at the salon were insinuating the possibility that he might be having an affair and using his job as an excuse.

Detective Zeneya had done his best to plead his case and for a moment he had a feeling that she was calming down. The jinx came when, in a low and subdued voice, he told her that he was with Detective Gunda and they were heading to Dedza to go and apprehend a suspect. The minute he uttered those words, his wife blew a gasket, called him an ungrateful pig and hung up the phone.

When he heard the beeping he answered the phone without even checking who was calling him.

"Look Mebo, I know you are angry. I don't think this is the . . ."

"Hello!" The familiar voice of Deputy Inspector General Sambani exploded on the other end of the line; "Detective Zeneya?"

"Yes sir! I am sorry sir I thought it was my wife sir!"

"Detective Zeneya, why am I seeing a suspect to a double murder at the funeral of my father?" Elijah exploded, ignoring the detective's apologetic explanation.

"Sir, I can only apologise. We . . . we are on our way there as we speak." Detective Zeneya stammered.

The detective was too scared to say the truth that all those hours spent watching Tosh, day and night, had finally taken their toll on his and his colleague. Whilst parked on the side of the road, near Walter's residence, both detectives had succumbed to sleep; a combination of fatigue and unbearable heat. Their suspect, Mr Lumbadzi, had come and gone right under their noses. When they woke up, Detective Gunda panicked, jumped out of the car and walked over to the gate asking the guards if Mr Lumbadzi had returned.

"Yes, the boss came long time ago. He left again to follow madam for a funeral in Dedza. He left together with the housemaid and a child about twenty minutes ago" An enthused guard said to a shocked Detective Gunda.

"I don't need apologies Detective Zeneya!" Deputy Inspector General was yelling on the other end of the line.

"I am sorry sir, we had to go back to headquarters and requisition for petrol so that . . ."

"Just get here detective, now!" Elijah yelled and hung up the phone while Detective Zeneya was still trying to waffle an explanation.

Tamanda shot out through the back door, weaving herself around women; most of them were laughing and talking jovially while cooking. They immediately stopped talking, their jovial faces turning sombre and sorrowful as soon as they saw her. Some of them, whose backs were turned to her, carried on joking and laughing, almost jumping out of their skins once they heard her voice excusing herself as she walked past. Tamanda was unmindful to the women's indifference to her father's passing. She didn't actually care that these were the same women who had been crying; faking to be experiencing genuine grief. Her mind was preoccupied with one thing; one person, Walter.

She hurried almost breaking into a run, along the parked cars. She shot past Walter's Ranger Rover and could see his unmistakable figure half way near the small brick house. He was talking to a woman; Stella, the housemaid, who was carrying a small boy. She broke into a run, wind blowing her black scarf off her face.

"Walter!" She yelled, slowing down into a walk.

"Yes?" Walter answered, turning round, "yes darling." He was surprised to see her standing there, almost in a confrontation stance.

"What's going on Walter?" Tamanda asked, her legs slightly apart, not sure whether she wanted to close in the remaining five or so steps.

"I think we certainly need to talk darling." He said, trying to gauge the temperature of this meeting; she was not the same Tamanda of last night.

"No, I think *you* should speak and I will listen. It might also be a good idea if you drop the darling bit. It sounds a bit empty and somewhat fictitious." She shot at him in an icy tone, her gaze holding his.

"I don't think this is the right place darling," He said in a calm voice, before turning to their house maid; "Stella, take the child to the small house."

"Stella, take that child back into the car!" She yelled, confusing the housemaid who looked at her and then at Walter.

"Darling please I beg you; don't cause a scene at your father's funeral." He pleaded, not sure whether the perspiration was due to the heat of the sun or heat caused by feelings of guilt.

"Walter, I said drop the darling term, it's starting to get on my nerves," She seethed, then, looking over her husband's shoulder, at the housemaid; "Stella why are you still standing there? What did I just tell you?"

"Stella, give me the child and go help out in the kitchen." He said, taking Prince from Stella's arms.

The confused housemaid gladly handed over the child and hastily walked back towards the mansion.

"Is that what you have been doing when I am not around Walter? Making babies and taking filthy photos with nude women?" Tamanda said in a raised voice, advancing towards her husband, closing the last few steps until she was almost face to face with him.

"Darling, there is no excuse for what I have done, for what I did. No words can explain how sorry I am and . . ." He said, taking one step back, he has never seen her feisty like this and wasn't sure what she was going to do next.

"Oh cut the crap Walter, you might sweet talk your way around these people who think you are the cleanest politician since Nelson Mandela, except that such nonsense is not going to wash with me. Do you hear me?" She yelled, taking one step towards him.

"Darling, I wish you would give me a chance to talk."

"Talk? Talk about what, Walter? How your mistress ended up dead? To talk about the detectives who are looking for you, or about the shooting that has left two men dead in Ndirande? What the heck do you want to talk to me about Walter? What? Do you want to confess that . . . that . . . that thing you are holding is your son . . . is . . . is . . . is that what you what to talk to me about? Why . . . how . . . how could you do this to me, to us? Is it because I can't have children Walter?" Tamanda was now sobbing, her anger turning into anguish.

Walter felt rotten and speechless.

"For better or for worse, Walter? For better or for worse . . . do you remember uttering those words? Is it because I can't give you an heir to your empire, Walter? Don't just stand there looking at me, talk! Say something!"

Walter kept looking at his wife, not sure what to do or how to respond. She had said so much, some of the things hurtful and some shocking.

"Shooting . . . in Ndirande? What are you talking about Darling? Who told you?" Walter's head was spinning, he looked at his wife and he felt her pain, he was disgusted with himself and wondered if there was a way to reach out to her.

"Don't ask me those questions Walter, why don't you ask them." Tamanda said pointing over his shoulder.

The two detectives saw Mr Lumbadzi, whose back was turned to them, arguing with his wife along the small path which connected the big house to the smaller brick house in the distance. The Deputy Inspector General had directed them where to find the suspect and that he would shortly join them as soon as they made the arrest.

"Mr Lumbadzi! I am Detective Zeneya and this is Detective Gunda, we are placing you under arrest on suspicion to the murder of Peter Zekazeka, also known as Tosh, and a Nigerian national by the name of Obafeni."

"Excuse me?" It was like Walter had just been hit by a sledge hammer, his eyes darting between his wife and the detectives.

"Mr Lumbadzi, you have the right to remain silent. Anything you say can and will be used against you in a court of law. You have a right to a lawyer, however if you cannot afford a lawyer, one will be appointed for you." Detective Zeneya recited the Miranda Rights to the baffled-looking Walter.

"Can I just have a word with my wife first detectives?"

"Did you hear what I just said? I am afraid I can't let you do that Mr Lumbadzi, you may hand over the child to your wife." Detective Zeneya said, taking out handcuffs from his belt.

"Darling, please . . . I am begging you, promise me you will take care of the child. Yes, you are right, he belongs to a woman I cheated on you with, but he is not my child. Don't hate him because of what I did Darling. Promise me." Walter pleaded, handing over Prince to a reluctant Tamanda together with the keys to his Range Rover.

She held him awkwardly in her arms, not sure if she should and watched in pain as the detective handcuffed her husband's hands.

"I love you Tamanda, I always have." He said as he was being whisked away by the two detectives.

Tamanda did not respond, she watched as the three men walked towards the parked cars. She heard a commotion behind her, turned around only to see a group of reporters and photographers running from the big house, down the gentle slope towards them. They had hoped to interview and take pictures of a promising future MP. They had come to see the man most people were saying; had the right calibre to one day be the president of Malawi.

However, seeing Walter in handcuffs was even a bigger scoop than what they had anticipated. The sporadic clicking of cameras started immediately, this was followed by a barrage of questions.

"Mr Walter Lumbadzi! Why are you being arrested?" One reporter yelled; shoving a recording device in Walter's face.

He ignored the question, and together with the two detectives, kept on walking with his head slightly bowed. During the two hour drive from Blantyre; Walter had prepared himself for a confrontation with Tamanda. Mentally agonised how he was going to explain last night to his wife; introducing Prince to her was going to be the toughest and he tried to think of a myriad of questions which were going to be spawned by the little boy's appearance. This was—as far he was concerned—the extent of his problems. Walter hadn't expected the quagmire he found himself him.

As the cameras clicked; he struggled to maintain his composure, it was obvious for all to see that he was shaken to the core.

"Is this the end of your political career sir?" Another, also armed with a voice recorder, chimed in.

"Mr Lumbadzi, is this arrest politically motivated?" A female reporter asked, taking long strides alongside him, being jostled by other reporters.

"Mr Lumbadzi, is this to do with the death of Tosh and Miss Nomsa Salala?" Another reporter asked. Walter froze in his tracks, and so did the two detectives, all three turned around to face the pack of chasing reporters.

"What did you just say?" Detective Gunda quizzed the reporter who had just asked the question; "Who gave you that information?"

"So it's true? You are arresting Mr Lumbadzi for the said deaths?" The skinny looking reporter pressed on, unfazed by the detective's threatening tone.

"Where did you get that information?"

"Were you having a secret affair with the deceased woman Mr Lumbadzi?" The reporter did not have to yell, all the other reporters had gotten quiet; everyone was looking at him.

"Okay, that's enough!" Detective Gunda yelled, propelling Walter towards the safety of the waiting Land Rover.

~ CHECK MATE ~

ELIJAH, WHO HAD been standing between two cars under the shade of the mango trees, watched the whole arrest unfold. He could not hear what the reporters were asking, the distance and the singing choir made that an impossible task; however, he had an idea what was being said. He grinned with satisfaction as Walter was bundled into the police Land Rover in front of reporters, photographers and most of the mourners. He had to remind himself that this was his father's funeral and it might not appear appropriate if he was to be seen smiling. From the corner of his eye he saw his sister walking towards the house, carrying the child. Now that his brother-in-law was out of the way, dealing with her was going to be easy; Elijah mused. She was emotionally distraught with everything that had taken place. Their father had instructed that, if for some reason Tamanda could not execute the duties expected of her as the one with the power of attorney, then he could step in.

With a sombre face he approached his sister; she looked up when he emerged from behind the parked cars.

"That is sad, the arrest that is. I am very angry at what he has done to you dear sister." Elijah said in a compassionate tone, gesturing with his head at the Land Rover which was slowly driving away, still surrounded by a horde of reporters and some mourners who had gone over to see what the commotion was all about.

"I am angry too, Elijah, but he is still my husband and right now I need to contact a lawyer." Tamanda, who was slightly startled to see her elder brother standing there, said flatly.

She was surprised that seeing her husband being arrested brought her pain, not satisfaction. Despite the events of the last twenty-four or so hours, it hurt seeing him being treated like a criminal. Tamanda hastily walked away from her brother, towards the house, to find the housemaid so that she could hand the child over to her.

"Are you going to take care of Prince? . . . eermm . . . I mean of the child?"

"What?" If he hadn't stuttered and corrected himself, she would have carried on walking.

She froze in her tracks, quickly recovered and doubled back to where her brother was standing.

"What did you just say?" Tamanda hissed, a slight frown forming across her face.

"I was asking if you are planning on taking care of another woman's child." Elijah repeated, slightly averting his eyes away from his sister's piercing look. He was shifting from one foot to another, and speaking all in a rush. Tamanda knew her brother too well, he was nervous; Elijah did that whenever his nerves were frayed, a lot of people didn't know this. She did.

"How come you know the child's name Elijah?" Tamanda yelled causing a few mourners who were within earshot to turn and look in their direction.

"What kind of question is that?" Elijah said and started to walk away from her.

"Elijah, don't you dare walk away from me. How did you know the boy is called Prince?"

"There is so much that I know about your husband that you don't sis."

"Elijah, just tell me how you know the child's name."

"Tamanda, you don't know your own husband. Walter is a monster." Elijah said; then hesitated, not sure if he had crossed the line with his remark.

"Elijah, don't tell me about what my husband is; tell me how you know the child's name? Do you know *who the mother is then?"

"I am not having this conversation with you Tamanda, because I know that you are distraught after witnessing your husband being handcuffed." Elijah said dismissively, taking long strides towards the house.

He disappeared inside, slamming the kitchen door so hard the women who were busy cooking looked up, startled, casting their gaze at Tamanda. She looked back and they looked away, pretending to busy themselves with what they had been doing before.

Tamanda thought of chasing after him, but stopped herself. The last thing she wanted was to have an exchange with her brother right in front of their grieving mother and relatives. She shifted Prince to her left side, fished the phone out of her bag; turned it back on and dialled Walter's number.

Walter was sitting next to Detective Zeneya in the back of the Land Rover, his handcuffed hands clasped together on his lap. A few eager reporters and photographers were still pursuing him, running alongside the slow moving car which was negotiating its way around the other parked cars.

"Mr Lumbadzi, is this the end of your political ambitions?"

"Do you think you have let down the people of Blantyre; especially those of Ndirande?"

"Mr Lumbadzi, are you going to fight this?"

Walter ignored them, he was struggling to clear his mind of clutter; trying to isolate the face of the skinny reporter who had startled him with the question earlier on. He was certain he had seen that face before; he couldn't remember where. His thoughts were interrupted by the beeping of his Mobile phone; he looked pleadingly at the detective sat next to him. With his hands handcuffed together, he couldn't get the phone out of his pocket.

"Is it okay if I answer this call or at least check who is calling?" He asked whist raising his bound up wrists.

"No, it's not okay Mr Lumbadzi, you are under arrest and you cannot take or make any phone calls until we get to the station, you have to be processed first and they you will be allowed a phone call," Detective Zeneya said, dipping his hand into Walter's pocket, confiscating his phone; "I am sorry Sir, I have to turn it off."

Tamanda snatched the phone from her ear, looking down at it in disbelief. Had he just switched off his phone on her? She fumed, speed-dialling his number again; nothing. Was he angry with her because of the things she had said to him? She thought, craning her neck and standing on the tips of her toes to see if she could still see the Land Rover.

The Land Rover hadn't made it outside the perimeter of the farm; she could see a cloud of dust bellowing from the tyres as it slowly itched towards the main road. Tamanda dashed round to the rear of the mansion where women were manning various boiling pots; she managed to locate Stella amongst the women.

"Go with the child back to the small brick house Stella." She ordered the maid, as she handed Prince to the bemused housemaid.

"Okay madam." Stella said, gingerly taking the little boy into her arms.

Both, the boy and the maid, stood there; watching Tamanda as she dashed off to where Walter had parked his Range Rover.

She reversed hard, almost slamming into a parked pickup, engaged into *drive* and floored the accelerator causing most of the mourners to look up, wondering what the commotion was all about.

The police Land Rover had joined the main dirt road and was now gathering speed; Tamanda floored the accelerator of the powerful Range Rover, catching up with the slower police vehicle.

She started flashing her headlights and blowing the horn loudly.

Detective Gunda looked at his rear view mirror at the speeding madman who was erratically flashing his headlights right behind.

"Go on just overtake if you are in such a rush!" He yelled then paused when, through the thick dust, he managed to make out the car and the personalised plate; *Lumbadzi 3.*

"Isn't that your car Mr Lumbadzi?" Detective Gunda said gesturing with his left thumb over his shoulder.

"It must be my wife." Walter answered, looking behind; "I am sure she is the one who was trying to call me."

"Just pull over on the side; I will see what she wants." Detective Zeneya said to his colleague.

They watched as the female figure, dressed in black jumped out of the pursuing Range Rover and started running towards the parked police Land Rover.

"Excuse me Dr Lumbadzi, but what do you think you are doing?" An upset Detective Zeneya jumped out of the Land Rover, confronting Tamanda.

"Detective, was my brother informed of this investigation on my husband?" She went straight to the point, ignoring the detective's question.

"Dr Lumbadzi, I cannot discuss official matters with you."

"Detective Zeneya, I am only going to ask you this once," She said, standing a step away from the detective; "Was my brother aware of the investigation on my husband?" She finished in an icy voice. She could tell that the detective was uncomfortable having a woman standing that close to him.

"Yes, the Deputy Inspector General is fully updated about this investigation. In case you have forgotten, he is, after all the Deputy Inspector General of police." Detective Zeneya said, taking two steps back.

"Yes detective, I am aware of that small fact." She retorted unfazed by the detective who was struggling to regain his composure.

"If that was all you wanted to find out, am afraid we have to go, we have a long drive ahead of us." Detective Zeneya started to turn around; eager to get away from this stubborn and feisty woman who made him more uncomfortable than Mebo, his wife.

"Detective, how many cases have you investigated this year?" Tamanda shouted.

"What?" Detective Zeneya, who was about to jump back in the Land Rover, paused, turned around to look at Tamanda.

"Let me make it easy for you detective; how many cases have you been reporting directly to my brother?"

"Dr Lumbadzi, you are overstepping your boundaries."

"Detective, I haven't started overstepping my boundaries yet, and trust me; you don't want me to overstep them."

"Dr Lumbadzi, what exactly is it you want?" Detective Zeneya asked in a mellowed down tone.

"I just find it a bit curious that you are reporting directly to the Deputy Inspector General, something you should be reporting to your immediate superior. Don't you think that's a bit odd Detective? I am sure it would make nice news headlines, wouldn't you say?"

"Dr Lumbadzi, what is it that you want from me?" Detective Zeneya, clearly ruffled, asked.

"For starters I want those handcuffs off my husband."

"That's preposterous; your husband is under arrest."

"Does my husband look like the fleeing type to you?"

"Can you remove the suspect's handcuffs detective?" Detective Zeneya said to his colleague, then turned to face Tamanda with an exasperated look; "What now Dr Lumbadzi?"

"That Blackberry you showed me at my house yesterday morning, is it still in your possession?"

"Dr Lumbadzi, that Blackberry is evidence to a crime."

"Detective, is the Blackberry still in your possession?"

"Yes, Dr Lumbadzi. What about it?"

"Do you mind if I take one more look at it?"

"There is nothing of interest to you Dr Lumbadzi apart from those photos and messages concerning your husband."

"Can I see the Blackberry please or do I need to call your Deputy Inspector General to requisition for it?" Tamanda shot at the detective, the underlying threat laden with sarcasm not lost on the policeman.

"Can you please pass me the envelope containing the Blackberry?" Detective Zeneya instructed his colleague; he reached into the middle console compartment and took out the manila envelope.

Tamanda grabbed it from the detective; she immediately started scrolling down the list of dialled numbers, a frown on her face. Most of them were to her husband's numbers and some of them didn't look familiar to her. She couldn't believe how many calls the woman had made to her husband. Most of the dates were when she had been away; outside the country. She was trying her best not look at Walter; she had to control her anger from clouding the task at hand.

"Dr Lumbadzi, what is it you are looking for?" Detective Zeneya asked, sounding agitated and slightly nervous.

There was something about this woman that he found unnerving; the detective thought. He smiled resignedly, not even his wife gave him this much grief and ignored him as if he wasn't even there.

Instead of responding to the detective, Tamanda started going through the phone log; scrutinising all incoming calls. She was mentally deciphering each string of numbers, eliminating them one by one as she scrolled down. She was aware that Walter and the two detectives were looking at her curiously; she did not look at neither of them. After ten tense minutes, she stopped. Her eyes bulged out of their sockets; she had found what she was looking for.

She blocked the Blackberry's number; then dialled back the number she had just come across. It started ringing on the other end.

Tamanda stood, tapping her right foot on the side of the road, waiting. For the first time she looked up at her husband, he was looking down at her from inside the backseat of the police Land Rover.

After what appeared to be an eternity a person picked. Tamanda stopped tapping, her suspicions were proved true as the familiar agitated voice exploded on the other end of the line.

"Hello! Who is this calling me private?"

"It's me dear brother."

"Tamanda? What . . . how . . . why are you calling on father's phone?"

"Elijah, you are the one who should be telling me why you have been using father's phone."

"You just don't stop do you?"

"To think that you blamed father's forgetfulness when we thought he had lost his phone and yet you were using it in secret."

"Tamanda, you need to come over here, now!"

"If I come are you going to tell me why you had used father's phone to call the owner of this Blackberry?" Her angry voice ricocheted on the side of the road; even the two detectives could not believe their ears.

"Tamanda, you listen to me, this is way out of your league you hear me?"

"Elijah, what is way out of your league is you trying to frame my husband!"

"What? Don't think for one second, that just because you are my sister I can't have you arrested!" Elijah yelled on the other end of the line, struggling to sound threatening.

"Elijah, you used that woman didn't you?" She countered, unfazed by her brother's ranting.

Inside the car, Walter flinched whereas the two detectives exchanged looks.

"Moreover, the disgusting thing is you had the audacity to steal father's phone to carry out your pathetic personal vendetta." She carried on.

"Tamanda, who is there with you? You need to come back here so that we can talk about this cordially." Elijah's tone was slowly turning into a whisper.

"I don't want to talk about anything with you Elijah, what you need to do is tell these detectives to release my husband!"

"Are you out of your mind? Your husband is a suspect to a double homicide."

"If you want my husband arrested, there has to be a proper investigation and trust me, if he is going to go to jail for those deaths, he won't be the only man sinking!" She seethed.

"Sis, wake up will you! Your husband was cheating on you!" Elijah yelled.

"Last time I checked you were not my marriage councillor or is cheating now considered a police matter?" Tamanda yelled and handed the phone to Detective Zeneya.

Walter couldn't believe what he was hearing; he looked at his wife who looked back at him. Certain things started to click in his mind; he had seen that skinny reporter—the one who had asked him specific questions—once with his brother-in-law at a dinner party huddled up at a corner. He hadn't paid much attention to the two of them.

Was Nomsa a setup from the get go? Walter felt nauseated and dizzy he almost didn't hear the detective talking to him.

"You are free to go Mr Lumbadzi. We might call you to come to the station if we need you to give evidence." Detective Zeneya, who had just finished talking with the Deputy Inspector General, said while holding the door open for Walter.

He hesitated slightly before jumping out of the Land Rover; then standing on the side of the road, staring at his angry wife. As soon as the police Land Rover drove off, Tamanda handed

Walter the keys to his Range Rover; their fingers touched slightly and he felt like saying something. He longed to hold her hand, to apologise for everything; however, she turned around and started going back towards the mansion.

"Tamanda, you are not planning on going all the way back on foot?"

She did not answer, she did not even turn around to acknowledge him; Tamanda kept on walking, her hands clenched into fists, her head held high.

"Come on sweetheart, get in the car please." He pleaded with her.

She did not stop; increasing her pace, almost breaking into a run.

Walter thought of running after her; he decided to get in the car. He made a U-turn and before long he was driving alongside her.

"Sweetheart, get in the car please." He pleaded with her through the rolled down window.

"Walter, leave me alone," she said in a flat emotionless tone; "and please do not attempt to go back to my father's funeral."

"Tamanda please, what will people think when they see you arriving back there on foot?"

"Is that your biggest worry right now? You are worried what people will think when they see your wife walking?"

"At least, let me drop you off darling."

"After everything you have done, after all that you have put me through and exposed me to? After you have destroyed the trust I had in you, Walter. Your biggest worry is that people will see me walking?"

"Tamanda I didn't mean it like that sweetheart."

"You know what Walter? Cut the crap okay! I suggest you go pick up that little boy of yours and return back to Blantyre." She yelled, her whole body trembling with rage.

With long strides, she walked away from the car; diverting from the main dirt road into a small foot path, a shortcut that meandered towards her parent's mansion.

He stopped the car and watched her disappear into the tall brown grass; he clamped his eyes shut, feeling nauseated and hollow inside. The humiliation of being arrested in public paled in comparison to what he was feeling soon after staring into his wife's eyes and seeing the hurt he had caused.

~ HEART UPON MY SLEEVE ~

IT WAS BOILING hot inside the packed minibus; Hendrina was struggling to make sure that her right thigh wasn't brushing against that of the man sitting between her and the driver.

'What a way to start a Monday,' she thought while stealing glances at the man. He looked unkempt and had a body odour which she found repulsive; a mixture of sweat, bad breath, lack of soap, all culminating into a total breakdown of personal hygiene. However, resting on the man's lap was that morning's newspaper, with a captivating headline.

Hendrina resisted the urge to ask him if she could borrow the paper; he looked the type who would take things the wrong way and assume that she was trying to encourage him on. As much as she didn't want to stare at the man's lap, her eyes were drawn to the headlines on the front page.

Walter Lumbadzi Arrested in a Triple Homicide.

Beneath it, was a picture of her boss; he was handcuffed and looking a bit withdrawn.

She stole a sideways glance at the sweaty face of the man, debating whether she should chance it and borrow the paper; feminine pride and a bit of fear prevailed. Hendrina decided to wait until she got to work; the men in accounts department always had newspapers. She didn't believe what she was looking at anyway, she would definitely read the *fake* story from the comfort of her office; Hendrina thought, forcing herself to peel her eyes from the man's lap.

She felt like telling the smelly man that the headline was not true; that Walter Lumbadzi was actually her boss, perhaps the most decent man the in whole country. She was certain that his political enemies were out to get him, she so much wanted to grab the newspaper and scream out; telling the whole minibus not to believe what was printed in the paper. Instead she grabbed the ends of her short skirt, pulling it down her knees, to try and cover her exposed thighs. It was a futile attempt.

The man slowly turned around, his red eyes gloating over her slender legs. His mouth was twisted into a grin, a few teeth were missing, and from the gap came a gust of bad breath; a mixture of garlic and yesterday's beer.

Hendrina looked away from him, staring outside the window, thankful that her stage was coming next. She could see the company's white van that always came to collect staff from the stage for the ten minute drive to where the offices were located.

Mr Lumbadzi's designated parking space was empty; Hendrina noticed as Samson pulled up. He was not yet in, which was normal; it was only 07:00, the boss always arrived around 9:30am. Hendrina hurried inside; her morning routine always started with the ladies room, on the second floor. She would freshen up, reapply her makeup and spray some perfume before heading to her office.

Today she was going to deviate from the norm; she would start with the accounts department. She was so desperate to grab herself a newspaper and read the whole story. First stop was going to be the accounts department; on the third floor.

The accounts department and the hallway were separated by a glass wall. As Hendrina half walked half run, she could see a crowd of people milling around one of the desks. It didn't take her long to realise what they were looking or rather reading. She was getting angry; she decided against going in, she felt like telling them to go back to work and stop believing in lies. Instead she marched on towards her office.

"Hendrina, have you heard what happened on Saturday?" Yvonne from personnel department, who was coming up the stairs, stopped in front of her and asked.

"No, I haven't heard, Yvonne!" Hendrina snapped.

"The boss was arrested while at the funeral of his father-in-law." Yvonne whispered.

"Were you present at the funeral, Yvonne?"

"No, but . . ."

"I didn't think you were, Yvonne."

"I just thought you would want to know what everyone is talking about Hendrina."

"Listen to me Yvonne; if you were not at the funeral, then I don't want to listen to your hearsay!" Hendrina spat out, clearly annoyed.

"It's not hearsay, Hendrina; it's all over the morning papers."

"Is that all you people do around here? Read papers and start gossiping?" Hendrina yelled, breaking into a run towards the flight of stairs. Yvonne looked slightly shocked, shaking her head and shrugging her shoulders.

Hendrina slammed the door behind her. She slowly walked over to her desk, slumped into her chair and started sobbing silently. If only she could call her boss, just to find out why people were spreading these malicious rumours about him; Hendrina agonised, looking at the antique wall clock on the far end of the office.

Mr Lumbadzi was going to walk in at the usual time, she was certain about that. Hendrina told herself that she was going to open the door for her boss and then during lunch she was going to laugh and chide the other staff who had believed the lies printed in the paper.

Yes, a complete lie is what all this was about, propaganda to tarnish the good image of her boss; Hendrina whispered. She opened the side drawer of her desk and took out a tissue; drying her eyes, telling herself to get a grip. He was fine.

She took a deep breath, peeped at the small photo of her boss which she kept hidden in her drawer under envelopes, a smile formed across her face. Hendrina got up and headed to the ladies room to fix herself; she had to make sure that she was looking stunning by the time Mr Lumbadzi arrived.

She always compared herself to Dr Tamanda Lumbadzi, the woman was beautiful and she knew how to dress. She was the one who took care of him at home; but here at the office, that role fell to her, Hendrina thought, walking past the accounts department. The number of people milling around the newspaper had grown. They all turned around when they heard her loud high heels pounding against the floor; they immediately went back to whatever they had been reading as soon as they noticed it was her.

After a flight of stairs, a perspiring Detective Gunda was ushered into the plush office by the lady from the reception. Wiping his brow with a handkerchief, he looked around the office, his attentive police eyes taking in each and every detail.

Two days ago, the detective had seen Mr Lumbadzi's magnificent mansion, surely nothing was going to surprise him; he thought. Detective Gunda quickly realised how wrong he was the moment the taxi drove through the gigantic sliding gate. As far as he was concerned the Walter Lumbadzi epitomised the phrase; '*how the other half lives.*'

It was the first time coming to the premises of *Lumbadzi Investments*; he wouldn't have guessed that the man they had just placed under arrest owned all this. There were stories within the police force that if *Lumbadzi Investments* had existed during the era when Press Corporation Limited was a business behemoth, the two would have gone head-to-head. Detective Gunda always dismissed these as baseless exaggerations; he didn't think that any private company in Malawi would ever grow to the size and magnitude that Press Corp had reached, at the height of its success.

He found himself revaluating his scepticism by the time he got out of the taxi and entered the glass doors. He had always thought *Lumbadzi Investments* was a haulage business; wrong again. Judging from what he was seeing; the transportation business was a small segment of the whole enterprise. He had to give the man credit for building what was mini industrial site away from the main road; away from prying eyes.

Entering the reception area reminded the detective of exclusive office complexes he had visited in South Africa; the ambience, the cool air conditioned environment felt like heaven to him. Detective Gunda smiled at one of the four ladies behind the hotel-like reception.

"I am here on business to see Mr Lumbadzi."

"I am sorry Mr Lumbadzi is not in the office; may I please take your name."

"Mr Gunda." He responded, deliberately omitting the detective part.

"Just a minute Mr Gunda, let me call his secretary, please have a seat." The lady said gesturing to a set of black comfortable looking leather couches.

"Thank you." Detective Gunda replied then walked to the nearest couch.

"Mmmh, that's strange; she is not answering. Let me try her mobile." The lady said loud enough for him to hear that she was trying her best. He smiled, wishing he owned a comfortable couch like this. Going home at the end of a shift would be such a treat, if one knew that such a sofa was waiting for him; he thought as he wiggled himself deeper.

"Yes Mr Gunda, she says you can go in; my colleague here will usher you to her office, it's on the third floor."

"Thank you." Detective Gunda heaved his enormous body out of the low comfortable couch.

After going up a flight of stairs and walking along a carpeted corridor, the lady from the reception came to a door with the letters *private* emblazoned on a silver plaque. She held the door open for him and stepped aside.

"Mr Lumbadzi's secretary will be with you in a minute. Make yourself comfortable." The lady said courteously; she left, closing the door behind her quietly.

Detective Gunda did not have to wait long. The door opened and a tall beautiful lady, with the body of a twenty-one year old athletic, walked in. She smiled and frowned at the same time; not too sure who this man was.

"Good morning Mr Ganda, can I help you." Hendrina asked, her eyes raking over the giant man who rose to his feet as soon as she entered.

"Good morning madam, my name is Gunda not Ganda, Ezekiel Gunda."

"I apologise, Mr Gunda. I thought the receptionist had said Ganda."

"That's okay, Miss . . . ?" He said; letting the sentence hang.

"Miss Munthali, I am Mr Lumbadzi's secretary." Hendrina answered, before asking her own question; "What can I do for you Mr Gunda?"

"I was wondering if I could see Mr Lumbadzi."

"I'm afraid that's not possible, the boss is not in right now; and you will need to book an appointment before you can see him." She said, pacing over to her desk and pulling out her diary to see Walter's availability.

"Miss Munthali, it is very important that I see your boss."

"I am sure it is, Mr Gunda, but like I said; he is not in and you will need an appointment. How does Wednesday afternoon sound?" Hendrina asked; her eyes were going through the diary.

"Miss Munthali, I am a police detective; as a matter of fact, if you read today's paper, I am one of the detectives who arrested Mr Lumbadzi on Saturday." The detective paused, noticing the secretary's face change colour.

"You . . . you are a police officer?" Hendrina gasped.

"Yes Miss Munthali, and like I said it is very important that I see your boss."

"He . . . he is not here; I have no idea where he is, detective. Why do you want to see Walter . . . I mean . . . Mr Lumbadzi?" Hendrina swiftly corrected her slip of the tongue, her eyes darting to the detective's face to see if he had noticed.

If he had, then he was good at concealing his reaction; his face was black. Hendrina was overprotective of her boss; she had an uneasy feeling about this man, especially after seeing her boss's name smeared in the paper. That had put her on the edge; her composure and nerves were a bit frayed.

"Can you try calling him and telling him that I'm here?" Detective Gunda asked, ignoring her question.

"Mr Lumbadzi doesn't take it kindly being called at home, especially in the morning."

"I thought you said you didn't know where he was?"

"I thought you said you arrested him? Shouldn't you know where he is?" Hendrina shot back, her composure slowly returning.

"It was a brief arrest; you haven't read today's papers have you?"

"I saw the headlines, but didn't bother to read the nonsense." Hendrina surprised herself by the high pitch of her voice; she couldn't hide the loathe she felt for the police.

An avid follower of politics, as far as she was concerned; the police had an axe to grind with her boss. It was common knowledge throughout the country that the incumbent MP was fairing very bad against her boss; this wasn't going down well with the regime.

"I have something for Mr Lumbadzi; something I feel will exonerate him." Detective Gunda smiled whilst holding up both arms in a sign of 'I come in peace'.

He slowly walked towards Hendrina's desk, still smiling.

"You are not making sense detective, just hold on." Hendrina lifted up her finger, gesturing for the policeman to stop talking.

Detective Gunda looked at the small raised hand in front of his face; he chuckled to himself. He had the impression that Mr Lumbadzi liked surrounding himself with good-looking but feisty women. On Saturday he had to deal with his wife and now his secretary was indirectly telling him to shut up. Since he had not come here in an official capacity, he simply shook his head subtly and walked back to his seat while she dialled the number.

As he sat down, the detective prayed that the secretary manages to get hold of him; he couldn't leave the package with her. It was vital that he meet Mr Lumbadzi and personally hand him the envelope, which he had concealed inside his jacket.

On Saturday, after parting ways with Detective Zeneya, who had to dash home to see if his marriage was still in play; Detective Gunda's conscious had been bothering him. The way the whole Lumbadzi operation had been conducted; the breaking of police protocol of bypassing the Senior Detective, the concealing of evidence and the obtrusive skinny reporter, it didn't sit well with him.

He was about to retire soon from the force and he wanted to do so with a clear conscious. Unlike his colleague, who still had ten or more years with the police; Detective Gunda didn't have to fear for his job that much.

After taking a nice cold shower; Detective Gunda went out searching. His quarry was the skinny reporter, the one who had been asking very direct questions about details no one was supposed to know, during Walter's arrest. He managed to find him at Kamba's Bar; a favourite drinking spot in Blantyre.

After threatening him and telling him that Dr Lumbadzi was about to drag her own brother and those involved in the Lumbadzi affair to court. The reporter, who, at the time was slightly drunk, capitulated.

"Yes the woman was a set up."

"You are referring to Nomsa, right?"

"Exactly, that's her name." The reporter responded, then went on talking about the day he approached Nomsa to set her up with Walter.

Their plan hit a wall when eventually the woman fell in love with Mr Lumbadzi. As much as they pressured her, making threats that they were going to take her son away from her if she did not comply with the requests; Nomsa did not bulge.

Although Elijah never disclosed, the reporter had a feeling that forces higher up were aware of the animosity between the Deputy Inspector General and Walter Lumbadzi. They used this to their advantage in order to try and halt Walter's political rise.

They are people high up who strongly believe that Mr Lumbadzi is connected and was assisting the opposition party; the Patriotic Front, in neighbouring Zambia. Since the PF came into power, there are those within our government who believe that the regime in Zambia is returning the favour by assisting Mr Lumbadzi's political aspirations here.

"If you follow me home, five minutes away from here, I have something which might interest you." The skinny reporter said between burps.

True to his word, ten minutes later, he handed to the detective a thick envelope containing private emails, photos and dates between Walter and Nomsa. A story he was supposed to follow and expose, about fertilizer shipment, but the cargo vanished.

"It's all in there detective, everything; take it." The skinny reporter said; his fingers were trembling very bad, struggling to light a cigarette.

This was the same envelope Detective Gunda was now carrying, hidden inside his jacket as the secretary was trying to reach Walter Lumbadzi.

Walter had tried his wife's phone countless times; it was still switched off. He hadn't slept all night; reading the handwritten notes from Nomsa. Even with such proof, who would believe a note from a former prostitute who had died of drug overdose? There is no way Elijah was going to admit to anything, and Tamanda's assertions would simply be viewed as an ongoing family feud. Tamanda might have prevented the prospect of him spending a night in jail; nonetheless, Walter knew that it was just a matter of time.

When he arrived back in Blantyre on Saturday; Walter chose the bedroom next to the master bedroom for Prince. The boy was already asleep when they pulled up outside the house; he watched as Stella tucked him into bed.

"Make sure you give him breakfast when he wakes up." He said to the housemaid as she was leaving the bedroom.

"Yes sir."

"I don't want anyone waking me up or disturbing me tomorrow. Don't bring me anything to eat. Is that clear?"

"Yes sir." Stella answered in a low voice before shutting the door, gently.

He gently run his hand on the boy's cheek, whispered goodnight and left the bedroom. He stared at the door leading into the master bedroom; that was his and Tamanda's sanctuary.

He still had the stack of papers he had taken out of Nomsa's house; he couldn't bring himself to taking them with him into their master bedroom. Walter entered the bedroom adjacent Prince's, gently shutting the door behind him; he sat on the edge of the bed. He decided he was going to spend the whole Sunday locked up in this room.

Apart from the romantic poems and notes, there was one piece of paper on which she had scribbled down what appeared to be a confession;

"Walter, I am writing this because I am ashamed to tell you in person what a bad person I have been. I never thought I would end up falling in love with you and I never thought you would turn out to be such a wonderful man. You have been nice to me, you changed me and you made me feel good about myself. I am crying as I'm writing this because I always thought being a prostitute is the lowest one can get. I was wrong. Being a traitor is. I will try to make things right though, even though you are married and love your wife, I feel there is still a small space in your heart . . ."

Walter looked at the crumpled up paper. It was obvious that even though Nomsa was writing this, she had no intention of showing it to him. He thought about the night at the hospital; she had wanted to tell him something, could this have been it? He agonised, wondering what she meant by traitor.

"Why didn't you finish writing?" He whispered, his eyes wondering over to the stack of papers, most laden with emotions and conflicts she was experiencing, then back to the note he was holding.

He had passed out on the bed feeling rotten and had woken up feeling the same way. It was Sunday afternoon, he stretched himself; wandered into the bathroom en-suite clutching onto Nomsa's notes. Sitting on the edge of the marble bathtub, he re-read the scrawny scribbling. After close to an hour, he wandered back into the bedroom; slumped back on the bed and passed out.

He could hear Stella knocking on the master bedroom; the maid had no idea that he had spent the night in a different room. He looked at his watch; 07:45am, Monday morning—he groaned, stretching himself.

The maid was most likely up here to inform him that breakfast was served. Walter stomach rumbled with hunger; however, he had no appetite, his mind was still in turmoil.

He knew that Elijah had definitely sniffed blood; there is no way his brother-in-law was going to give up that easily, even with the confession note which was still next to him, on the bed. It was obvious, the Deputy IG was going to come down hard at him; the death of Nomsa, Tosh and the Nigerian would most likely give him an impetus to do just that. On top of this Elijah had uniform on his side; the courts of law would most likely look in favour of the policeman.

Walter felt like he was on the Titanic; his political career was most likely doomed, if he went to jail, his business empire would take a hit and most importantly, his marriage was teetering on the brink. The one person who was always there by his side in times of turmoil like these was the same person he had wronged.

"Oh! My darling Tamanda, my dear Tamanda, what have I done?" He whispered into the palms of his hands.

He then scratched the stub on his chin; he had no urge to shave, eat or speak to anyone except his wife. How he wished he was a drinking man; he needed something to take the pain away, a release.

The ringing of his phone startled him; his face lit up, checking the caller ID, hoping and wanting it to be his wife.

"*Hendrina—Secretary.*" He read, his shoulders sagging in disappointment.

She was probably calling him to find out where he was. He needed to tell her to cancel all his meetings and appointments for the whole week and the next.

"Hello?" He answered the phone, surprised that his voice sounded croaky like a frog. He needed a drink to wet his throat; Walter thought, swallowed a mouthful of saliva.

"Oh! Good morning, Mr Lumbadzi." Hendrina's voice was clearly that of excitement and relief.

"Good morning Hendrina."

"Oh sir, I'm so glad . . . it's so nice to hear your voice sir."

"What is it Hendrina?" Walter cut her off.

"There is a man, a detective here sir. His name is Mr Gunda." Hendrina paused, enjoying the moment, the sound of her boss's voice sending a chill of excitement all over her body.

No matter how many times she had heard that voice of his; it never failed to make her smile. If only he knew how much she loved him, if only he knew that she would do anything, even work for him without pay. If only Walter would take the time to . . .

"Yes, what is it Hendrina?" Walter's booming voice interrupted her thoughts of fantasy.

"He says he has some information which you might be interested in." Hendrina said startled by her boss's impatient tone.

"Can you ask him what kind of . . . actually, can you just put him on the phone!"

"Mr Lumbadzi would like to talk to you, detective." Hendrina said, handing the phone to the officer.

"Hello, this is Detective Gunda, sir." He said as soon as the secretary handed him the receiver.

"Yes, detective; what is it now?"

"Sir, it would be best if we could meet."

"You can talk to my lawyer, detective; I have been advised not to say anything to you people."

"Sir, I'm not here on official capacity." Detective Gunda lowered his voice, turning around, shielding the phone from Hendrina.

"Excuse me?"

"Sir, I have some information which you might find helpful. The whole thing was a set up."

"I already know that detective. In case you have forgotten we were together when my wife blew your vendetta mission wide open."

"Sir, I have more information; do you remember that reporter?"

"Detective, put my secretary back on the phone."

"Okay sir." Detective Gunda was startled by the sudden request; "Mr Lumbadzi wants to talk to you Miss." He said handing the phone back to Hendrina.

"Yes sir?" Hendrina said with a smile.

"Find one of the drivers, preferably Samson, to bring the detective to my house."

"Okay sir, I will do that straight away."

"And, Hendrina . . . ?"

"Yes sir?" She answered, her heart skipping a beat at the way he pronounced her name.

Walter Lumbadzi had a way of saying her name which was different from anyone else. The way his tongue stressed on the 'r' it always sounded as if there were two or three 'r's, it felt so sweet to hear him call her.

"Is the detective right next to you?" He asked in a low voice; she could tell he wanted to tell her something meant for her ears only.

Two years of working for him they had developed a certain telephone rapport. There were times he would talk to her over the phone about a visitor he didn't want to see, whilst the visitor was right there in her office. She loved times like these, she felt so connected to him; their minds working as one. I only . . .

"Hendrina! Is the detective right next to you?" Walter's voice snapped her out of her daydream.

"Not really." She answered, without dropping her voice; he understood that it was okay for him to talk and the detective wasn't going to pick up anything.

"Good. Is he alone?"

"Yes sir, I believe so."

"Okay. Is he carrying anything with him or on him?" He asked and waited.

He knew that this was a difficult question for his secretary. If the detective had something with him or on him; there is no way she was going to be able to say whatever it was, without the policeman realising that they were discussing him.

"Yes sir. Do you want the documents in a brown A4 envelope?" Hendrina responded, hoping that her boss was going to understand what she was trying to say.

"What?" Walter was confused by her response, he was about to snap at her angrily when she repeated the same thing.

"In a brown A4 envelope sir, I wanted to know if you want me put the documents in a brown A4." Hendrina repeated, conscious that the detective was looking at her, his sausage like fingers fastening his tight fitting jacket, hiding the brown manila envelope which was showing earlier on.

"Oh, I get it. He is carrying a brown envelope. Thanks Hendrina." Walter said in a mellow tone; smiling at how she had managed to relay the message to him.

"You are welcome sir. When are you . . . ?" Hendrina was about to ask but her boss had hung up the phone.

For the two years Hendrina had worked for Mr Lumbadzi, she had heard so much about his house from the drivers. She always longed to see it; to see if what she had often dreamt about corresponded to the real thing.

The minute the guards at the gate let them in, Hendrina's lips parted in awe; reality was ten times bigger, better and more magnificent than what she had envisioned in her dreams.

As the car pulled up to the front; she saw him, her boss was standing by the terrazzo steps, his hands on his hips. It was the first time seeing Mr Lumbadzi in a pair of jeans and a T-shirt. He looked so stunning, so handsome; Hendrina almost got out of the car before it came to a stop. Both Samson and the detective looked at her; she was the first one out.

"Hello sir, this is Detective Gunda." She smiled, gesturing to the detective who was still trying to wiggle out of the car.

"Hendrina? What are you doing here?" Walter asked, surprised at the sight of his secretary.

"I . . . I . . . the way you sounded sir, I thought you might want me to be here." Hendrina stammered; lowering her face, feeling embarrassed.

"No, Hendrina. I asked you to tell Samson to bring the detective here." He said shaking his head, turning his attention at the detective who was approaching him, his hand extended.

"Good morning sir." Detective Gunda extended his chubby hand.

"Good morning detective. Please do come in." Walter grasped the policeman's hand.

"Thank you sir." Detective Gunda answered with a smile, slowly going up the steps.

"Samson can take you back now Hendrina; cancel all my appointments for the week." Walter, paused by the top of the stairs, speaking dismissively whilst looking at Hendrina.

"Okay sir." Hendrina said with a slight tremor in her voice.

She wondered if her boss could see in her eyes what she felt; but he had turned around and had just disappeared through the large front double door.

Hendrina walked back to the car; she sat in the back seat, looking at the white mansion. She wondered which one of those many windows was the master bedroom. Which one contained Walter's bed? She had visualised his bedroom a thousand times, she had even lied on his bed on so many occasion, wearing her pink lacy lingerie, enjoying the silky feel of the expensive beddings against her skin, enjoying the . . .

"What now, madam?" Samson's voice, from the driver's side, startled her.

"Back to the office, driver!" Hendrina snapped.

~ RECONCILIATION ~

THE DAY SHE walked away from her husband by the roadside was the worst day of her life. Despite fact that Walter had been released and allowed to go back home, Tamanda refused to return back to Blantyre with him. She opted to stay in Dedza with her grieving mother; so as to think of the way forward.

Throughout that week he was calling her nonstop; she did not answer his calls, crying herself to sleep every night, Tamanda hardly ate her foot and opted to stay locked up in her bedroom most of the time.

Walter surprised her by showing up at the mansion, seven days after the funeral; the day before the whole family was due to go back to the cemetery and lay fresh flowers on the Chief Justice's grave in a ceremony called *kusesa*.

When Elijah, who hadn't said a word to her since the day of the arrest, saw Walter's car pull up he got up from the veranda abruptly.

"You are crazy Tamanda, you are mentally unstable." He hissed and marched inside the house, slamming the door behind him.

The whole family had been sitting outside, praying and remembering their departed father and husband. Silence ensued as soon as Elijah left, they could still hear doors, inside the house, slamming shut.

"Mother, do you think Elijah is right?"

"What do you mean, Tamanda?" Mrs Mkiche, who was sitting between Tamanda's two older sisters, asked in a soft voice.

"Because of the feelings that I have for my husband, I mean, after everything he did to me, I am starting to think that maybe I am crazy." Tamanda said, looking at her mother who was sat in front of her.

"My daughter, crazy is part of love. You should know that, when we are in love, we all do certain things that we wouldn't do under normal circumstances."

"In other words, Tamanda is crazy?" Mathews, the youngest of the boys, asked; his eyes were also looking at the approaching car of Walter.

"Love makes us crazy and only those people outside that circle of love are able to see and wonder why someone would go ahead and do the things that they do."

"You mean, by fighting for his release?"

"Exactly what I mean my daughter."

"Sometimes you talk just like dad. It's as if you have always shared the same mind." Tamanda said; noticing a faint smile dance across her mother's face.

"Go and welcome your husband." Her mother said, gesturing to where Walter had parked; he had gotten out and was standing next to his car.

With heavy feet, Tamanda walked towards Walter; inside her head, she was trying to compose what to say to him. Her brain had never been so taxed with so much; her husband's infidelities, the passing of her father and Elijah's actions in the whole affair.

It was all too much; nonetheless, she had to face her husband.

Walter looked at his wife who was approaching him like a storm; she was still dressed in black like she had been the day of the funeral, the day he got arrested.

It had been the longest week of his life; the return trip to Blantyre, with Prince and Stella the housemaid, was a moment to reflect on what he had done. In his mind, the events of what had happened kept playing over and over, like a movie.

He was now certain that the reporter, who had asked him a barrage of unnerving questions, was the same skinny man he had seen talking to Elijah at a dinner party, some months back. He was also the same man who had dropped off Nomsa, when they first met at Ku Chawe Inn, no wonder he hadn't seen her paying him; although at the time this hadn't registered.

As Tamanda got nearer, he debated with himself if it was necessary to bring this up; the conspiracy concocted by her brother. On second thought, maybe it would be better just to concentrate on them, instead of talking about things that would make him appear as if he was trying to justify the wrongs he had done.

The two of them walked in silence to the small brick house, conscious that the other family members were looking at them. As soon as they entered the empty house Tamanda confronted her husband, telling him how much his actions had hurt her; leaving a permanent scar on their marriage. Despite the fact that Elijah had used threats and coerced Nomsa to have a relationship with Walter, Tamanda argued that it was his own fault.

"Walter, you shouldn't have set the ball rolling by taking your cyber friendship into reality."

"I cannot argue with you on that one my dear." He spoke with genuine remorse; "I wronged you in so many ways sweetheart, all I ask is for you to forgive me and let me rebuild the trust that I broke."

"I forgave you the moment I saw you being arrested sweetheart."

"I appreciate that sweetheart." His voice was full of remorse.

"I may never forget what you did, but I forgave you a week ago; after all that's what the bible teaches us." Tamanda went on.

Walter looked up at his wife, not sure if he heard her correctly when she mentioned the bible. He chose not to comment, right now he just wanted to hold her in his arms; to smell her and feel her heart beating against him. A cold chill snaked the length of his body when he thought how close he had come to losing her, to losing his life.

They left the small brick house, strolling hand in hand towards the mansion. He was holding her hand tighter than usual; afraid of losing her. He never loosened the grip until they were inside the big mansion.

"I love you so much my beautiful wife." He had said to her as she retrieved her hand from his and walked over to the other side of the bed.

She had her back to him and was looking outside the window. He could see she was shaking; she wanted to cry. Walter walked over to where she was; standing right behind her, gently placed his hands on her shoulders. He was expecting her to brush his arm off. She didn't.

He felt her taking a deep breath and holding it in, like someone who wanted to take a plunge in a pool. He gently turned her around, almost like a ballerina, until they were facing each other. It dawned on him that the spot they were standing on was the very same spot he had stood when this bedroom was nothing but brick masonry sticking out of the earth as foundation. The exact same spot he had stood with his late father-in-law, the day he reassured him he would never treat Tamanda the way his father treated his mother.

Walter extended both his hands, reaching out for hers. She accepted them, accepted him back and he clasped them, rubbing his right thumb against the wedding ring on her finger.

"Thank you Tamanda, you have such an amazing heart."

"I don't know why I love you this much, Walter." She said with tears in her eyes, she made no attempt to wipe them off.

"Lately I have been wondering if I deserve to have such a wonderful person like you as a wife." He spoke slowly, letting go of her hand and wiping off her tears with his thumb.

"I am so sorry for what happened . . . for what I put you . . . put our marriage through." He went on, his voice trembling, his eyes blinking, tears forming around them.

She heard the touching sincerity and pain in his voice; it was the second time he was apologising. Tamanda felt herself wanting to cry; instead a smile began to tug at the corners of her mouth, and then tugged harder.

She burst into a melodic laughter, that of someone who had just found something precious they thought they had lost forever. She threw herself at him, tilting her chin up to his. Her laughter was snuffed out by the kiss that followed; her hands slowly came up, hesitating just around his neck, then she held him there.

Still laughing, still crying; feeling so many strong emotions.

~ TRUE LOVE ~

Eight months after her father's burial, Tamanda kept having recurring dreams; she would hear echoes of conversations she used to have with her father. Sometimes these dreams would happen during her daytime nap and on some occasions, she would be wide awake, sitting all alone. Whichever; her father's voice would sound as if he was standing right next to her.

On this particular day, Tamanda was curled up on the couch, her novel by Desmond Tutu lying on her belly. Prince was playing on the carpet with his toy train. She could not see her departed father, but she could hear his voice loud and clear. A conversation they had years ago was replaying itself inside her head. It sounded so real causing her to look around, hoping to see him standing behind the couch.

"You only find out how you honestly love someone when fierce gusts of wind and torrential rains are pounding on your relationship." Her father's booming voice resonated.

It was a conversation they had, just a few days after getting married to Walter.

"Dad?" Tamanda's question was loud enough for Prince to pause; he looked up at her, smiled and then carried on playing with his toy train.

"It is easier to tell your husband how much you love him when things are okay."

"Yes, father,"

"However, when dark clouds cast an ominous shadow over your marriage and when an earthquake is shaking the very foundation of your love."

"I'm listening, father."

"My daughter, only then will you ever realise how deep and true your love goes for the other person, especially when those tribulations come in form of infidelity." Judge Sambani went on in his trademark booming voice.

Back then she hadn't paid much attention to him, as far as she was concerned this was just one of his many mumbling sermons. She remembered the exact day her father had said this to her.

"You see that?" Chief Justice Sambani was gesturing with his head at brick foundation they were standing on.

"What father? The bricks?" Tamanda quizzed whilst looking down at the brick masonry that was barely sticking out of the partly overgrown ground.

"Yes my dear daughter, the bricks; those bricks are the foundation of what I am about to build."

"I am not following you dad."

"Once the house comes up, that's what people will talk about, that's what everybody will see. Except that it is what they don't see, the foundation, which is more important."

"Okay, I see now." Tamanda nodded her head smiling.

"The foundation has to be deep and strong, for the house to last forever. It you have a weak foundation, you have nothing." Her father said, looking intently into her eyes.

"I know what you are trying to say father, you don't have to worry; me and Walter, we love each other dearly." Tamanda said while looking at the brick house where, she could just make out the figure of Walter, surrounded by his new in-laws.

"That is very good my daughter, what you and your husband have right now is a beautiful thing. But it's like a house that will one day be shaken by an earthquake." He paused clearing his throat; "Make sure the foundation of your relationship is very deep and so strong that no matter what happens, what you have will not be shaken and cause irreparable cracks to your marriage." Her father said, spreading his arms, an invitation for a hug.

"I love you dad." She said, smiling.

"Are you okay, mom?" Prince asked; his eyes looking at her quizzingly, his little brain wondering why she was talking to herself.

Looking back now, to that sunny day, each and every word her late father said was resonating with some painful clarity. She always knew that she loved Walter. However, after everything that had just taken place prior and after his arrest, a lot of cosmetic layers had been peeled off, exposing only that which was real; love in its raw state.

Tamanda's feelings for her husband went deeper; he had shaken and eroded much of the trust she had for him. Nevertheless, deep down, she still strong feelings for Walter.

That evening, when Walter came back home, the two of them were sprawled on their favourite couch. She did not tell him about her recurring daydreams and voices of her father, instead, Tamanda snuggled into his chest, feeling his arms around her. She resisted the urge to look up into his face; if she did, they would end up kissing. She so much wanted to feel his lips on hers, but decided against showing such explicitness in front of Prince; the boy was lying on the floor, with his eyes glued on the plasma screen.

Tamanda smiled, raising the novel she had been struggling to read all day; she paused, squeezing Walter's right arm with her left.

"Listen to this sweetheart."

"What's that?" He mumbled, rubbing his feet against hers.

"It's a quote from the book I'm reading."

"What is Reverend Tutu telling you sweetheart?" He asked, casting his eyes on the book's cover.

"He claims that, and I quote; *most people would have been filled with revulsion had someone gone and set up an electric chair or the gallows or the guillotine as an object of reverence. Well, look at the Cross. It was a ghastly instrument of death; an excruciatingly awful death reserved for the most notorious malefactors. It was an object of dread and shame, and yet what a turnaround has happened. This instrument of horrendous death has been spectacularly transfigured. Once a means of death, it is now perceived by Christians to be the source of life eternal. Far from being an object of vilification and shame, it is an object of veneration*, end quote" Tamanda read, exhaling gently while looking up at her husband.

"That is powerful darling. What is Tutu on about?" He asked, smiling back.

"He is talking about transfiguration, not of Jesus but of human beings."

"Oh?"

"What do you mean by '*oh*?'"

"You surprised me that day I came to Dedza, saying that you had forgiven me because that's what the Bible teaches us." He said with a smile.

"Why, I can't mention the Bible now?" Tamanda quizzed, smiling back at her husband.

"That's not what I'm saying; it's just that I get the feeling you have finally found faith, that's all." Walter said; he was gently rubbing his hand on Tamanda's hip.

"I don't know, Walter."

"You don't know what, sweetheart?"

"Lately I feel like our relationship has undergone a similar process; a metamorphosis, so to say."

"I know, I feel closer to you sweetheart." He said, then he cleared his throat; "I just wasn't connecting our closeness to religion."

"It has to be darling, because at one point, I thought we were going to separate; but now I feel so close to you." Tamanda's smile was widening.

"You surely have found faith, haven't you sweetheart?"

"I think so, sweetheart; I think it happened the day I got back from South Africa."

"You mean the time you sat next to the talkative pastor, the one who was petrified of flying?" Walter asked.

"I think so, sweetheart. For some reason, it is from that day that I start analysing everything that happened between us."

"You mean the discovery of female underwear in the boot?"

"That and so much more, Walter; I have often thought of why when we were supposed to have gone our separate ways, the opposite happened. I mean, here we are, fiercely drawn together."

"I have thought of that too, why you didn't walk out on me when I had given you all the reasons to."

"Exactly and how does one explain that if one removes God from the equation?" Tamanda spoke in a very soft voice, her mouth curved into a beautiful smile.

"Mama! Mama!" Prince yelled from the middle of the living room, interrupting their conversation, before Walter could answer.

The young boy was pointing at the big plasma screen; at the cartoons, Tom and Jerry, which were locked in a fierce cat and mouse chase.

Tamanda dropped the book flat on her belly; she looked up at the three-year old boy who was smiling and running towards them, almost bumping into the low glass table in the middle of the living room. He started yanking on her blouse whilst pointing at the cartoons.

"Yes darling Prince, what is it?" Tamanda asked, fully aware of what the boy wanted her to do.

"Mama, chase." Prince said excitedly.

"No, please no Prince, I am tired to be chasing you around the living room," Tamanda pleaded with a smile; she looked up at Walter, whose eyes were shut as if he was in a deep sleep.

"Honourable Lumbadzi, you better cut that out, don't you pull a fast one on me."

"I'm fast asleep, trust me; I'm sleep talking." He said without opening his eyes

"Well, you better get on your knees and start sleep chasing the boy because I have a date with Desmond Tutu." Tamanda said.

She lifted the book closer to her face; it was almost touching her nose. With her face burying in between the open pages, Tamanda was struggling not to laugh.

"Not the Tom and Jerry chase again, I am so tired after . . ." Walter groaned.

"Oh no you are not going to pull the political card on me sweetheart." Tamanda exploded into a loud laugh.

She knew that Walter was going to come up with a trademark excuse; she started pushing him off the couch, trying to dump his body onto the floor.

"Okay, you chase him today and I will chase him tomorrow." Walter protested; digging his feet into the couch and clutching onto the armrest to prevent his body from going over.

"That's what you said yesterday Honourable MP. I have been playing Tom and Jerry with him all day, while you were having it easy with your constituents, telling them how many bridges you are going to build."

"Did I say that yesterday?"

"Yep, and the tomorrow of yesterday is now. Come on Honourable; it's your turn to play Tom the cat." Tamanda said.

She was still struggling to shove Walter off the couch whilst Prince was yanking on his shirt, helping her.

"I thought you just told me that our marriage has gone through a metamorphosis?"

"Exactly, you are no longer Honourable Lumbadzi."

"I am not?"

"No, you are now Honourable Tom the Cat; so go do what Tom does best. Let's see if you are capable of catching Prince the Mouse." Tamanda coaxed him whilst winking at their son.

She shifted her body to the other side of the couch, still trying to shove her husband off the couch. He did not bulge; instead he started making very loud snoring sounds. Both, Tamanda and Prince started laughing at Walter's funny pretence.

"Come on sweetheart, get up and be the cat." She pleaded.

The more she did, the louder Walter snored and the louder Prince laughed. She simply gave up and started snoring too.

Despite his efforts of pretending to be asleep, Walter could no longer suppress the smile, his lips were twitching. Tamanda was still trying to topple him from the couch onto the floor;

he struggled to open one eye without being noticed, looking at the big screen on the far end of the living room. They both saw him; the laughter of Tamanda and Prince at his snoring antics was both mesmerising and touching. He looked slightly away from the two of them, trying to dry a tear that had started to cascade down his left cheek. He was crying; it all felt perfect, they were a family; one unit.

Tamanda treated Prince as if she was his biological mother; she had thrown a wonderful party four months ago when he turned three. Most of his young friends, from school, came to their mansion. They were accompanied by their parents; some of whom were delighted at the chance of meeting Walter Lumbadzi.

Prince had acclimatised himself to his new surroundings; both at home and school. There were times when he wondered if the little boy had any recollection of his past life, he would often stare into his little eyes hoping to find something there.

"Daddy! Daddy!" He would often startle him.

It felt natural and right whenever the boy said Daddy or Mummy; both of them looked at him as their son.

He had thought a lot about Prince during the afternoon, while at his constituency, in the heart of Ndirande. He was mobilising people to construct a new health clinic facility and, as had been the case for the past eight months, the women came carrying their young ones on their backs. Every time his eyes wandered to where little boys were playing noisily, while the men were offloading problems that needed fixing, Walter thought of Prince. At times he had to remind himself to pay attention to what the men were talking about; they had elected him as their MP and they looked at him as their messiah.

So far in a space of less than a year Walter had delivered, and already people in Ndirande and beyond were touting him to run for higher office. This was the same township he had vowed never to return to; however, the new Walter embraced it with both hands. He was channelling all his energy into improving the lives of those who needed help.

He used his childhood, his painful past, as motivators to represent and speak vociferously for his constituents in Parliament. With his British friend, Graham, pulling the strings in England, assistance in form of money and equipment was finding its way into much needed projects in his constituency. Every time he visited Ndirande, he felt like he was coming home and at the end of the day, slowly driving out of this bustling township, he always felt a sense of satisfaction and a bit of sadness.

While wrapping up the meeting, Walter's eyes again wandered to where a group of young boys, about the age of Prince, were running chasing each other playfully across the open field. A smile formed across his face; he thought of their son at home with his wife. Both would most likely be waiting for him, for their daily game of Tom and Jerry.

His smile widened as he contemplated on a way how he was going to avoid running on all fours like a cat once he got home. He will pretend to fall asleep; he thought as he indicated left before joining the main road.

"Dad, cry . . . Mama, why dad cry?" Prince, who was clutching on to the TV's remote control, quizzed whist tugging on Nomsa's blouse and pointing at Walter.

"Dad is happy, Daddy is crying because he is happy. Isn't that so Daddy" Tamanda beamed, her beautiful dental structure exposed, as she gently wiped Walter's tears with the back of his hand.

"That's right," Walter sniffed, looking at Prince's curious face, "tomorrow you—young man—and me are going to Ndirande together." He said to their son, pulling him closer until all three of them were locked into a warm hug.

~ END ~

~ GLOSSARY ~

- *Abwanoni*—grasshoppers which are roasted and eaten as a delicacy.
- *Apongozi*—father-in-law or mother-in-law.
- *Bwana*—Boss.
- *Dedza*—a small town; located about 85 km south of Malawi's capital, Lilongwe, off the M1 road to Blantyre. The town is based around a bypass loop of tarmac road connected to the M1. Much of Dedza is rural countryside.
- *Kusesa*—a practice that generally marks the end of the mourning period. It is done one to three days after burial.
- *Malawi*—a landlocked country in southeast Africa (formerly known as Nyasaland). It is bordered by Zambia to the northwest, Tanzania to the northeast, and Mozambique on the east, south and west. Malawi is separated from Tanzania and Mozambique by Lake Malawi. Malawi is over 118,000 km² (45,560 sq. mi) with an estimated population of more than 14 million. Its capital is Lilongwe, the largest city is Blantyre and the second largest city is Mzuzu.
- *Mwaswela*—an afternoon greeting.
- *Nsima*—Malawi's staple food made from ground maize (corn) flour

~ BY THE SAME AUTHOR ~

MAKALA AMOTO: MADE IN MALAWI
Rinzi Peter Phoya

Published in 2010 by Authorhouse Publishing
ISBN: 978-1-4520-8293-6 (sc)

Shasha didn't bother lying to me, he came straight out; "I was online when I stumbled across this Company's website which claims for $19.99 only, they can manufacture an authentic academic Degree which can be delivered to you in five business days. Listen to this; if you pay by Visa Credit card they throw in a free gold plated frame for your Degree. Since I don't have a Credit card, I had to send them cash that's why I didn't get the frame but the Degree arrived this morning."

"So you bought your Degree?" I asked in disbelief and Shasha calmly answered; "Yes. And this website claims that for $50 they can send you three Degrees: Law, Medicine and Accounting, unfortunately I could only raise $19.99—that's why only graduated with a Law Degree."

That was over a month ago, today Shasha is now the senior partner and proud owner of SAL (Shasha Attorneys at Law) a legal firm which everyone is now talking about in Malawi. His client list comprises of the crème de la crème of Malawi's wealthiest. I sure some of you have already heard about this amazing legal firm.

MAKALA AMOTO 2: MALAWIANISM
Rinzi Peter Phoya

Published in 2011 by Authorhouse Publishing
ISBN: 9781456787820

Our pockets were filled with all sorts of wild fruits. The eight of us had agreed to walk over to the river, the part where girls would often take their bath. The intention was simple; sneak up on them, conceal ourselves in the tall bango reeds and enjoy the free view whilst chewing on our fruits.

For some unknown reason Borobonya, my cousin and also our lead, took a wrong turn. That's how we stumbled upon the clearing in the forest around Che Ng'anga's hut. Clay pots of different sizes were scattered all over, most of them filled with indescribable concoctions. What fascinated me most were the clear glass bottles, especially the contents inside. They contained bundles of wood and some even had bricks inside.

We walked in silence towards the hut as if being pulled by an unseen force until we were standing just a few steps away from the opening. There was no door, just a gaping hole with two little round windows on each side. The ruffled up straw-thatched roof, gave the hut a spooky humanoid face resembling a toothless old woman with her mouth menacingly open. It was dark inside. I was scared.

Borobonya was fearless, the only one amongst us who could drink milk straight from a cow's udder and bite its nipple hard once he was full. The cow would violently kick and thrash its massive hooves in pain missing Borobonya by centimetres.

That would tickle my cousin into bouts of hysterical laughter, the same way he was laughing now.

From inside the hut, Borobonya's laughter stopped. He emerged holding a big glass bottle. As he got closer I was filled with horror with what was inside the glass bottle.

THE 'THIRD' INSTALMENT

MAKALA AMOTO 3—MALAWI'S FINEST
Rinzi Peter Phoya

Just when you thought your lungs couldn't be tortured any more. Just when you thought you had finished drying your tears of joy; Makala Amoto—the protagonist—with his twisted sense of humour, returns with his family, friends and the famous Torpedo-2000. Get your plates out and prepare to be barbecued with hot sense of humour—about politics, family, homosexuality, religion and of course Escom.

COMING OUT SOON

WHISPERS & TEARS
Rinzi Peter Phoya

"Is this the Griffin you have been talking about?" Lord Browning yelled gesturing to the monitor with his head whilst crushing the remaining half of his cigar in the glass ashtray perched on his mahogany desk.

Lauren Browning, his daughter and only child, was standing next to the massive book shelf. Her hands were clasped in front to stop them from twitching, a futile attempt. She was trying her best to stay calm and started wishing she hadn't tied her blonde hair in a knot. In the past she has used her hair as a mask to cover part of her face so as to hide the anger she felt. But she hadn't expected today's family tête-à-tête to turn so confrontational. Right now her father was pushing all the wrong buttons inside her.

At twenty years old, Lauren was no longer the little girl depicted on the family portrait despite her controlling father always treating her as if she still was. She looked at her angry father who was still crushing the obscenely expensive cigar in the ashtray as if he was trying to kill it.

"Yes Daddy, he is the Griffin I was telling you about." She answered in a defiant tone despite her efforts of trying to sound cordial.

"But, he . . . he . . . he is black." Lord Browning stuttered angrily whilst walking towards the minibar and pouring himself a shot of Hennessy from an expensive looking crystal decanter.

"Yes Daddy I know that, in case you haven't noticed, he is also a human being and . . ."

"Yes Lauren my dear, but you could have at least told me that he is black." Lord Browning cut her off sternly avoiding eye contact with his daughter. Instead he walked back towards the double glazing windows, staring outside briefly then sinking his massive frame in the plush leather chair behind his mahogany desk.

"Why Daddy, I don't recall ever telling you the race of the boys who have been my acquaintances in the past!" Lauren retorted in a raised voice since the conversation began.

"Don't play lawyer with me Lauren, this is different." Lord Browning calmly answered sensing the trap his daughter was trying to set for him.

"How different Daddy?"

"When you said Griffin, I assumed he was . . ."

"You assumed he was white?" Lauren finished the sentence for her father, not bothering to disguise the underlying sarcasm.

"No . . . I mean yes . . . come on, the name Griffin . . . how was I . . ." Lord Browning's hand was shaking profusely causing the ice cubes in . . . [To read the whole story and more, get *Whispers & Tears*]

Whispers & Tears is a compilation of short stories about romance, relationships, tragedy and then some. Experience a unique way of storytelling. Stories told with simplicity and clarity.

COMING OUT SOON

"Thanks to you for the first time I had to be part of a book; your book; Malawian own; Makala Amoto: *Made in Malawi*, and I got all copies. God has truly blessed you so you can be a blessing to others. As many have said; your respect for women is indescribable, especially our culture/tradition where women have been and some are still being looked down, disrespected, lied to, brutally abused, emotionally wounded and not valued. They should learn it from you and women appreciate you; we want more of you; you are a kind that gives us hope and courage to be the best we can be despite the disappointments and God will give you a reason to celebrate all the days of your life. Remain blessed."   ~ Angelina Digolia.

Posted on my Facebook wall on 28 Dec. 2011

Rinzi Phoya is a Malawian Writer. He has published two novels; Makala Amoto: Made in Malawi and Makala Amoto 2: Malawianism.

He lives with his wife—Sandra—and their two children.

This is his third novel.